Lawrence Robinson' ... tions such as *Arena*, ... *Weekly*. He worked ... moving to Hollywoo... has sold a number o... independent production companies and is the author of a non-fiction book about soccer. *Thirty Bytes of Solitude* is his first novel and he is currently working on a second for Piatkus Books. He lives in Los Angeles. And he spends entirely too much time online.

www.britwriter.com

Thirty Bytes of Solitude

Lawrence Robinson

PIATKUS

Visit the Piatkus website!

Piatkus publishes a wide range of best-selling fiction and non-fiction, including books on health, mind, body and spirit, sex, self-help, cookery, biography and the paranormal.

If you want to:
- read descriptions of our popular titles
- buy our books over the Internet
- take advantage of our special offers
- enter our monthly competition
- learn more about your favourite Piatkus authors

VISIT OUR WEBSITE AT: www.piatkus.co.uk

All the characters in this book are fictitious and any resemblance to real persons, living or dead, is entirely concidental.

Copyright © 2005 by Lawrence Robinson

Lyrics from 'A Long December' © 1996 by Adam F. Duritz used by kind permission.
EMI Blackwood Music Inc./Jones Falls Music BMI. All rights reserved.

First published in Great Britain in 2005 by
Piatkus Books Ltd of
5 Windmill Street, London W1T 2JA
email: info@piatkus.co.uk

This edition published 2005

The moral right of the author has been asserted

A catalogue record for this book is available from the British Library

ISBN 0 7499 3604 5

Set in Times by
Action Publishing Technology, Gloucester

Printed & bound in Denmark by
Nørhaven Paperback A/S, Viborg

Acknowledgements

For their support, friendship and donated lines, my heartfelt thanks to Amanda, Gilly, Shawn, Gareth, Debbie, Evee, Dave, Greg, Kenny, Babs, Stephen and Kev; for so many other reasons, Jenny.

Thanks also to Glen Hamilton for that letter; Paul Douglas and Dave Taylor at *.net* magazine and Mark Hooper at Arena for encouraging the madness; and a huge thank you to Emma Callagher and everyone at Piatkus Books for taking the chance.

For their emails, I'd like to thank Tracey from Burbank, who I almost met once, and the blind date I refused to kiss after three drinks at the Cat & Fiddle on Sunset who then wrote about me on her web site, accusing me of being either married, gay or an axe murderer. Finally, to Lisa, for rescuing me from any more nights at the Cat & Fiddle.

For my dad

A computer lets you make more mistakes faster than any invention in human history – with the possible exceptions of handguns and tequila.

Mitch Ratcliffe

Prologue – Eight Bits to a Byte

I'm heading north on Pacific Coast Highway, a journey along the very edge of America. The windows of the bus are closed but as I put my head back and shut my eyes, I can imagine the warm air buffeting around my face. It's a drive I've done a thousand times before, usually in an old camper van, with the roof open and 80s retro thumping out from the radio.

Palm trees drift in the summer breeze, the ocean spits hordes of relentless surfers onto the beach. It's a scene from any episode of *Baywatch*. A dozen Pamela Andersons skip across the sand, plastic breasts bouncing like excited puppies. The bus continues into Malibu, near where Jim Rockford slipped in and out of his trailer. Names, places synonymous with glamour and stardom; places I dreamed of back in cold, grey England. And now I am experiencing them first hand. I am living the dream that brings so many people to this bizarre, extraordinary corner of the planet. I am in the land of movies, perfect bodies and endless sunshine. Lucky, lucky me.

The Hispanic gangster next to me coughs and raises

a tattooed hand to his mouth. The chain that connects us pulls sharply on my handcuff, biting the skin around my wrist. I wince. He wipes the mucus from his hand onto the underside of the seat.

'You been to County Jail before?' he says. I shake my head. 'It fuckin' sucks, homes.'

I'm cold, tired, and scared. Very scared. This cannot be happening. I've always seen my life in LA play out like a movie, complete with outlandish coincidences and sudden plot twists. But this is not my movie. Someone has written a 70s exploitation piece and slapped it in the middle of my romantic comedy. Tarantino has rewritten *Pretty Woman*. It doesn't fit. I'm Hugh Grant à la *Four Weddings*, not Hannibal Lector, for God's sake. Somebody shout 'cut!'

But the great movie director in the sky isn't listening. So I'm stuck here: a star-struck Englishman with all the criminal tendencies of a cocker spaniel, on his way to Los Angeles County Jail. For the first time since I've been in LA, I'm truly missing England.

If only I'd never logged on ...

Byte 1 – Error Messages

The message just keeps coming back at me. *Internet Explorer Script Error. Cannot find 'x-%24home%24://null/.' Make sure the path or Internet address is correct.* I click [OK]. And again. [OK]. [OK]. *Internet Explorer Script Error. Cannot find 'x-%24home%24://null/.' Make sure the path or Internet address is correct.* It is correct. [Cancel]. [Erase]. [Back]. [Reload]. [Control-Alt-Delete]. Load you bastard, load. For the love of God, I just want to send an email!

My neighbour's staring at me again – the one with the shaved head and bushy sideburns who spends all day sitting on his balcony smoking cheroots. He looks like a Mr Potato Head who's been put together all wrong: ears down by his shoulders, a thick moustache pinned in front of each one. I should close the window. The sight of an Englishman supping hard liquor at 11 am on a Monday and screaming obscenities at his computer screen clearly unsettles him. I spent all weekend working and now I need some down time. I've earned a drink. Or at least that's what I keep telling myself. There is the letter as well, of course: that single sheet of plain white paper with 12-

point Courier type, folded into thirds. I know it's supposed to make me feel happy or sad or something else, but it doesn't. Every time I look at it I just feel hollow.

I drain my drink down to the ice and pour another. Mr Potato Head's eyes are still locked on me. I need to reboot the server and run the disk defragmenter. I'm not exactly sure what that means or why it fixes things but it always seems to work, even if it usually takes a whole afternoon to run. But I don't. I unfold the letter instead. I picked it up from my mailbox this morning. It must have been sitting in there for three or four days, skulking in the darkness behind a bank statement, waiting to snap shut like a bear trap.

'A Judgement was entered in the register of the Court in the above-noted case number,' the Courier type reads. 'Judgement Dissolution was NOT docketed in the circuit court judgement docket.' I email the attorney to find out what that means.

'It means,' he writes back, 'that your divorce was finalised on the eighth.'

We've already been divorced for a week. Like I said, I know I should feel happy or sad or something. But I don't. There are none of the side effects you normally associate with divorce: no emotional devastation, no anger, no sense of betrayal. It's all been clean and amicable; easier than cancelling a magazine subscription.

Now all I need to do is forward the email to her. I try turning the computer off and then on again. I kill another vodka-and-tonic in the time it takes the sign-on screen to reappear. I log on. Damn, it's slow. I try retyping the email but can't remember exactly what I wrote the first time. I want it to sound neutral – our marriage is over, there's no real reason for us to ever communicate again, have a nice life, etcetera – but say it in such a way that it doesn't sound like I care too much or don't care enough. I try it a few different ways but it never sounds quite right. I finally give up and click send. *Internet Explorer Script Error. Cannot find 'x-%24home%24://null/.' Make sure the path or Internet address is correct.* For the love of God!

I step outside onto the deck for some air. The sun is warm on my face. When I crane my neck over one side I can just make out the strip of green that separates Ocean Boulevard from the sudden drop down to PCH and Santa Monica beach. In the distance, the Pacific Ocean glimmers like a pool of freshly spilt ink. Mr Potato Head watches me. I look over and raise my glass to him. He huffs and retreats inside. Neighbours apart, if there's a better place to live in America, I've yet to see it. The apartment has the ocean on one side, the bustling Third Street promenade on the other, and the boutiques and restaurants and tree-lined pavements of Montana Avenue on its doorstep. All rent controlled. We found it a few weeks after we were married and couldn't believe our luck. The landlord had already had a dozen or so applications that morning but he instantly took a shine to her and said we could have it without going through the formality of a credit check. We moved in that same afternoon, three pieces of furniture between us.

The phone rings. I half expect it to be her – maybe the email went through before the computer crashed. I leave the door to the deck open and run in to snatch it up. It isn't her; it's the editor of an Internet magazine calling from London. He sputters out question after question.

'How are you? Are you OK? Do you need any help?'

I frown and ask him what the hell he's talking about. He adopts the tone of a concerned parent. He's just received a disturbing email from me telling him we're divorced. 'Is this your way of saying you don't want to write for me anymore?' he says. I laugh. 'It's LA, isn't it?' he goes on. 'It's finally getting too much for you.'

It's a conversation we've had a lot in recent months. I know where it's headed so I make a facetious remark about his judgement being clouded by another pub lunch.

'Stop gibbering and for once listen to me!'

The grey-haired patriarch of online journalism, the kindly old man permanently clad in tweed, the man all freelancers affectionately refer to as 'Uncle Ralph', is actually shouting at me. I've never heard him so much as raise his voice above a chirp in the three years I've worked for him. Now he's shouting. He's concerned. My submissions are becoming increasingly bizarre and fragmented, he tells me. I'm not producing Internet articles anymore but rather disturbed ramblings from 'the dark side'. I try halfheartedly to defend the work but then he reads from the latest copy I submitted. It's supposed to be a five thousand-word piece on the future of e-commerce in the United States. Three thousand words of it are nothing more than an account of a rum-drenched conversation with a man who may or may not have been a former marketing executive at eToys. The rest is incomprehensible. It's gabbling, demented stuff.

Some of it isn't even in English.

'It's unprintable, unreadable,' he says. 'You need a holiday.'

'No, I need a regular pay cheque. Freelancing's killing me.'

There's a long pause. 'OK,' he says at last. 'I think I've got an assignment for you. One that should keep you out of trouble for a while.'

'What is it?'

'Live online for a month,' he says. 'And we'll run a daily column on the magazine's web site.'

'What do you mean: "Live online"?'

'Completely immerse yourself in cyberspace, with no human contact and no communication with the outside world except through the Internet. That means no using the phone, no television, no shopping, no going out to bars, no dialling up for a pizza – unless you can do it online.' He takes a breath. 'See, told you it would keep you out of trouble.'

'And I report back every day?'

'Exactly,' he says. 'An Englishman living in the States on the Internet.'

I'm not convinced. A month online? Cut off from all humanity for thirty days?

'Just do it for as long as you can,' he says. 'We'll run the column for as long as you can stay online. It's pure gonzo journalism, right up your street.'

'Mmmm,' I'm still not convinced. 'But what's the story?'

'The story's whatever you want it to be,' he says. 'And we'll pay double the usual rate.'

And suddenly I'm convinced. Sold to the ex-pat divorcee with unpaid attorney bills. 'Love it,' I say. 'When do I start?'

'Now. As soon as your PC's back up.' He tells me to hang up the phone. 'And I don't want to hear your voice,' he says, 'for at least a month.'

And that's it. For the next thirty days it will be just me and the PC and the one-bedroom apartment in Santa Monica.

I let the idea sink in. Hell, is this really what I travelled six thousand miles to do? Is this really why I left England and came all the way to America: to live in solitude on the Internet? This can't be the American Dream, can it, to spend all day, every day plugged into the Net? Hell, I'm not even sure I know what the American Dream is supposed to be.

'You need an American Dream, buddy,' the cabby at LAX tells me that first afternoon I get off the plane. 'You're in the City of Angels.'

He's a heavy-set Latino, either drunk or high. I tell him I'm more interested in the little devils than the angels. He doesn't get it. He thinks that's maybe a place near Fullerton.

He pulls out into the seething traffic around the airport and I wind down the window and let the warm, stale air brush my face. I stare wide-eyed at my first piece of America: palm trees, long cars and thin girls. Everything blonde and sunny. I read somewhere that when then-Soviet-supremo Nikita S. Khrushchev first flew into Los Angeles he looked down at all the swimming pools shining in the sun and said, 'Now I know Communism has failed.' I can imagine many things failing in the face of Los Angeles, but never hope. It's an eternally optimistic city and I am filled with enormous expectation as the taxi bounces me north through the land where you can be anything and do anything –

all you have to do is decide what that anything is going to be. American Dream or not, I have arrived, I am in Los Angeles. It's a long way from London and advertising and everything I've ever known but it immediately feels like home.

I'm here because of a girl and a pub and a web site. In fact they're the three reasons why I've done most things in life.

The web site is LAtourist.com, the pub is the Dog and Duck on Frith Street and the girl is Roxy Hepburn. One of the account managers spots her first, standing with her back to us at the far side of the bar. She appears to be on her own, so Nervous Bob decides to approach. Poor thing, little does she know she is about to be bludgeoned by the world's most enormous personality. I choose to await his likely rejection from the comfort of the window seat. It's not that Nervous doesn't have a lot to offer. He is clever, funny, earns bucket loads of cash and, contrary to popular belief about fat men, is hung like a stallion. The only reason he carries the moniker Nervous is that every time he has to present a client with a new ad campaign, he deteriorates into a squirming schoolgirl, pacing the office floor, panicking about market share and product positioning. In every other respect, certainly in any social environment, he is a triumph of self-confidence. A lot of that confidence is wasted, by his own admission, because he's always drawn to unattractive women. He attributes it to the only piece of advice that his father ever gave him about the opposite sex. 'Go ugly early,' he told him. He said there weren't enough good-looking women to go round so Nervous should go straight for the ugly ones. But, as it had been pointed out to

Nervous on several occasions, his father probably didn't mean *all* of them.

The window seat suddenly fills up as Nervous crashes down next to me. 'She's attractive,' he says. 'And she's French. Doesn't speak a word of English.'

'So what were you saying to her?'

'Le singe est dans l'arbre.'

'The monkey is in the tree?' Even for Nervous it's a terrible line.

He shrugs. 'That's about all I remember from school. It seemed better than asking her for a baguette or directions to the nearest train station.'

I start to laugh. 'So what did she say?'

'No idea. I don't speak French, do I.' And with that he dissolves into roars of laughter and rolls off to the bar for more drinks.

I'm still laughing to myself when she sits down. 'Your friend off to find his monkey?' she says.

The only accent she has is an American one. She pushes back her golden-brown hair and fixes me with piercing blue eyes and a dangerous smile. Some women generate an instant aura of danger that for whatever reason I find irresistible. And danger seeps from this woman like snakes from Medusa.

I hold her gaze for as long as I can before breaking out into broad grin. 'His German is even worse,' I say. 'All he can say is: *Durch die luft und um die ecke. Through the air and round the corner*. A real ice-breaker.'

She pushes her tongue against the inside of her cheek as she stifles the urge to laugh. 'So. What's your usual line then?'

'Oh, I don't know, something tried and trusted, like "Haven't we met before?"'

She screws up her nose and shakes her head, chin down, eyes up: puppy-dog cute. I resist the enormous urge to clamber over and embrace her.

'Or, depending on my level of intoxication,' I say, 'I might throw in a snappy one-liner like: "If I owned a restaurant, you'd be dish of the day."' This time she groans and mimes pushing her fingers down her throat. I grin. 'Maybe explains why I'm sitting on my own.'

'Maybe.' And she leans forward and seductively wipes her finger across my cheek. 'You look great,' she says.

I stare at the piercing blue eyes and shrug. 'I'm losing my hair.'

'Oh, please.'

'And I'm putting on weight–'

She leans forward again and brushes the back of my hand with hers. 'It's a compliment. Take it.'

'Thank you. So do you,' I say. 'Look great, I mean. Not fat and balding.'

She smiles. 'I've still got the earrings, look. And the bracelet you gave me . . .' She flashes the chunky silver jewellery I bought her all those years ago from a Greek island. And then she smiles that dangerous smile again.

Roxy and I used to live together in a small one-bedroom flat near Chancery Lane, long before I started working with Nervous. She had what a psychologist might refer to as 'an intense, co-dependent personality'. Everyone who knew her called her 'fucking mental'. Our neighbours were twice driven to call the police when they heard her screaming late at night. The first time was due to a particularly energetic bedroom performance after we'd been apart for a week. The second time she was drunk and tearing up the flat. She found a girl's telephone number in my jacket pocket and went berserk. A pensive, rain-soaked cop viewed the aftermath and said it reminded him of the final scene in *Carrie*. Shards of broken glass were embedded in her hands and knees where she'd smashed a dozen or so picture frames. Blood was splattered across the walls and carpet like ruby paint on a Jackson Pollock canvas. It was fruitless trying to explain that the phone number was for a woman who wanted to buy my car, so I took the approach made famous by the armies of France and beat a hasty retreat. I barricaded myself in the bathroom and struggled to dislodge the short paring knife she'd wedged up to the hilt in my thigh.

Two days later we were back together again. I walked in to find the flat filled with party balloons and huge banners screaming apologies. A series of cryptic tags and romantic notes led me through the swell of balloons and into the bedroom, where she was waiting for me, wrapped in nothing but delicate strands of snow-white lace.

Then on Christmas Eve she got drunk again and tried to use a gas heater to blow up the flat. I told her she needed help and went to see an Italian movie at the art house cinema near Russell Square. When I returned, the shelves and cupboards were stripped of her things and a card in the shape of a snowman was waiting for me in the spot where her face cream used to sit. It read simply: 'I'm sorry. I've gone back to the States. Happy Christmases. Always.' And I hadn't seen or heard from her since.

Roxy Hepburn. It isn't her real name of course. She

was born Sharon Eckersley, English dad, American mum. But she changed her name to Roxanne after the Police record. When I explained to her the song was about a hooker, she revised it to Roxy. It was her way of trying to rewrite the past, to reinvent herself as a glamorous somebody with no memories of a bitter, squalid childhood. And I guess that's where the anger came from. She could never fully escape being plain old Sharon Eckersley.

We both lean against the frosted glass of the window, eyes fixed on one another, sizing each other up. I ask her what she's doing back in London. 'Here for an audition,' she says. 'And to look up an old boyfriend.'

She tells me she spent the afternoon trying out for an Anglo-US TV pilot, a spin-off of the stage musical *Starlight Express*. It sounds horrible.

'How did it go?' I ask.

She shrugs. 'I nearly walked out. I felt like the chick from *Flashdance*. All the other girls were fresh out of dance school or they'd done TV and movies. They all knew each other, they all had the latest gear. I just turned up in my sweats, you know. Felt like the girl from the wrong side of the tracks.' She pauses a moment. 'I won't even get a call back. Fuckers.'

I say something encouraging then bring up the subject of her temper. She explains it away with some sweeping California shrink-speak, something about her jealousy and insecurity and how she's been 'working through those issues' with her analyst. I nod and finger the scar on my thigh.

'You're a nut, you know that?' I say.

'Yeah,' she replies. 'But a loveable nut.' I shake my head in mock despair and she leans across and very lightly kisses me on the mouth. A tickertape parade erupts in my chest.

'I've missed you,' she says. More tickertape. We kiss again.

'How long are you in London for?' I ask.

'I go home tomorrow.'

'Tomorrow? Can't you stay any longer?'

She shakes her head.

'Why?'

'Because I've got a seat booked.'

'Change it.'

'It's not that simple,' she says. 'I'm with someone.' And with that the parade screeches to a halt and I'm left standing alone, knee-deep in scraps of rain-soaked confetti.

'Where is he?'

'At the film festival,' she says. 'He's a producer.'

'Oh ... are you ... serious?'

'We're engaged.'

I glance down at her left hand. There's no ring. She follows my gaze with hers. 'I don't wear it,' she says. 'I'm sorry. I didn't mean to ...'

I shrug and tell her it's OK. 'Do you love him?' I ask. 'Of course you do, you're getting married. Stupid question–'

'It's not like that. I don't love him like I loved you. But he's a good friend. He takes care of me. And he loves me.'

'So did I.'

'Did you?' she says. 'I thought it was just because of what happened with Katie.'

The casual mention of my sister's name takes me by surprise and I stand up and move away from her. 'You want another drink?'

She calls after me, but I am intent on reaching the emotional safety of the bar. She follows me up, pulling on her coat. She's leaving.

'I didn't plan this,' she says. 'I never expected to feel the same way about you. The wedding's in LA. I thought you might want to be there. I understand if you don't.' And she sets a subtly embossed wedding invitation down in front of me.

She waits for me to meet her gaze before speaking again. 'I'll say this only once. I wish it could have been you, I really do. It was wonderful to see you again.'

She's nearly at the door before I stop her. She turns expectantly, but all I can muster is a 'good to see you too.'

She nods. 'LA would be good for your screenwriting, you know. You've got a whole bunch of talent.' She looks around at the drab pub. 'Why waste it here?' And with that she is gone. All over again. But this time she's left more than a Frosty-the-Snowman Christmas card.

I drag Nervous back to the ad agency and make him show me how to log onto the Internet. The Net is still in its infancy, something only geeks and Americans are interested in. Like skateboards and pop tarts. My computer experience hasn't progressed beyond an Atari console and a prehistoric desktop with floppy disks the size of LP covers. The modem spits out the now familiar *dunk, dunk, ccckkkkk, ccckkkkk-ddddddddddd* tones and Nervous hands me the mouse and the keyboard and I step through the looking glass for the very first time. It's a seismic event rivalled only by the first time I put my hand up a girl's sweater. So this is what all the pale kids with duffel bags and hooded jackets were doing while I was playing football and falling over in the pub? They were conquering the world and looking at nude photos of celebrities. Blessed are the meek, for they discovered the Internet first.

I run my first search: for a web site on California. I click on the top link and up springs a picture of a girl trying to rollerblade on the second O of the Hollywood sign. Rollerblading! On the Hollywood sign! I am instantly hooked, on both the Internet and Los Angeles. Three days later I am in the back of a cab at LAX holding a brand new laptop with no particular plan other than being somewhere I've never been before.

That was eight years ago. In those eight years I've had seven apartments in six different cities, sixteen roommates, eleven phone numbers, five cars, six computers, one marriage, one divorce, six speeding tickets, twenty-two parking tickets, eleven jobs, written for sixteen magazines, five newspapers and half a dozen web sites; sold two books, eight screenplays and been in thirty-three states, seventy-four hotel rooms, six jail cells and four courthouses and I'm still no closer to uncovering the American Dream than when I started. The cabby was right. I need to have an American Dream.

Maybe I'll find it on the Internet.

Byte 2 – The American Dream

Outgoing Email:

> To: <Address Book>
> From: <BritWriter>
> Subject: Call of the Wild
>
> Salutations friends, comrades and others. As of today I am on assignment, so I will be unable to have any further contact by phone or fax. My mission is to trawl through the furthest reaches of cyberspace and uncover the American Dream. Please tell those unfortunate 'disconnecteds' – namely my grandmother and that vile technophobe Johnny Lager – that I will not be returning their calls for at least the next few weeks. (God knows how long my quest will take. Legend has it that the American Dream can be somewhat elusive.)
>
> My daily dispatches will be posted on the magazine's web site. Feel free to email messages of encouragement, but please, no pictures of wide-open spaces or scantily clad females. And,

as ever, no crazy talk of short people or the French. The isolation is likely to leave me in too fragile a state for such unpleasantness.
Happy thoughts. See you on the other side.
BritWriter

America's a strange place. It balances on the technological edge, a place where half-crazed computer freaks unveil mind-boggling gadgets that redefine the frontiers of existence at the rate of about nine a day, only to have them rejected by war-starved generals with huge necks and tiny brains for failing to destroy small countries at the flick of a switch, or thrown out by vapid corporate marketing executives who spend all day worshipping the gods of flashing neon and then vomit in the face of anything that can't be sold in less than three words by large-breasted women in red Lycra swimsuits. Or maybe they're the smart ones. They've found their American Dream and they're milking it for every cent. I think it was Zelda Fitzgerald who claimed the American Dream was founded on the infinite promise of American advertising (and all its bosoms and swimsuits). If nothing else her theory can at least provide a starting point to my search for the American Dream. Hell, after eight years in the US, I am ready to believe it's possible to get a flat stomach in just three minutes a day, remove any stain without scrubbing and get whiter teeth overnight.

'Horse shit,' reads the response. 'People are so busy dreaming the American Dream, fantasising about what they could be or have a right to be, that they've all forgotten how to interact with each other. That's why we're all so goddam lonely. We're all living in a self-imposed isolation.' It isn't the answer I was hoping for when I put the question out there in a couple of chat rooms. But it's better than the first two replies: 'Piss off, faggot,' and 'I'll show you where the American Dream is, honey. Cost you sixty bucks and you pay for the room ☺.'

I should have seen it coming. Advertising is a low trade, full of miscreants with the moral fortitude of pimps and pornographers and tabloid journalists. I know these things; in London I wrote copy for print advertorials, that mutant hybrid of the soft-sell ad and objective feature. They were slick tales about health products doused in exclamation points and deceptive catch phrases and testimonials with all the integrity of a Republican manifesto. It was Nazi-style work that would've shamed Joseph Goebbels. I'd shower five times a day but could never scrub the stench of it from my pores. I quit after a couple of weeks for the more worthy pursuit of standing by traffic lights begging commuters for change. Or at least I should have done, if only I could've shaken the ugly realisation that everyone lives by selling something.

I was a copywriter, one of Thatcher's children, a whore to the money god. To some it may have sounded like a glamorous occupation, certainly a lucrative one. To me, it was about as creatively fulfilling as shaving carpet. It wasn't writing, it was word management: I simply moved words about, shepherding them from one sentence to another like war-ravaged refugees. Then in the evenings I would hurry home to watch movies or write screenplays and lose myself in some other world where people did something meaningful. Or at least something incredibly violent. Meaning and violence became synonymous after a soul-shredding day transposing words.

I call in sick the day after I see Roxy in the pub and use the time to print out copies of my newest aliens-invade-earth screenplay and draft my resignation letter. It is meant to be funny, but I doubt if the head of the agency ever sees it that way. 'I've moved to Los Angeles to sell a screenplay,' I write. 'And no, I won't remember any of you when I'm famous.' That is it. It will certainly create a buzz. I've failed to give any proper notice, my actions are totally bereft of professionalism and it almost certainly means that I will never work in the industry again. But that suits me. If there is no coming back, there can be no turning back.

The cab weaves in and out of heavy traffic, moving slowly north from LAX. I grip the wedding invitation in my hand and think of Roxy. It's less than an hour before her wedding. I figure she's probably sitting in front of a mirror right about now, doing her hair or her make-up. Outside dozens of waiters in silver vests are putting the finishing touches to the reception tables spanning the length of the lawn. Sunlight twinkles on the aqua-blue of a swimming pool. She'll be wearing white of course. Not fluffy meringue white, more of a snug, tailored ivory. With black shades and a pearl necklace.

But what about him? What is her fiancé like? Suntanned, fit, handsome? I picture him as a George Hamilton type, oily-handsome. I look at my watch again. The minutes are slipping away. Traffic has ground to a halt on the 405. I ask the cab driver how long he thinks it will take to get there. He laughs and shrugs and mumbles some madness about surfing in Malibu.

'Where you from anyways?' he asks. 'Australia?'

'England,' I say.

'England,' he repeats. 'I was close. I knew someone from England once. Tall guy, brown hair.'

He looks in the rear view mirror at me to see if I know who he's talking about. I shrug. 'Gee, what was his name?' he continues. 'Chris I think. Yeah. Chris something. From England. Nice guy.'

He looks at me again. England has a population close to 60 million but he still expects me to know everyone there, at least every bloke called Chris. I shrug. He seems disappointed. 'You on vacation or here to stay?'

'I don't know, really,' I say. 'I want to be a screenwriter and–'

He lets out a sudden snort. 'Ahh, you're here to stay,' he says. 'I'm a writer too.' He leans forward to open the glove box and pulls out a huge manuscript, about ten or twelve inches thick.

'My book,' he says. 'I started it ten years ago. 'Bout halfway through.'

'Ten years?' He's serious. 'What's it about?'

'It's about nuclear fusion,' he says with a straight face. 'Explains all the equations. Combine x with z over four to get T seventy-eight.'

'What's T?' I ask.

'Can't tell you,' he says. 'See, this is an ideas town. You got a good idea, there's always someone who wants to steal it. You know nuclear physics?'

He glances in the rear view mirror and I shake my head. 'CIA were researching it in the desert,' he continues. 'Had to close it down through budget cutbacks.' He holds up the manuscript again. 'Would've cost them over three and a half million bucks to find out all this. Now I'm the only one who knows. See, cab driving is just a sideline. 'Till I finish the book.'

I look at my watch again and tune him out. He's rattling off more improbable equations and chuckling to himself but I'm more concerned about the time. Roxy will be in the back of the white limo right about now, pulling up outside the church. She'll chew on her bottom lip as she so often does. Then she'll have to frantically check her lipstick. The door will open and she'll emerge, film star-confident, embracing the camera flashes, basking in the attention.

The cab rounds a tight bend somewhere off Montana. And we pull up across from the chapel. It's larger than I had imagined. Not as regal. But the limo is out front. It's white and it's empty. Roxy is already inside. A wave of icy-cold sweat suddenly flushes over me. What had played out in my head so easily is now so real. And so very far from being easy. Dozens of cars fill the adjacent parking lot. There are hundreds of people in there. Hundreds of pairs of eyes will be fixed on me and no one will be secretly rooting for the scruffy Englishman. What the hell am I thinking?

The cabby's growing impatient. He probably needs another fix. I pay him an extra twenty to wait, but doubt that he will. His glassy eyes and nuclear fusion/CIA gibberish suggest he is less than reliable. I straighten my shirt and snatch a glance at my reflection in the glass partition. My eyes are bulging with fear but the adrenaline pumping through my veins has banished any trace of jet lag.

I edge up to the chapel door. *The Wedding March* fades as I approach. Roxy will be at the altar now. Standing next to the George Hamilton person, chewing her lip again. I try to follow the ceremony from outside. I can just make out the priest's monotone voice. I decide to wait for the moment when he asks if anyone knows of any reason why these two people should not be joined in matrimony. That's my cue. The priest drones on. I shift uncomfortably. Then a dreadful thought suddenly strikes me. What if they don't do that 'does anyone know any reason why' bit at wedding ceremonies in America? Why had I presumed they'd be the same as in England? I can't wait out here and miss my chance.

I pull down the sunglasses from the top of my head – I don't want anyone to see the fear in my eyes – and push open the door. It opens directly into the red-carpeted chapel. A few people in the last row steal glances back at me. I duck behind a large speaker in the corner and peek at the altar. And there is Roxy, her face shielded in a white veil and the George Hamilton next to her. Only he isn't a George Hamilton at all. He's a lot younger and not a handsome man by any means. He's more of a Steve Buscemi: crooked teeth and google eyes. I swell with confidence. For about three seconds. And then the priest says it. 'Does anyone here present know of any reason why these two people should not be joined in holy matrimony?'

Only all I hear is the 'Does anyone here' part. And the rest passes like a dream. If it was a movie, it would have to be shot in slow-motion, like the baby carriage dropping down the station steps in *The*

Untouchables. I'm aware of the syrupy sweat trickling from my brow and caking the rest of my body. My under-shorts are pasted against the inside of my thigh and I desperately want to adjust myself, maybe even scratch a little, when the priest hands me my cue.

I step from behind the speaker and yell out. I'd like to say it is a stirring, heroic yell, but my throat is dry with fear and I kind of just croak out her name. And I tell her that I love her. It's innocent and soppy and heartfelt. And Roxy turns to me and I wait for her to run to me, to jump into my arms, to add the happy ending. But she just pushes up her veil and screams. And all I keep thinking is, why put so much bright red carpet inside a church? And the unfamiliar face under the veil continues screaming and screaming at me. And then other faces crowd in and the red carpet swallows me up.

I wander back to Montana in a daze. I want to be back in London. I don't like America one bit. Several buttons have been torn from my shirt and the side of my face stings. Some of Steve Buscemi's friends threw me out of the church. I figure they spared me a more severe beating when they saw the wedding invitation in my hand. It was obvious the mistake was genuine. Mulholland not Montana. I make plans there and then to track down that fat, laughing, junkie cab driver and kill him. Three and a half million bucks worth of nuclear fusion equations will die with him. I look at my watch. By now, the *other* wedding will be over. And Roxy will be married.

I walk into a grocery store for something to drink. But I just keep pushing the cart up and down aisles filled with strange-sounding products like Corn Dogs and Quick Grits and Grape Nuts and somehow three hours pass before I notice the manager following me. 'Yes, can I help you?' he keeps saying. The other staff eye me warily. I grab a bottle of water and head for the checkout.

Two girls are standing in line ahead of me, their cart full of beer and wine and Bacardi and lemons. They turn as I wheel up with my single bottle of water.

'How do you turn a fox into an elephant?' they both ask me at the same time.

I stare at them a moment, trying to figure it out. 'Is it a joke or something?'

'Yeah, it's a joke,' the taller one laughs. 'Where are you from–'

'Australia, right?' the other one says.

'England. London.'

'So how long you been in LA?'

'What you doing here? You an–'

'Actor? Or a–'

'Director?'

'Or a writer?'

They speak like a nightclub double-act, finishing off each other's sentences. It's like trying to have a conversation with a pinball machine. They introduce themselves as Bubble and Squeak, names they think any Englishman should immediately find hilarious. Bubble is the smaller of the two, pale and wiry and softly spoken, the Chong to Squeak's Cheech. Squeak is a livewire. She's a handsome nurse with a deep tan and infectious laugh. They are both from Philadelphia, have known each other for years and now live together in West LA. And they're having a party.

I swap the water for a couple of bottles of vodka.
'So what's the punch line, anyway?' I ask.

'Punch line?' says Bubble.

'How do you turn a fox into an elephant?' Squeak prompts her.

'Oh, right.' Bubble starts.

'We don't know,' says Squeak, 'that's why we were asking you.'

'This guy keeps leaving the first half of jokes on our answer machine. It's driving us crazy trying to work out the punch lines.'

'So why don't you just call him back?' I say.

'No way,' says Bubble.

'That's why he does it,' says Squeak. 'So we'll call him.'

'The guy's a real cheeseball.'

'We met him in a drag bar downtown.'

'And he wrote his number on the back of his pay slip.'

'His pay slip! How cheesy's that?'

'Soooo cheesy,' says Bubble smiling. 'What a loser. Let's go party.'

Who am I to argue?

An hour later I am standing by a heart-shaped swimming pool in the middle of an apartment complex just off Santa Monica Boulevard drinking vodka shots and talking to a girl in a red dress and black Doctor Marten's. She looks like a model down on her luck and talks like a self-help guru. Her face is fixed in a constant smile. I can't work out if she's deliriously happy, badly constipated or suffering a rare side effect to the barrel load of collagen that's recently been pumped into her lips. She asks me what I'm doing in LA. I tell her I have a thing for

American women. The smile doesn't waver. She asks me if I want to go up to her apartment and see her pet snake. I'm not sure if there's some Freudian meaning to this that I've missed, but agree anyway.

No, she really means a pet snake. I stare at an empty cage by the kitchen door. The snake must've escaped, she decides. It does that sometimes. She shrugs and hands me a bottle of olive oil and a roll of cellophane. I can't work out how this is going to help catch a seven-foot python.

'No, you wear it,' she says, like that should somehow explain it all. 'It's very good for the skin.'

I always thought it was healthy to eat a salad not dress like one. Then she removes the red dress. She turns her back to me and I stare down at her naked shoulders and the soft curve of her bum. She's not wearing any underwear.

Like most guys, I've been fortunate enough to experience a few inexplicably great moments with women I've just met, but never regularly enough to ever make me take a moment like this for granted. I figure it's probably the accent that's induced her to suddenly behave like she's in a men's body spray commercial. Or maybe she just recognises that I'm the male lead in this movie, the one writing itself furiously inside my head, and well, this is just what happens to male leads. Either way, I figure I'll do my best to forget about the seven-foot python lurking somewhere in the room and see where this leads. I pour the oil over her naked body and wrap the cellophane around her and don't think about snakes or Roxy for the rest of the evening.

LA's like that. When something bad happens there's always something good lurking around the next corner waiting to cheer you up. It's like a self-healing mechanism that keeps the whole city constantly cheerful. God understands that no one in LA has the constitution to deal with unpleasantness. That's why the weather here is always a balmy seventy degrees. The American Dream is a fair weather creature.

Former Dot-Com Shifts From E-Biz to G-Strings

Web Site Helps Jailbirds Get Back Together

Pennsylvania Reverend burns Harry Potter Books in the name of God

Reuters.com headlines

I need to devise a plan for my search. I can't just rattle around the Net and hope to stumble on the American Dream, so I start by checking out the news sites in the hope of gleaning a few clues from the morning's headlines. Then it suddenly dawns on me that by plugging in the URL AmericanDream.com I could save myself a month's work.

Alas, AmericanDream.com is home to the world's largest shopping mall, a Canadian one at that. I toy with the notion that the American Dream has indeed migrated north and is hiding out in a ladies' shoe store near Montreal, but the ramifications are too awful to contemplate. The American Dream with a French-Canadian accent. Dear God.

I try a few variations on the address: AmericanDream.co.uk sells jukeboxes, American-Dream.com and .net are under construction. A search on

Google for 'American Dream' uncovers little more than e-commerce sites for real estate and recreational vehicles.

It's not the most auspicious start to my search but then this is only Day Two. I have many more to go. I am in it for the long haul. To hell with the obvious places, I decide. If the American Dream is somewhere so obvious that someone like me can find it in a couple of days, it would never have been lost in the first place. And it is lost, of that much I am certain. With Pennsylvania reverends burning books, you can be sure the American Dream is not where it should be.

Thankfully, there's room for everything on the Net so I'll just have to look everywhere: every news site, every lame personal web page, every porn site, every chat room, every last forgotten bit of flotsam floating through cyberspace.

If the American Dream is out there, by God, I intend to find it.

Incoming Email:

> To: <BritWriter>
> From: <Nervous>
> Subject: Re: Call of the Wild
>
> Thought the following might give you a chuckle. It does mention French people – but only very briefly and there's nothing to suggest they're short.
> Happy hunting,
> Nervous

The following people are stranded on desert islands in the middle of nowhere:
2 Italian men and 1 Italian woman
2 French men and 1 French woman
2 German men and 1 German woman
2 Greek men and 1 Greek woman
2 English men and 1 English woman
2 Bulgarian men and 1 Bulgarian woman
2 Japanese men and 1 Japanese woman
2 American men and 1 American woman

One month after being stranded, the following things have occurred on the islands:
One Italian man has killed the other Italian man for the Italian woman.
The two French men and the French woman are living happily together in a ménage-a-trois.
The two German men have a strict weekly schedule of when they alternate with the German woman.
The two Greek men are sleeping with each other, and the Greek woman is cleaning and cooking for them.
The two English men are waiting for someone to introduce them to the English woman.
The Bulgarian men took a long look at the endless ocean and one look at the Bulgarian woman and then started swimming for home.
The two Japanese men have faxed Tokyo and are waiting for instructions.
The two American men are contemplating the virtues of suicide, while the American woman keeps on bitching about her body being her own, the true nature of feminism, how she can do

everything that they can do, about the necessity of fulfilment, the equal division of household chores, how her last boyfriend respected her opinion and treated her much nicer, and how her relationship with her mother is improving. But at least the taxes are low, and it's not raining.

Incoming Email:

>To: <BritWriter>
>From: <gifts@1-800-4champagne.com>
>Subject: Confirmation of your order
>
>Your Order # is 746881-S
>Veuve Clicquot Champagne, Gift Wrapped, Quantity 1
>Next day delivery, New York
>A reminder: Federal Law requires that both you and your gift recipient must be at least 21 years of age.
>Thank you for using 1-800-4champagne.com!

Byte 3 – Hollywood Ending

Incoming Email:

> To: < BritWriter >
> From: < Abby >
> Subject: The Big 3-0
>
> OK, so I've been travelling all week with what feels like double pneumonia, my car died on the interstate, I'm turning 30, and this is the scene of my last 24 hours (please don't use it in one of your screenplays):
>
> EXTERIOR. MANHATTAN STREET – DAY
> After a gruelling five-hour flight from 'Frisco and a two-hour traffic jam leaving the airport, I finally arrive back at my apartment. The Indian cab driver turns to hand me my change.
> CAB DRIVER: You no married?
> ME: No.
> CAB DRIVER: How old?
> ME: I'm 29. 30 tomorrow.
> CAB DRIVER: Oh, no. You look at least 35.

Maybe cause dat you have a big body.

CUT TO:

INTERIOR. KITCHEN – THIS MORNING
The stick-thin Russian cleaning lady has just finished the laundry and she looks me up and down as she's getting ready to go.
MAID: You gaining weight?
ME: (panicked) I don't know? Am I?
MAID: Yeah. You look bigger in the hips.
ME: I've been sick and travelling a lot . . not exercising so much . . you know . . summer's coming, I'll lose it.
MAID: Yeah. You better. It's not good look for you.

Fuck me. I'm never eating again.
Abby
P.S. Thanks for the champagne!

Outgoing Email:

To: <Abby>
From: <BritWriter>
Subject: Re: The Big 3-0

Happy birthday! What's all this fat nonsense about? You may be a number of things, Abby (unhinged, 30, an alien abductee) but fat ain't one of 'em.

'Weight, David, is a feminist issue.'
'Why?'

> *'I don't know, but it just is.'*
> *— The Full Monty*

PS. Spare me this madness and tell me where the American Dream is.

Incoming Email:

> To: <BritWriter>
> From: <Abby>
> Subject: Re: The Big 3-0
>
> It's in the worm at the bottom of a bottle of tequila. Or at least it sometimes seems that way. I'm drinking the champagne now. Have bookmarked the magazine web site to keep up with your column. Seems strange, like hearing your voice every morning.
> Abby

Outgoing Email:

> To: <Abby>
> From: <BritWriter>
> Subject: Re: The Big 3-0
>
> Is hearing my voice every morning a good thing or a bad thing? At least you don't have to hear it if you don't want to, right.

Incoming Email:

> To: <BritWriter>
> From: <Abby>

Subject: Re: The Big 3-0

I don't know (whether it's good or bad). It's just strange, that's all.

Incoming Email:

To: <BritWriter>
From: <Abby>
Subject: Re: The Big 3-0

Sorry. That last email sounded rude. Of course it's good to hear your voice. I'm just tired, been having a hard time of it lately. Travelling is getting me down. Thinking about moving. New York's making me hard.

Outgoing Email:

To: <Abby>
From: <BritWriter>
Subject: Re: The Big 3-0

And your last check-up?

Incoming Email:

To: <BritWriter>
From: <Abby>
Subject: Re: The Big 3-0

Being online all day is going to drive you nuts, you know that don't you. I've told you before – words are not substitutes for people.

Outgoing Email:

> To: <Abby>
> From: <BritWriter>
> Subject: Re: The Big 3-0
>
> Don't be evasive.

Incoming Email:

> To: <BritWriter>
> From: <Abby>
> Subject: Re: The Big 3-0
>
> Not too good. Liver panel was all wrong and my white cell count was too high, red too low. Went for a re-test. They're supposed to call me with the results today or tomorrow. Trying not to think about it.
> You arranged some medical insurance yet?

A cold shiver barrels down my spine. Medical insurance. Bugger. I woke up this morning with a dull pounding behind my eyes and an ugly rash around my groin which I foolishly assumed were respective side effects of sitting in front of a computer screen without wearing my glasses and sleeping with a grubby barmaid from the Valley last week without wearing a full-body bio-hazard suit. Now the Woody Allen paranoia hackles are up and I've got three hours to live and no medical insurance. Then I feel guilty, guilty in a way that Woody Allen's characters never seem to. My neuroses seem even more pathetic in the light of what Abby's going through. I imagine her sitting at home on her own, waiting for a phone call that could spin her life out of all recognition. I can almost hear the rain tapping against the window as she sips champagne and eyes the five blue reminders tattooed on her leg and wonders if it's time, if the doctors were right after all.

At the age of fourteen, she feels a sharp pain running the length of her left leg. The doctor says it's a muscle strain, she should rest and maybe take an aspirin. But even to a fourteen-year-old it doesn't much feel like a muscle strain; it's too painful, too persistent. Two years and five doctors later she finally has an MRI. The scan reveals a malignant tumour in the muscle tissue of her thigh. She has Alveolar Soft Part Sarcoma, a rare cancer that attacks the tissue of the legs and abdomen and often spreads to the bones and brain. It takes two surgeries to remove the tumour, another to replace the muscle so she can extend the leg, then six months of radiotherapy to mop up the remaining cancer cells. Rather than have the doctors realign the radiation machine at the beginning of each treatment, she agrees to have a line of blue dots permanently tattooed on her leg.

By the time the doctors finish, it looks like a shark has taken a mouthful out of her thigh. But she is alive. Still, the prognosis isn't good: two out of six patients with the disease survive for a year; one out of six for as long as five years. Beyond that, things look bleak. All she can think of is living long enough to taste champagne on her twenty-first birthday.

Today, on her thirtieth, she's tasted birthday champagne more times than anyone expected and the only reminders are the scars, the tattoo marks and an annual check-up with the oncologist. She is lucky; or blessed; or deserving, depending on how you view such things as being decided.

As an experiment, I plug her symptoms into the diagnostic program at the Harvard Medical School site. It suggests there may be a serious problem and she should visit a physician immediately. I feel relieved. What it took five doctors two years to determine now takes less than two minutes on the Internet.

Cancer. Just the word resonates with doom. Someone said it kills in only two ways. Quickly and slowly. For my older sister, Katie, it has all the speed of a tortoise ageing. She's thirty-three at the end but has been dying for nearly three years.

The last time I see her is on a Friday evening in late February. She's back at our parents' house in St Albans, back in the room she'd gown up in as a child. The doctor is just leaving as Roxy and I pull up, edgy from the rush hour commute out of London. It's near the end, the doctor tells us. Hope is gone; it's now just a matter of time. Deep down we'd all known for months that any chance of remission was slim but secretly we'd been clinging to the faintest of hope, holding out for a Hollywood ending.

I tell my parents to take a break, to get some air; Roxy and I will sit with Katie. My father's eyes are red from crying, tears still fresh on his cheeks. I've never seen him cry before. It makes my heart ache just to look at him. He takes my mother's hand and lures her and the dog outside for a walk.

Katie's asleep. I pace her bedroom, moving in and out of the evening shadow. Her hair is shredded from chemo, her face wizened and drawn. Her left arm lays draped over the covers, the morphine plunger attached to her wrist like a pass to some foetid nightclub. I want to rage. I want *her* to rage. But it is not to be. She is facing death with the same passive equanimity that she faced life. Roaring and raging at the inevitable will not bring comfort to anyone.

'You know what I regret most?' she says, suddenly awake.

Her once crackling green eyes are fading like dusk and even her precise enunciation has withered. She sounds how she looks: on the brink. 'The places I never went to,' she says. 'Africa, Antarctica, Los Angeles. There were so many places I never got to see. Can you believe I never went to LA?'

I fight back tears and nod lamely. For weeks now I've been renting travel videos from the local library, videos of places she's been to but wants to see again – Rome, Athens, Sydney – and those she's only ever dreamed of: Rio, Tokyo, Cape Town. And LA. I spend whole weekends watching them with her, one after the other, each accompanied by her rasping narration: how she watched the sun set by the Trevi Fountain in Rome or the streets of New York she recognises from *Annie Hall* and *Taxi Driver* and *The French Connection*.

I drop next to her on the bed and clutch her fragile hand. The skin is pallid and clammy, like candle wax on an autumn branch.

'You want to watch a video?' I ask. 'We haven't seen the one on Shanghai yet.'

She shakes her head. 'I want to see a movie,' she says.

I check my watch; the local video store closes at seven. 'At the cinema,' she says. '*Aliens* is showing at the Odeon.' She's serious. Mum and dad would never allow it of course, which is why she's asking me, now, while they're out.

'We'll leave them a note,' she says, anticipating my objection.

I stare at her. '*Aliens*?' is all I can manage, the single word laced with incredulity, partly because I can't believe she's really considering going out and partly because I hate sequels.

'You know, I was talking about you with my therapist the other day,' I say.

'Oh, yes?'

'Yeah. He reckons the strong influence you exerted over me as a child is the reason why I've allowed women to dominate me in later life.'

'Nonsense,' she says. 'I forbid you from seeing him again.' And she breaks out into a broad smile and then rasps and coughs.

I know I have to take her.

Roxy helps me to dress her. The bones protruding from her nightshirt take us both by surprise. She's half the weight she was just a few weeks ago. I carry her to the car and she feels like she could break at any moment. Her birdlike limbs twitch with cold and the electronic plunger on her wrist whirs softly, pumping morphine into her bloodstream. She's hurting.

Roxy drives and I sit with Katie in the back. Moonlight claws through the rear window, circling her frame, emphasising her frailty. Roxy's the only person who would ever consider this a good idea.

I wonder if I would have even tried it without her.

Fortunately, the cinema's half-empty. I seat Katie at the back nearest the aisle and drape my jacket over her. She grimaces as she shifts in her seat and presses the plunger on her wrist. It whirs and she relaxes into the hit of morphine. I ask her if she's OK. She forces a smile. 'I want to stay, if that's what you mean,' she says, still the big sister talking down to her kid brother.

'Just let me know if you want to go,' I say.

'Sssssh,' says Roxy the other side of me. 'It's starting.'

Katie winks at me and rests her bony hand on mine.

The first act of the film is everything I had been dreading: clunky dialogue and macho posturing from the marine characters, coupled with the all-too-regular whir of Katie's morphine. I monitor her breathing, counting the seconds between each breath. Four, five. Sis? Rasp. Her fragile chest heaves and she breathes.

More B-movie dialogue. Bill Paxton to female marine: 'Do you ever get mistaken for a man, Vasquez?'

Vasquez: 'No, do you?'

Then, by the time the nest of aliens wriggles to life, Katie's breathing and morphine appetite have settled down and I'm totally engrossed in the film.

'This is great,' I whisper to Katie.

'Told you,' she smiles. 'Now Sigourney's going to kick some ass.'

Roxy drives back to my parents as fast as she dare. It's late and the roads are clear and the film went on a lot longer than any of us thought. My parents are going to kill me.

'Do you think they'll make a third one?' Katie says. 'A third *Alien* movie?'

'I hope so,' I say. 'That was so good.' She suddenly drops her head. 'What is it?' I ask.

She looks up and I see there are tears in her eyes. 'I just realised,' she says. 'If they do make another sequel, I won't ever get to see it.'

My parents run out as we pull into the drive. Neither of them look at nor speak to me. Instead they cover Katie with a blanket and carry her between them into the house. She turns to look at me from over my dad's shoulder. And smiles. Then the front door closes and she's gone. I can't face a scene with my parents so Roxy and I quietly head back to London.

We talk little. There's nothing to say. I'm secretly fantasising that Katie can somehow muster the strength to blast away at the tumours eating her body in the same way that Sigourney Weaver blasted away at the aliens. But by the time we get home there is already a message on the answer machine from my dad. His voice is barely recognisable.

'Call me,' he chokes. Then the line goes dead.

I don't need to call him. I already know. There is no Hollywood ending.

'People choose illusions,' Robert De Niro once said in an interview, 'and these illusions are created by movies.'

My illusion was that there was some link between Katie and Roxy. Roxy knew Katie; she was there that night, something no other girlfriend could ever claim. She's the only person who could possibly understand why the opening credits of *Alien 3* always bring tears to my eyes. Sure, it's a strange reason for impulsively shifting my life six thousand miles across the globe. But it's the only one I've ever been able to manage.

Byte 4 – Sun Up on Santa Monica Boulevard

The dazzling sunlight pouring through the open blinds wakes me up that first morning in LA. Cellophane Girl is lying next to me, still wrapped in a few strips of plastic wrap. I have a pounding headache and a bad taste in my mouth and I immediately regret that it's not Roxy lying there. The sheets feel damp with olive oil and sweat and there's an empty bottle of vodka next to the bed. I sit up and swing my feet over the edge, then remember the missing snake and quickly pull them back up again. I nudge Cellophane awake.

'Where's the snake?' I whisper.

'In its cage,' she grunts. 'Remember?'

I rub my head. No, I don't. She rolls over and slips an arm around me. 'That was a nice thing you did for Cleo,' she says. 'You're a sweet guy.'

Did I miss something? 'Who's Cleo?' I say. 'The snake?'

She sits up. 'My friend. You met her last night.' She stares at me, looking for a glimmer of recognition. There is none. I have no idea what she's talking about. 'You bought her car,' she prompts. Still nothing. Apparently the second half of the evening just passed me by without stopping to make even a cursory deposit at the memory bank.

Someone whistles from a passing car. I shield my eyes against the sunlight and pull Cellophane's pink satin robe tighter across me. And I stare at what can only be described as a huge heap of metal, parked at an odd angle outside the apartment building.

'How ... how much did I pay for it?'

'Seventy five hundred,' she says again. 'She wanted a thousand but you insisted she take more so she can start her web site.'

'Web site ...?'

'To reunite old lovers. You were very keen on the idea. You seemed adamant she take it.'

'Adamant? I was drunk.'

'Yeah,' she says. 'That too.'

I look down at the certificate of ownership in my hand. Apparently, the huge heap of metal is, in fact, a beige 1969 VW camper van with a rag top roof and two-speaker radio. I doubt it's worth $100, let alone $1,000 or the king's ransom I drunkenly ponied up for it. Strips of cardboard rest in lieu of glass in the side windows. There's no rear bumper but rather a rusty iron girder that someone has clumsily welded to the back. It's possible that the paint work was originally beige – maybe a decade or two ago, before it was engulfed in layers of white and puce primer – but it would take an autopsy from the automotive equivalent of *Quincy* to say with any certainty.

The last owner is listed as 'Petra Lader.'

'Who's Petra?' I ask Cellophane.

'Dunno,' she says, 'One of Cleo's aliases I guess.' She tells me how the handbrake came away in my fingers last night so Cleo replaced it with a house brick tied to a length of rope. 'She said you need to drop the brick behind the front wheel when you park to stop it rolling away.'

'That should be interesting when you valet park it in Malibu or Beverly Hills.' Bubble has ventured out to admire my purchase. Squeak, as ever, follows close behind, eyes squinting in the sun.

I open the side door and offer them a tour.

'The seat pulls out into a bed,' says Cellophane.

I try it. She's right. I feel marginally better. $7,500 for a $100 van with a foldout bed. At least I'll never be stuck for somewhere to sleep. I pull out a road map of North America and a worn copy of *Nineteen Eighty-Four* from under the mattress and wonder if there's any significance.

'What's this?' Bubble has hold of a black wig she's pulled out of a cupboard.

'Cleo,' Cellophane says. 'She likes to dress up, change her appearance.'

'I'm not surprised,' says Squeak. 'If she's involved in many deals like this.'

I fetch my trousers and my empty wallet and get behind the wheel.

'Where are you going?' says Cellophane.

'To look up that girl I told you about.'

Cellophane frowns. 'Isn't she married?'

I shrug and start the engine. It farts like a baby. I pull out the choke and try again. Another baby fart. On the third attempt it finally springs to life with all the verve of a two-stroke lawnmower engine.

Bubble and Squeak can barely contain their laughter. 'You know its got out-of-state plates, right?' Bubble says.

'No. What does that mean?' I ask.

'It isn't registered,' she says.

'Great.'

'And you haven't got any insurance?' says Squeak.

'No. How do I get insurance?'

'You need a licence,' says Bubble.

'OK. Where do I go to get a licence?'

'The DMV,' says Squeak.

'Nearest one's in Santa Monica.'

'But you need to have a green card or a work permit.'

My head flits between the two of them as they volley off instructions. 'So I'm screwed then?' I say.

'Yep,' says Bubble.

'Welcome to America,' says Squeak. 'Just don't get pulled over.'

I can't do anything but laugh. Cellophane says I must be crazy and goes inside to feed the snake. Bubble tells me to stop by later if things don't work out with Roxy.

'You're welcome to stay with us,' Squeak says. 'Seeing as you've got no money left for a hotel.'

'And that bed doesn't exactly look comfortable,' says Bubble.

'My cousin once stayed for three months,' Squeak adds. 'It'll be fun.' I thank them for the offer and say I'll keep in touch whatever happens. I then pull up the house-brick handbrake and tentatively steer the huge heap of white and puce metal into the traffic.

I hunt for the RSVP address on the wedding invitation Roxy had given me. It takes me most of the morning to find it, hidden on a side street just off Wilshire Boulevard at the edge of Beverly Hills. But it's not a house or an apartment or even an office. It's a mailbox.

I try the phone number listed on the invite. It's a voicemail. I don't recognise the voice but leave a message anyway. Then I wait half an hour and try again. I leave another message, this time including Bubble and Squeak's telephone number.

I drive the camper van back to their apartment in West LA and sit by the phone and wait for it to ring.

Much like Abby has spent the last couple of days.

Outgoing Email:

> From: <BritWriter>
> To: <Abby>
> Subject: Re: The Big 3-0
>
> Have you heard anything yet? Let me know if you do. I'm sure everything will be OK.

After a check-up when she is twenty-six, Abby is so convinced the cancer has returned that she sits in a bar all day, waiting for the doctor to call, easing her nerves with strawberry margaritas. The call never comes so she drives home in the rain, drunk. Her cell phone rings and in her haste to undo her seatbelt to reach for it, she loses control of the car on the wet road. She hits the brakes, the wheels lock into a skid and the car mounts the sidewalk and ploughs into a wall. Abby catapults through the windshield and lands twenty yards away. Paramedics have to revive her twice on the way to the hospital. Surgeons work on her for fourteen straight hours to save her life. It then takes another eight operations over the next three years to reconstruct her face. She takes twelve months off work after the crash to recuperate then, in her first week back, she boards a flight to Europe for a sales conference. A fire erupts in one of the engines during take off and the plane has to make an emergency landing. Abby is the last passenger on board when fire billows through the hull. Miraculously, she escapes again, with only minor burns where her stockings melted onto her legs.

'You're Captain Scarlet,' I like to tell her. 'Indestructible.' But she never knows what I'm talking about.

Incoming Email:

> To: <BritWriter>
> From: <J2>
> Subject: Voice Message
>
> You have one new voice message.
> Click to download

While I'm online I forward my phone to an Internet voicemail number so voice messages are emailed to me as electronic files. This one is from Abby. Her voice echoes, like she's calling from the bathroom or under the bedcovers.

'I know you can't answer this but I couldn't face typing it. The doctor called.' She takes a breath. 'It's OK. The second test was better. They want me to come in and get tested a third time, but ... but they don't think they'll find anything. They think I'm anaemic. Just need to take some iron and vitamin supplements.'

Another pause while she catches her breath. 'Sorry. Take care. Bye.'

She hangs up, having beaten the prognosis by another year. And I'm filled with something that exceeds admiration.

Byte 5 – Rejecting Rejection

The Immigration and Naturalization Service web site estimates that there are about six and a half million illegal aliens living in the US, forty per cent of them in California. Hordes of Mexican immigrants spend their days baking in the sun outside the DIY stores and van rental places, begging for work, dreaming of some better life. Arabs and Eastern Europeans head to Koreatown for fake drivers' licences and taxi permits and long summer nights getting lost on the LA freeway system. The British pubs in Santa Monica heave with ex-pat construction workers and nannies and wannabe actors and musicians who've all slipped in under the INS radar.

After six months in Los Angeles and a series of investment decisions to rival the purchase of a $100 van for $7500, I'm broke, my credit cards are max'd and my tourist visa has expired. Without a work visa I can't get a California drivers licence or insurance, so every time I hear a siren or glimpse a black-and-white in the rear-view mirror, my heart skips a beat and my forehead erupts in beads of icy sweat. I'm on the expressway to a stomach ulcer. Then there's my accommodation. I'm living in the walk-in closet off Bubble and Squeak's living room. Even though I haven't found Roxy, I still don't want to return to England. I just need work, any kind of work.

Bubble introduces me to a literary agent at a Halloween costume party. He's wearing a small table hanging from his waist with a lamp, a pair of women's panties and a condom attached.

'What d'you think of the costume?' he says, grinning widely to expose unnaturally white teeth. 'I'm a *one night stand.*'

He dissolves into hysterical laughter at this. He's a small man in his forties with wrinkle-free skin pulled taut across his face.

'He's had some work done,' Bubble whispers to me. 'Tell him he looks good.'

'You look ... good,' I say and he immediately stops laughing.

'You're damn right I do,' he says.

'This is the writer I was telling you about,' says Bubble. 'The English writer.'

'Aha.' He eyes me with suspicion then presses a business card into my hand. 'Drop by the office tomorrow,' he says. 'Bring something for me to read.'

He turns and moves on to another group of people by the buffet table. 'So whaddya think of the costume?' I hear him say. 'I'm a one night stand.' And he dissolves into hysterical laughter again.

I walk into his office the next afternoon clutching a script. He sits me down in front of his desk and reels off a well-worn spiel on the nature of the agent/writer relationship.

'I'll tell you what I can do for you and what I can't,' he says. 'I can get your work under the noses of the people who count. I can get my phone calls about you returned. And I can negotiate the best possible deal on your behalf. What I can't do is write the scripts for you. You're the writer, I'm the agent. Clear?'

I nod and he grabs my script and flicks through the pages, as if that will somehow provide him a mystical insight into its worth. 'So pitch it to me,' he says.

I swallow hard and begin. 'It's about a woman who comes to believe that her husband is an alien serial killer who's terrorising the city,' I start.

'An alien serial killer? I like it. But can the kids dig it?' he says. 'Is it hip?'

'Well ... ' I say. 'It's hip-ish.'

'And it's an upbeat ending, right? None of this limey, art house "let's make the audience suffer – kill the hero at the end" bullshit? Life's sad enough without spending two hours in a dark movie theatre being made to feel worse. We want happy. We want uplifting. We want action. We want American. Which means no frigging soccer, by the way. I know what you people are like.'

'It's an alien movie. There's no soccer,' I say.

'Cause no one over here gives a crap about fucking soccer,' he says. 'You look cut ... do you work out?'

I glance at the photo of his wife and kids on the desk and decide he's just making small talk.

He calls me the following Monday. He read my screenplay over the weekend and thinks he can sell it for hundreds of thousands of dollars.

'It's an outstanding script,' he says. 'I want to send

it to Sean Young. Maybe even *Jodie*. I wouldn't let it go for less than two hundred and fifty thousand.'

In the meantime, he says, he'll pay me cash to work part-time in his office as an assistant, answering phones and reviewing scripts. He also suggests I check out the web site of a unique LA employment agency called 'The Job Connection'. It proclaims to offer the 'weirdest jobs in Los Angeles', things like hot tub tender, gravedigger, shell sorter or dockhand. It's all low paying work, the kind of jobs no American or legal immigrant would ever consider. I sign up for a month's membership. The site is updated with new vacancies every afternoon. The first one I respond to is for a window cleaner at a chain of Venice Beach apartment buildings.

A hip twenty-something woman with a tie-dyed shirt and matching orange shades greets me at the door of the first building.

'Hi, I'm Suzy,' she says and hands me a bucket of cleaners and rags. I follow her up two flights of stairs and along a dark narrow hallway with fading pictures of movie stars and the faint aroma of incense.

'It's real simple,' she says in a West Coast drawl. 'We just have to clean the vacant apartments before we rent them out again.' She opens the door to an apartment and points to the windows. 'You've got long arms so you can reach outside as well. Cleaner on with one rag, off with another. Do all the windows in here, then apartment thirty-four at the end of the hallway, and number forty-one upstairs. Any questions?'

I shrug and go to speak, but she cuts me off. 'Good. Let me know when you're done.' And she's gone.

I look around at the old apartment. It's clean but weathered with old sash windows, the type I could imagine Scrooge leaning out of on Christmas morning. I try to slip one of the windows up but it jams half way. I jiggle it again. The moveable sash part is loose in the frame. I sit on the open ledge and start cleaning the outside of the adjacent window. I balance a bottle of cleaner on the ledge and buff the final pane with the clean rag. I stretch to reach a slight smear in the far corner and my elbow knocks the cleaner. It topples off the ledge. I bite my lip in horror as it drops and smashes clean through a car windscreen parked on the street below. Shit!

I grab the open window to haul myself inside. The window jiggles, wobbles and instead of moving up or down, slips out of the frame and starts to fall inward. I reflexively extend my leg in an attempt to catch it but the glass lands plumb on my outstretched shoe and shatters. I gasp again and the frame slips off my leg and hits the floor, spraying fragments across the room.

I stand up, crunching glass under my feet, and look around at the mess. I make a pathetic attempt to piece some of the shards back into the frame, but it's useless. The door swings open and I look up to see Suzy step into the room clutching the bottle of cleaner retrieved from the car. Her mouth hangs open in silent disbelief. My gaze moves from her back to the glass littering the room and I try to muster an explanation. But there is none.

'Dude,' she says at last. 'That's not what I had in mind ...'

The Job Connection office is a tiny, smoke-filled

space in West Hollywood, overflowing with ashtrays. Following the window-cleaning debacle, the owner thinks it important that I come in and meet him.

As I stand by the door he draws heavily on a cigarette and barks down the phone. 'Asshole!' And he hangs up. 'Prick,' he mutters and I look around, not sure if he's talking to me.

He's a heavy-set guy in his mid-forties, thinning hair pulled back in a ponytail, dark facial hair cut into a square beard, leaving his appearance somewhere between coffee house poet and child molester. I introduce myself and he waves me over to the chair in front of his desk. He stubs the cigarette out and flicks through a file while he lights another.

'You ever use a pizza oven?' he asks without looking up.

'No, but–'

'Need experience,' he says and flicks over the page.

I cough from the thick smoke. 'I didn't think anyone in LA smoked anymore?'

'They don't,' he says. 'I smoke enough for the whole city. You gotta die from something right?' He looks up from the file and starts to tell me about a script he's writing. 'It's a comedy about a man who discovers that cigarettes are a cure for AIDS. So one of his patients has to decide whether he wants to die from AIDS or smoke ten packets a day and die from cancer. Some dilemma, huh?'

He seems to find this concept hilarious. I'm not sure whether to take him seriously or not, so I just smile thinly.

'How's your sperm?' he says.

'Sorry?'

'Your sperm? Cum? Jizzum? Ever been a daddy?'
I shake my head in disbelief. 'You getting laid right now?' he continues. 'Huh? How often d'you jack off?'

I try to think of any possible reason why he's asking me this. He beats me to it. 'If you're healthy and you can fill a test-tube every coupla days, you can make yourself two hundred a week easy,' he says. 'Fertility clinics need quality donors. You went to college, right? No jacking off on the days in between though. And no sex. Unless she asks nicely, right?'

He can obviously tell from the less-than-enthusiastic look on my face that bashing my cods for a living isn't really for me.

'Ah, so you're an uptight Englishman. What about donating your organs, then? You know, the ones you don't need.'

'I think,' I say, 'that I probably need all of them right now.'

'Oh ... Kay ... What about driving a bus on St Paddy's day? You do drive, right?'

I nod. 'Do I need special insurance?'

'Not if you don't hit anything. Just remember to give the owner head a couple of times.' My mouth drops. He smiles. 'Relax, British guy,' he says. Then winks. 'Once'll be fine.'

The bus turns out to be a red double-decker straight off a London postcard, filled with a bunch of drunks expecting to be ferried between Irish bars all day. Somewhat inevitably I end up drinking as much as they do and have to abandon the bus and thirty angry Irishmen outside a pub on Sunset. Another driving job follows: chauffeuring movie execs to and from Burbank airport. But again this lasts for just one evening after I get lost three times and then run out of gas on a deserted stretch of Sepulveda.

Every day I log onto the Job Connection site and try something new. And each new job ends in disaster. I am a copywriter and apparently not much good at anything else. I dress up as a British policeman, complete with plastic truncheon, to operate the elevator at a wedding fashion show but am fired within an hour after I catch the train of a model's dress in the elevator doors. I am a sausage salesman, a security alarm salesman and, ironically enough, spend a week as an assistant to an immigration attorney.

I'm turned down for a position that involves wearing a full-body turkey outfit and standing outside a restaurant on Thanksgiving in favour of someone else with, and I quote, 'prior experience.' Then I spot a vacancy on the site for a résumé writer. I feel confident that finally this is something I can do that without cocking it up, so email my application immediately. The following afternoon I receive a standard rejection email. Undeterred I respond to the rejection with a rejection of my own:

Dear Sir,

Thank you for your recent email detailing your rejection of me for the position of Résumé Writer. I would like to take this opportunity to inform you of my rejection of your rejection.

These past six months I have been fortunate enough to receive a high number of quality job rejections. While yours was certainly of a very high calibre, I have found that there are other companies that have been significantly more qualified to reject me than you. It is with this in mind that I feel that your rejection of my services does not meet with my needs at this time and I shall, therefore, begin employment with your organisation effective immediately.

On behalf of myself, I do wish you every success in your future attempts to offer rejection to would-be employees.

An hour later, the owner of a chain of JobPro résumé offices calls me up, still chuckling. He thought the rejection email was very funny and has already forwarded it to all of his friends. He has an empty office in Glendale, he tells me, and he wants me to run it for him. And no, he doesn't need to see a work visa or social security number.

The office is buried deep in the San Fernando Valley and in truth the whole enterprise consists of little more than a desk, a Yellow Pages listing and a 200-year-old photocopier. Oh, and a client list of some of the weirdest people in Los Angeles. But I'm finally able to earn enough cash to cancel my membership to the Job Connection site and concentrate on writing another screenplay while Jodie's considering the alien script.

It's 7 pm, my eyes hurt and I have a splitting headache again. I can't find any aspirin in the apartment so I order some from a local online grocery service along with a twelve pack of beers, three bottles of wine and a litre of Absolut. Then I add a bottle of extra virgin olive oil and some cellophane just for old time's sake. Five solid days online is taking its toll. All I want to do now is crash out in front of a movie and relax, maybe even wrap myself up like an oily sandwich. I click on to iFilm and start downloading a film about two girls who get lost in the desert and 'unearth repressed sexual desires'. It's come to this: scanning low-budget movies for something that may or may not contain a lesbian love scene. The fact that I seem to be making little progress in my quest isn't helping my morale. Maybe I shouldn't spend so much time picking at the scabs of the past. It just emphasises the solitude of the present.

The doorbell rings. I peer through the peep hole in the door for a fish-eye view of a lanky youth wearing a plastic nose and whiskers, clutching two bags of groceries. He hovers a moment then rings the bell again. I left instructions for the order to be left on the doorstep but he's obviously holding out for a cash tip. In the street behind him, I can just make out a fuchsia-coloured Volkswagon adorned with a huge baseball cap and a pink tail in the shape of a bottle opener. The deliver guy's nose swells up to obscure my view as his face leans closer to the peep hole. I duck down, holding my breath, then realise how absurd this is. I'm hiding from a struggling actor condemned to travel the streets of Los Angeles dressed as a giant purple hamster. I'm used to hiding form the landlord on rent day but not from a psychedelic Disney reject.

I'm just about to shout something threatening when I hear him drop the bags and walk off. I wait a moment or two longer then, with the speed of a hooker disrobing, I pull open the door, drag the bags inside and slam it shut again.

Mmmm. Booze.

Bugger. The order's wrong. Instead of aspirin he's

given me laxatives; instead of vodka there's gin. And there's no wine. At least the beers are right, even if they're warm. And he wanted a tip?

I flip the top of a Heineken and return to the movie. After ten minutes of slow panning shots across the desert and even slower conversations oozing with teenage angst, it becomes clear that the film will need a plot twist of immense proportions to feature any kind of love scene, let alone the kind of deviance I'm hankering for.

To hell with the movie. I just want to sleep.

Byte 6 – Memo to the Editor

One hundred and forty-two emails in my inbox this morning; 109 of them are spam: *Add 2–4 inches on your penis; Find out anything about anyone – Now!; Make Money Fast!; I'm 17 and my panties have just fallen off; You've Won $1,000; Hot Sex; Hot Farmyard Action; Free Hawaiian Vacation; Eat Shit & Die.* [Delete, delete, delete]. My email address is out there for sure. Every spammer in the US has my email. And a few in Germany. *Ich Bien Helga; Viewen Mein Pussy; Hotten Sexen Bitter.* [Delete, delete, delete]. *Cheapest Viagra on the Net; Last All Night; I Want You Big Boy; Hey, Sexy Here's My Pic.* [Delete, delete, delete].

Amid the debris is an email from an ex-JobPro client, Karina, an Iranian lady who insists on calling me 'English.'

Incoming Email:

> To: <BritWriter>
> From: <Karina>
> Subject: Nurse Complain Letter

English, I try to send you email week ago but I mix up everything. Now I am taking courses. For email, that's the reason I am sending to you email. I mean this is my complain letter to hospital that I want be translated on proper English. If you want to make changes, additions, please does so, to make the letter very professional, very beautiful. And I beg you I mean, make all your efforts to write my complain letter. English, can you please email to me back I mean as soon as you can. Yes.

She used to sit in the JobPro office eating jars of raspberry jam while outlining endless complaint letters she wanted me to draft to Senators, Congressmen and even the President, usually about the poor service she receives in restaurants.

'And then waitress say this, English ... I mean and it isn't right meal ... and I want you to write I not order fries. Or I did, but then I mean I change my mind ... And English, be very sure you say it isn't right meal and I mean I don't order fries and they were being discrim – discr – you know, against me for they hate Iranian lady. I mean in America always same. And, English, I mean I not order fries ...'

What makes her suspect that the declining level of waitress service at her local Denny's diner is a pressing matter for the most powerful man on earth is hard to say. But she keeps him well informed on the subject nevertheless.

I haven't heard from her for several months. She's been taking care of her sick father and now wants me to write a letter to the California Governor complaining about his treatment in hospital. She also thinks it important to cc the President on this one as well. Just in case the Governor forgets to mention it to him when they next meet on the Denny's waitress issue.

If there is a person who should encapsulate the classic Horatio Alger vision of the American Dream, it's Karina. She came to the US from a country where she had few rights and even less money, a place where she was persecuted for her sex and for her religion. She now owns two houses in California, claims huge social security benefits for her work-shy husband and exchanges regular correspondence with half of Congress. And all she can do is complain about waitresses and nurses.

Dammit, Karina, no wonder the American Dream is missing. It's running scared, like a bunny from a corn field with a tail full of buckshot, terrified you'll write three hundred letters to the President complaining that the American Dream is a lazy, overpaid bigot and could he please wire up an extra chair next time he's executing a jail full of political dissidents and handbag thieves. The American Dream is being dismembered by the very people who used to embrace it: immigrants and politicians and idealistic writers. Of course I can't find it. It's no longer there to be found.

I want to write a different column. I need to come up with a new idea, one that doesn't involve me spending all day online on a futile quest.

I have just the thing.

Outgoing Email:

From: <BritWriter>
To: <Ralph>
Subject: Memo: Idea for My New Column

Nervous Bob was involved in a curiously sordid evening in Kentucky recently, one that began in the darkness of a low rent strip club and ended with a hunk of twisted automobile and three naked people being towed from a ditch outside Louisville airport. 'My homepage horoscope said it was a good day to make spur of the moment decisions,' was the only explanation he could muster. I told him to stop with such gibberish. He's a degenerate beast and deserves to be punished. Nevertheless, I agreed to ask some of the finest legal minds on the litigious West Coast to consider his landmark case, Gullible Sagittarius v Charlatan Astrologer.

According to a news wire out of Madras, thousands of Indian couples are booking banquet halls for 18 November, simply because astrologers have selected it as the luckiest day this year for getting married. Not to be outdone, star gazers here are turning like packs of rabid dogs to financial astrologers, who chart both the planets and stock prices, to gain a crucial investing edge. These sites would have you believe that volatile markets and tumbling tech stocks have less to do with global economics, unrest in the Middle East or oil price fears, than with the conjunction of Jupiter and Saturn in the Twelfth House. They could be right. It would at least explain why TV astrologers always look so affluent, fat and smug.

This is an ugly and unsettling trend to be sure, but there is something very comforting in the removal of all personal accountability. I can hear newly enlightened readers now: 'Goddamnit, our marriage didn't fail because I slept with your sister, darling, but because we were hitched on the wrong day. It would all have been so different had we done it on the Thursday. And it was the Moon in Cancer that flushed our life savings down the wazoo with eToys and Pets.com. It had nothing to do with me possessing all the financial acumen of a high-ranking Enron executive.'

This is where the idea for my new column comes in. A tech horoscope aimed at all the lost souls out there on the Net, searching for guidance and meaning in their Pentium-riddled lives. 'Today, Taurus, is a good day to surf around for some travel ideas; Leo, why not contribute to a newsgroup or write some killer code?; and Virgo, you've been putting it off for long enough, time to change your ISP and order a little something online for your cyber sweetie.' If nothing else, it should at least increase the magazine's circulation in India.

Despite having little knowledge of astrology, I remain the ideal candidate to write the magazine's Horoscope due to my wealth of experience. Some years ago a Webmaster asked me to write monthly forecasts for his site. He didn't care if I could string a sentence together, much less if I knew an earth sign from a fire sign. However, the forecasts remain posted on the site. They read like 'real' horoscopes and come complete with lucky numbers and lucky colours (which is apparently important to horoscope aficionados). 'Love blossoms in the peak of summer, Aries,' I wrote. 'Do something different on the fourth and amazing things could happen. It's "independence" day, so ditch the red housecoat, get out of the backyard and go liberate that special someone. By the end of the day, you should have plenty to celebrate.'

Absolute piffle, of course, but the good news is I can't be sued. The case of Gullible Sagittarius v Charlatan Astrologer resulted in a judgement for the Defendant, although Nervous maintains that was only because the hearing took place when Venus was in ascension in the Twelfth House.

Nervous Bob used to be a round, jolly account manager in London, now he is a round, jolly software executive in Louisville, Kentucky. His emigration experience was the exact opposite of my own. By the time he arrived on the shores of the US, he had a work permit, expense account, corporate apartment and a company car. A web-based headhunter helped him land a job in New York selling computer software. He refuses to divulge her name or URL, though, on the grounds that he slept with her after his final interview. All he will confirm is that, yes, once again, he did go ugly early. The job later brought him to LA, then on to Louisville. That was his style. His nerves could never have coped with a murky foray into illegality and uncertainty.

Now he's addicted to a daily dose of hogwash from online soothsayers. He's actually letting their words dictate the course of his day. He'll decline invitations because his horoscope advises against travel, or he'll insist on going out when the stars foretell he's likely to meet the woman of his dreams.

And it has all come to this .. this depravity and sordidness ..

Incoming Email:

> To: <BritWriter>
> From: <Nervous>
> Subject: My girlfriend
>
> Nokia mobile phone – $24.95
> Call to buddy in Louisville -$2.10
> Discovering my girlfriend is a prostitute – PRICELESS
> Mate, that's the latest and greatest from here. As well as discovering that she's not a nurse but rather a stripper at the local ale-and-tits-house, I have a very strong suspicion she's been doing sexual favours for cash! Why do American women do this to us? Can't they just play fair? I miss London. I miss the time when I'd never heard of this girl or that Louisville strip joint.
> Reminds me of Roxy.
> Nervous

Roxy.
Roxy, Roxy, Roxy.

Byte 7 – The Crypt

It takes me about six months to find Roxy. I meet her again after she sends my parents an anniversary card and includes her email address. I think about it for nearly a week and draft more than a dozen different emails before I finally click 'send'. She doesn't email me back but the next Friday morning she turns up on the doorstep.

It's eight o'clock and I'm already halfway through my second Van Damme video of the day. The previous night I was out bar-hopping with Cellophane Girl. We meet a producer who specialises in straight-to-video action films. When I tell him I'm a screenwriter, he asks me if I have an action script.

'Yeah,' I lie. 'But it's back in England.'

He asks how long it will take to get it sent over. 'About a week,' I say.

'Great. Then drop it round next Friday and I'll give it a read.'

Now I have seven days to write a low-budget bombs-and-badger flick. We leave the bar and rent a pile of action films from Blockbuster. Cellophane watches the first one with me that morning, peering out from the foldout mattress in my closet-come-bedroom. Then she decides to start the 'angina' conversation again.

'What are your feelings towards me?' she asks suddenly.

I do have a slight hangover/action movie-induced stiffy but know that isn't what she means.

I shrug. 'You know.'

'Why won't you ever talk about your feelings?'

I sigh. We've been through this before. I never know what she wants me to say. I like her, she's cool and we have a laugh together (though not always at the same time).

'This is very difficult for me,' she goes on, 'being with someone who won't share his feelings.'

'Sorry,' I say.

'Well?'

'Well what?'

'What are your feelings?'

'You know.'

'No, I don't.'

I shrug and squirm and go to slip in the second video. She pulls it from my hand and stares at me with the question hanging in the air. 'I don't know what you want me to say.'

'How you feel.' God, this is uncomfortable. 'OK,' she says. 'You're a writer. Why don't we both write down our feelings?'

I start to laugh. 'You want me to write down my feelings?'

'Why is that so funny?'

'I dunno, it just is,' I say. 'Go on then. You go first.'

'No,' she shakes her head, 'because you won't do

it then.' I smile. 'Write them down later today,' she says, 'and I'll do the same and we'll swap.'

I'm laughing again. The whole notion of writing down my feelings just seems so ... ridiculous. I feel ... happy. I feel ... hungry. I feel ... horny. I feel every emotion beginning with h.

She stands up to leave. That's the end of this morning's angina conversation. 'You're not going to watch the next one?' I ask.

'Naa,' she says, 'all the violence is harshing my mellow. And I gotta feed the snake. I'll call you later.'

On her way out she indicates one of my screenplays sitting on the floor. 'Can I read it?' she says. 'I'm sure it's brilliant and I won't understand it. But I'd like to read it anyways.'

I smile. She's convinced that just because I have a British accent, I must somehow be more intelligent than anyone else. It's a misconception I've been slow in correcting. Despite her flighty persona and plastic lips, she has a real thirst for knowledge and loves to read. The first time we go out, she asks me to list my favourite authors. I rattle off a few names, the only one of which she recognises is George Orwell. The next time I see her, she proudly announces she's read both *Coming Up for Air* and *Nineteen Eighty-four*.

Nineteen Eighty-four was OK,' she says. 'Except for the title. He should've made it a date in the future. And the other one, it was just about a guy going fishing. Bo-ooring.'

I tell her I think there's a little more to it than that, but she isn't convinced, so she decides to tackle plays: *A Midsummer Night's Dream* and now my alien-serial killer script. I just hope she doesn't try to compare the two.

I hand her a copy of the script and she blows me a kiss and her Doctor Marten's march her out of the apartment.

A few minutes later Van Damme sends a bad guy crashing down some prison stairs and the doorbell rings. Bubble and Squeak are both at work so I expect it to be Cellophane returning to see the riveting conclusion of *Death Warrant*.

'Hi,' Roxy says. 'I got your email.'

And my mouth drops open. She's wearing thigh-high boots and a raincoat unbuttoned to the waist. It's obvious that underneath the coat she's naked save for a few strands of black underwear. There's a loud explosion on the TV behind me and for a moment I think it's my groin spontaneously combusting. I hold the door open and she steps inside.

My conscience raps on the inside of my head like an angry landlord on a squatter's door. *No, no, no,* it keeps telling me. *This is another man's wife. What kind of bad karma is it going to be if you – Oh, Lordy*! She slips the raincoat off and drops it to the floor. The voice falls silent and we fuck 'til noon.

She's left her husband and wants somewhere to stay. I wonder how Bubble and Squeak will feel about a second person living in their closet.

'I looked around for you,' she says as we lie next to each other on the foldout mattress. 'At the altar. You can see me in the wedding video, standing in front of the priest peering around the church. I really expected you to come rushing in.'

I tell her about interrupting the wrong wedding. She laughs.

'Maybe there's some higher force trying to keep us

apart? I mean, apart from junkie cab drivers. Maybe it just isn't meant to be.'

We lie in the closet for the rest of the day. Talking and screwing. Then Roxy decides she wants to go out for a drink. I tell her I don't know any place that has a dress code of thigh-high boots and black lacy underwear. She smiles her dangerous smile. She knows plenty such places.

She logs on to the Net and pulls up the web site of New York's infamous Vault nightclub housed in an abandoned subway station deep below lower Manhattan's meatpacking district.

'My friend's just opened something similar in LA,' she says as I stare open-mouthed at the screen. 'Their web site isn't up yet, but you wanna go check it out?'

Within the hour, we are carrying six-packs of beer along a dark alley in Venice Beach looking for a club called The Crypt. It's hidden in the vast basement of a derelict pub that was used to smuggle liquor into LA during prohibition. I palm eighty dollars to the doorman and he slips me a printed flyer outlining the rules of the club: 'The Crypt is a safe sex club,' it reads. 'This means no fellatio, no vaginal or anal intercourse, no exchange of bodily fluids, no drawing of blood.' That seems to rule out everything I generally associate with sex (and then some).

In the first of a myriad of dingy, stone-floored rooms, an older woman with exposed sagging breasts presides over a masturbating competition: two naked men beat themselves furiously to see who can ejaculate first. A polite smattering of applause from the circle of viewers greets the first drops as they hit the plastic sheeting covering the floor. A bearded man wearing only black ankle socks and polished loafers walks past. He's pulling on his flaccid manhood. I squirm nervously and grasp Roxy's arm. She smiles, relishing my discomfort.

I chug down a six pack, one after the other, hoping that the alcohol might put me at ease. We move on to the next room. A girl in a steel cage pleasures herself while a buxom dominatrix services a blindfolded man strapped to a wooden rack. She scrapes his testicles with what looks like a leather-handled cheese-grater. He yells out in pain. I feel nauseous and retreat to the bathroom. Next to the stalls a naked dwarf stands in a tin bath, ankle-deep in urine. He tells me I can piss on him for twenty bucks. I decline. Sexy lingerie and melted chocolate have always been my primary turn-ons. Dwarfs and urine just don't have the same appeal.

I leave the bathroom and find Roxy talking to her friend who owns the club. She's a middle-aged Hispanic, stark naked, stoned and tired looking. Rolls of fat are creased around her middle like a heavy mat pushed against a wall. She tells Roxy how great it is to have three guys performing oral sex on her at the same time. The bearded guy in the socks and loafers brushes past me again, still tugging on his little penis. No amount of beer is ever going to make this a comfortable experience. I grab Roxy's arm and pull her towards the door. This will all seem much funnier once I'm safely outside.

We hit the alley and I violently shake my arms and legs about, somehow hoping to physically shake off the whole aura of the Crypt. Roxy just stares at me and mutters something about the English being sexually repressed. I tell her if being uninhibited involves grotesquely fat women and naked men in loafers, I'll take that as a compliment, thank you.

By the time we arrive back at the apartment, I've recovered my sense of humour and have Roxy in stitches relaying my conversation with a 300-pound masked lady who told me she wanted to lick my bottom. As I push open the front door, Cellophane appears behind us. She glares at Roxy, then shakes her head and turns to me.

'I thought *we* were going out tonight?' she says.

'Were we? I didn't realise.'

'Did you write down your feelings?' she says. I glance at Roxy then shake my head. 'You bastard,' Cellophane says.

I struggle to find something to say. 'And you know what,' she says. 'I read your screenplay.'

'Oh, yeah?'

She stares me straight in the eye. 'Dude, you must've been a helluva copywriter. It was ridiculous,' she says. 'Could never happen.'

'You said that about *A Midsummer Night's Dream*.'

'And I was right. A man's head can't turn into a donkey's. It's just not realistic.'

'I think you're missing the point,' I say.

She turns away from me, the label from her skirt sticking out. Instinctively, I reach out to push it down. She swings round and slaps me hard across the face.

'Get off me!' she cries. 'You crazy pervert!' And with that she runs off in a blur of air-cushioned boots and clothing labels.

'Crazy pervert?' Roxy says. 'What did you do to her?'

'You saw,' I say. 'I just tried to push her label down.'

'You must've done something. She your girlfriend?'

'I've been seeing her. But this whole LA dating thing is hard to figure out. She was seeing someone else when I met her, some–'

'Yeah, well fuck you very much!'

'What?'

'Good for you, you're such a fucking stud.'

'What? What's up with you?'

'What the hell do you think? You fucking pig!' And she swipes me hard across the other side of my face. I back up and stare at her, trying to figure out where this is all coming from. The blue from her eyes has drained away and her face has turned a dangerous-looking puce colour.

'Roxy?' My voice is filled with confusion.

'Why the fuck didn't you tell me you were seeing someone?'

'I don't know, I just–'

'I'm gonna fucking kill her.'

'What?'

She barges past me to get to the stairwell. 'Roxy, please, calm down.'

'Get out of my fucking way. I wanna kill the bitch.'

'Roxy, stop it!'

'Let me go, you cunt! I'll fucking hit you. Now let me go!'

The raw anger shocks me. The irrationality of it all is downright unsettling, much worse even than anything I'd ever witnessed when we were together in London.

'What's going on?' Bubble is standing at the foot of the stairs, peering nervously up at us.

'We can hear you halfway down the street,' adds Squeak at her shoulder.

'Sorry,' I say.

Roxy smiles. 'We're having our first lover's tiff,' she says and slips her arm around my waist. 'It's my fault. He won't take me to a motel. I'm Roxy by the way.'

Bubble and Squeak introduce themselves then turn to me. 'What's the matter with you, boy?' says Bubble grinning.

'Take her to a motel,' says Squeak.

'Or you're welcome to stay here,' says Bubble.

'There's room for two in the closet.'

'If you're sure you don't mind?' says Roxy. I stare at her. The puce colour has vanished from her cheeks and the blue returned to her eyes. She's smiling, she's funny and she's charming. She's the girl I travelled six thousand miles to be with: dangerous, but not *Dangerous*. Bubble and Squeak shoot me glances. They like her.

An hour later, Bubble and Squeak head for their rooms and Roxy and I slip into the walk-in closet. I half-close the door and look at her. She's smiling.

'I can't believe you live in a closet,' she says.

'I don't mind it,' I say. 'Bubble and Squeak are so much fun to live with.'

'You sleeping with them?'

'For Christ's sake, Rox.'

'Not even Bubble?'

'No. They're my friends. What's wrong with you?'

She looks down and apologises. For everything. She explains her outburst away with more California shrink-speak. She's in a difficult place right now, she tells me, stressed out about her marriage breaking up, coming to terms with her 'new emotional state'. I think it probably has more to do with drinking on an empty stomach, but I simply listen and silently nod my head like a guest on *Oprah*.

She kisses me on the cheek and thanks me for being so understanding. I tell myself that I'm not going to have sex with her. I don't want to validate her behaviour. She kisses me again, on the mouth this time. And slips off the raincoat. The soft light streaking through the door highlights the black lace against her pale skin. There's another minor explosion in my groin. And I hate myself for doing what I do.

A week later, I move out of the closet. I pack up all my clothes and possessions into a single box and haul it into the camper van. I hug Bubble and Squeak. I feel like I'm saying goodbye to my parents before leaving for college. They'll keep the closet as I've left it, they say: movie posters on the walls, futon rolled up on the floor. It will always be there for me if I need it.

As I leave, I realise I'm leaving the only security I've known in this country. But then Roxy is the reason I came to LA in the first place and, God knows, her move must be much harder than mine. I'm bidding a tearful farewell to a closet. She's moving from a sprawling pad in the Hollywood Hills to the squalor of a one-bedroom fleapit at the edge of gangland in Venice Beach. From swimming pools to cesspools. More importantly, it's a move that's taking her from the glamorous Roxy Hepburn back to Sharon Eckersley. And that can never be a good thing.

But that's a story for another day. Literally. Right now I just want to check my email, to see if Uncle Ralph will go along with the new column idea and I can get my head out of this tailspin and get back in the real world.

Incoming Email:

> To: <BritWriter>
> From: <Ralph>
> Subject: Re: Memo: Idea For My New Column

In a word, no.
The publisher is already anxious about you having so much exposure with the first column. To start another column in your current state of mind would be asking for trouble. Besides, we like this one. Just take some time to relax, maybe get some sleep.
I'll check in with you tomorrow.
Ralph

Bastard.

Byte 8 – Email Menopause

Incoming Email:

> To: <BritWriter>
> From: <The Baron>
> Subject: <none>
>
> I'm supposed to be leaving for VC Central on the ninth. But the boat's been delayed cuz the guy with the greens is getting cold feet. Obviously, all I can afford is a bogey and, as we very well know, bogeys are not really seaworthy ... So, I need a place to hide out in LA. I get in at 3.10 pm your time on the nineteenth, flight VS007 ... You'll be done with your month online by then, right? Can you pick me up?
> Thanks pal,
> Baron Von Hairyback
> P.S. I've finally got a book on building web sites. There should be something to read on my site very soon.

I first met the Baron when he was working in

London and we kept in touch after he returned to his native New York. It's safe to say that in any properly organised society he would have been legally put to sleep by now. But, alas, until the rest of the country is run the same way as Texas, random euthanasia will probably remain outlawed. And the Baron will remain on the loose.

The Baron is an enigma. He's a frustrated artist, with no creative bent; a poet with no desire to write; an Internet entrepreneur with no bright ideas and even fewer technical skills. But he has one true talent, albeit a much-maligned one in today's 'God is a greenback-how much for my granny-did you spill my pint' society. The man truly knows how to live.

Two years ago he had an early thirties menopausal meltdown, quit his high-paying job on Wall Street and embarked on a cross-country trip to Los Angeles, with only the vague objective of learning how to surf. By the time he hit the Golden State, however, that objective had morphed into travelling the globe – preferably in a boat – and documenting the entire experience on a web site.

But, like I said: no technical skills. His web site is up and despite an introduction that promises he'll 'make it interesting', two years have passed and he still hasn't worked out how to load content. Instead, he has only a series of deranged, narcotic-induced emails as a record of his voyage. 'I'm not sure ... but I think I'm in Tibet,' he wrote on one occasion. 'All I know for certain is there's a strange pounding in the front of my head. I have to stop the smoking and drug-fuelled drinking binges before I end up joining Ollie Reed in that great tavern in the sky.'

He's sailed solo across the Pacific Ocean; navigated

a 120-foot rigger through the ice flows of Antarctica; ridden a camel across North Africa and a mule along the banks of the Amazon. He's zig-zagged across the US, travelling every dusty two-lane highway, sheltering at the remotest outposts and the largest cities, gathering stories as vast as the territory. His savings have dwindled but his enthusiasm for the wild outdoors and a life on the move has never wavered. He is truly a free spirit. To paraphrase Hunter S. Thompson, he's found a way to live out there where the *real* winds blow. To sleep late, have fun, get wild and drive fast on empty streets with nothing on his mind except falling in love and not getting arrested ..

If anyone is likely to know where the American Dream is, it's the Baron.

The first time he visits me in LA he is still living and working in New York and I have been living with Roxy for just a couple of months. I commute to the JobPro office in Glendale every day in a futile attempt to earn money as quickly as Roxy seems able to spend it on furniture. The apartment we share in Venice is cramped and the roof leaks when it rains and the walls rattle whenever the next door neighbour flushes his toilet. To me, it's straight out of *Barefoot in the Park*, just quirky enough to be romantic but without the unpleasantness of real poverty. Roxy, however, is living a different movie: *Wall Street* or a Whit Stillman film, all designer art and couches too expensive and too uncomfortable to actually sit on. I suggest borrowing the fold out mattress from Bubble and Squeak. Roxy suggests I make Karina pay more for her crazy letters. She has a point. And it's not worth arguing about. At least I'm not living in a cupboard anymore.

Then the Baron turns up. Roxy hates him. She says he's a 'flash cunt' who has too much money and does too much blow. It's true, Wall Street and commodities trading have been good to him and he has a taste for expensive suits and even more expensive narcotics. But even then he hardly ever sees the sun rise over Manhattan on a weekend. Every Friday night he flies, drives or sails out of the city and doesn't return until late Sunday night or early Monday morning, his restless urge sated at least until the next weekend.

This weekend it's a flight to Los Angeles. When Roxy and I walk into the bar in the Marina, he is already supping pink champagne and chilled vodka shots, eyes constantly scanning the room for single women or a mirror. He greets me warmly, flashing his newly bleached teeth and asks how everything is and says he thinks he might be in with one of the barmaids. It's only a moment or two before he turns to say hello to Roxy, but a moment of not being the centre of attention is like a lifetime of persecution to Roxy.

'And how are you, Roxy?' he says.

She holds his gaze a moment, then turns to me and very deliberately says, 'Are you gonna get me a drink or what?'

I'm at the bar, watching the barmaid chill vodka over crushed ice, when I hear the glass smash. I spin round to see Roxy holding a broken champagne flute at the Baron's neck.

'I'll fuck you up!' she screams.

The Baron freezes, palms up, the smile long gone. I run over and pull the glass from her hand.

'He was making fun of me,' she says.

The Baron looks stunned. 'I only asked how the acting was going,' he says.

She lunges for him again but the bouncer and I hold her back. The Baron stares shell-shocked as I lead Roxy out of the bar.

I don't say anything or even glance over at her as we drive back through the Marina, but I can feel the anger emanating from her. I turn left on Washington and head towards the ocean and suddenly she punches me in the face. I pull the van over. A car horn blares and the stretch limo I cut across swerves to avoid me.

'What the hell!' I yell.

She goes to hit me again and I grab her wrists. Anger washes across her features until they are hardly recognisable. It's like watching the family lap dog suddenly enveloped by rabies.

'Why do you have to do this?' I say. 'All that's going to happen is we'll fight, say a lot of shit we don't mean then spend the rest of the weekend making up. Can't we just skip to the making up part?'

Her expression softens and I can see the Roxy-I-followed-across-the-globe slowly emerge from the cloud of rage. I let go of her wrists.

'I'm sorry,' she says.

'Look,' I say after a few moments, 'if you want out of this, you just have to say.'

She shakes her head. 'I love you. I want this to work.'

I nod and she leans on my shoulder. I let her. Traffic flows past, headlights arcing across the wing mirrors. I stare at the ocean in the distance. I can taste the salt in the air. Roxy moves her head and slips her arm across my lap.

'My mum didn't watch the commercial,' she says at last.

'What?'

'I phoned her earlier tonight,' she says, 'to see what she thought. She said she didn't see it. *Home Improvement* was a re-run so she watched a movie on HBO instead. She didn't even tape it.'

Roxy had landed a spot in a McDonald's commercial. It aired the previous night on network television before the end credits of *Home Improvement*. We watched it with Bubble and Squeak, the four of us huddled round my portable TV like a wartime family waiting for news from the frontline. We cheered wildly when she appeared on screen and drank cheap California champagne. It was a two-second shot of her on the beach playing volleyball but we couldn't have celebrated more if it was the lead in *Titanic*. Her mother couldn't have given a shit either way.

'She probably just forgot,' I lie. 'I taped it. We can make her a copy.'

I've only met her mother a handful of times, but she has an ugliness that touches her soul. She's an obese woman who rarely moves from her chair in front of the television. She's addicted to home-delivery pizza and prescription painkillers. Roxy's father died when she was five. He lost control of his car in the rain and drove it into a ravine. Looking at Roxy's mom, it would be easy to understand if he'd done it on purpose.

She watches television, she eats, she spits grievous obscenities at anyone who ventures near. Including her only child. She didn't go to Roxy's wedding, she never phones her and she can't even be bothered to flick the channel over for two seconds to watch her in a commercial. Away from Roxy, I always refer to her as Saturn, the cannibal Roman god that Goya famously depicted devouring his infant child. That's exactly what she is. A Baby Eater.

When Roxy was seven, her appendix burst in the middle of the night so the Baby Eater called an ambulance. When it arrived, even the paramedics were shocked when she waved goodbye to her daughter and went back to bed. Some time after the operation, Roxy was discharged from hospital. The Baby Eater was too busy to pick her up so she got a taxi home. She sat on the doorstep for three hours watching blood soak through the dressing, waiting for her mother to return.

The Baby Eater.

More car headlights flick across the mirrors. It's getting late. I start the engine again.

'You could drop the tape off to her this weekend,' I say.

'Yeah, maybe,' Roxy says. Then she hugs me. 'I'm sorry for hitting you.' I nod. 'And I'm sorry for hitting your friend,' she says.

'Maybe you should tell him that.'

'I will,' she says, looking me straight in the eye. 'I promise.'

But she never does.

The next day I drive the Baron back to the airport. He's still totally at a loss to explain why she attacked him. 'Do you love her?' he asks eventually.

I shrug. 'It's just that temper of hers ... ' I stop and glance at the Baron. He smiles. He knows what I'm talking about.

'How are you supposed to tell, anyway?' I say. 'If you love someone?'

'I think you're supposed to get a sort of sick feeling

in the pit of your stomach.'

'Really?' I say. 'I thought that was Indian food.'

He laughs and peers out of the window at the grotty store fronts along Lincoln Boulevard.

'I found this letter the other day,' I say.

'From her husband?'

'No. Worse. From Reggie Kray.'

'Reggie Kray!?' the Baron screws his face up, an expression somewhere between shock and hysterical laughter. 'He's still in prison.'

'I know. The letter was from Parkhurst. She'd written to him after she read that book, *The Profession of Violence.*'

'You're kidding me! What for?'

'She liked the book.'

'Then why did she write to Reggie Kray and not the author?'

'God knows. She thinks he should be released.'

Reggie Kray was one half of the Kray twins, notorious London gangsters in the 60s. His brother Ronnie died in prison in 1995 and Reggie was still serving a life sentence for the murders of George Cornell, a rival gangster, and Jack 'the Hat' McVitie, a low-rent hoodlum infamous for pushing his wife out of a moving car and leaving her paralysed.

I found the letter under the bed when I was searching for a shoe. I saw the prison stamp on the envelope and couldn't resist taking a peek. In it, Reggie thanks her for her kind words and asks her to help petition the British government.

'He's a gangster,' the Baron says, definitely laughing now. 'And a murderer.'

'I know.'

'What are you doing, man?' he says. 'I used to

really admire you. Now look at you. No job, no work visa, and living with a married bird. A *crazy* married bird.'

He can't understand why I've thrown away a perfectly good career to feed an ambition as ethereal as screenwriting. 'You're turning into a collection of bad decisions,' he says. 'Come stay with me in New York. I can sort you out with an ad agency there. Get you legal. Put your life back together again.'

'I'm done with advertising.' I say. 'That's not what I want to do.'

'What about money?'

'It didn't make me happy when I had it.'

I drop him in front of the terminal entrance. 'You know,' he says, leaning against the van, 'there are two theories to arguing with women. One–'

'Mate,' I say, shaking my head. 'Not now. Save it for another time, huh?'

'OK, but think about coming to New York, yeah?'

'I will.' He knows I won't though. There's nothing to think about. He's only made me more determined to make everything work.

The Baron is half right. Not about the writing; I've had some luck with the screenwriting. I finished writing the action script in seven days for the direct-to-video producer from the bar. He liked it. His only note was he wanted some yoga in there 'to show the central character has a spiritual side'. He's drawing up a contract. It isn't much money, certainly not enough to impress the Baron or sustain his coke habit for more than a few weeks, but it's a sale, something to build on, and I enjoy screenwriting far more than I ever did copywriting.

It's the situation with Roxy that he has down. She

is crazy. I thought the conversation in the van that night might change her behaviour, but things only ever work out like that in the movies. One character gives an impassioned speech and the other character has a moment of epiphany and is a totally different person by the next scene. Roxy's apologetic state fades faster than a Sunday morning erection. She hates being poor, sees no honour in being a starving artist. And she practises violence like it's a bodily function. I stupidly assume that the rage that led her to thump a knife into my leg all those years before in London would have dissipated with age, along with the need to wear hot pants and boob tubes. But as her persona edges from Roxy back to Sharon, her propensity for rage mushrooms.

Every time I leave the apartment, she's convinced I'm seeing someone else, usually Bubble, and shouts and screams and bawls her eyes out until I promise to stay. The incident in the bar with the Baron is just one of several. When a night club barman refuses her another drink, she smashes a glass and threatens to cut off his testicles. In a late night diner, she stabs a guy with a kebab skewer for staring at her and, in another drink-fuelled incident, she's arrested for punching a traffic cop. And on each occasion the overriding emotion I feel is gratitude: gratitude that it isn't me on the receiving end.

At night, when she falls asleep and the apartment goes quiet, I sit at my desk and stare at the computer screen and aimlessly surf the Net, hoping to stumble upon the answer to a question that isn't even fully formed yet.

The last time I saw the Baron was nearly a year ago.

He has a layover in LA for a few days and we decide to take a road trip into the Nevada desert. I notice then how much he's changed since he quit his job and began travelling. All his worldly possessions now fit into two backpacks. The designer clothes have gone, replaced by torn shorts and well-worn hiking boots. His Wall Street crop has grown into a scraggy shoulder-length mop, his face is weather-beaten, lips constantly chapped from the sun and wind. He no longer scours every room he enters for a glimpse of his own reflection. He reads books voraciously, drinks the cheapest beer he can find. And is just about the happiest person I've ever met.

We drive along Nevada Highway 375, the 'extraterrestrial highway', that runs alongside the infamous Area 51. Hours pass without us seeing another vehicle. We stop for a few drinks at the Little A'Le'Inn restaurant and bar in the small town of Rachel, the only outpost of civilisation for a hundred miles in either direction, then drive on until darkness falls.

We pitch a tent at the edge of a dry lake and huddle around a hastily made campfire as the desert temperature plummets. I sup on a can of weak domestic beer and savour the surroundings. The stillness is eerie. We're engulfed in a blanket of nothingness. The only light is from our small fire and the stars above; the only sound from the wind and the occasional scuttle of a lizard or desert fox. The sense of solitude is as overpowering as I can ever imagine.

'I ever tell you about my two theories for arguing with women?' the Baron says.

'No.'

'Damn. I've been trying to remember them.' I

laugh and open another beer. 'You know, you're the luckiest guy I know,' he says. 'You're doing something you love, regardless of how much money you make.'

I remind him of the conversation we had in LA when he told me I was turning into a collection of bad decisions.

'What can I say, buddy?' he says. 'I was wrong. I think everyone has that meltdown where they just want to throw everything away and follow a crazy dream. It just happened to you earlier than it did to me.'

He tells me how he recently sailed solo from Japan to Hawaii, spending endless days alone at sea.

'The solitude was overwhelming,' he says. 'Days could pass without me seeing even a sign of human life.'

One morning in the middle of the Pacific Ocean, surrounded by nothing but water and sky, he was gripped by a bizarre desire to look back at his yacht, to see the boat as the ocean saw it. So he jumped over the side and clung to the rope and watched the boat slowly drift away from him. The sight so inspired him he seriously considered letting go of the rope and merging himself forever with the ocean.

'At that moment, that was my only ambition, my only dream,' he says. 'To let go.'

I never fully understood what he meant until today, eight days into my month of solitude. The easiest thing for me would be to walk away from the computer right now and step outside and break the solitude. But my response to anxiety or depression (in this case induced by the burning solitude) has always been to turn inwards, to cut myself even further off.

That's how the Baron felt on his solo voyage. The remedy to his solitude wasn't companionship but even greater solitude. He wanted to become one with the ocean around him.

Of course, none of this ever makes it to his web site. If it did, it may help explain the mad rantings that pop up in my inbox every couple of weeks. As the locations become more remote, the Baron's emails grow steadily more bizarre. The latest concerns the alleged sighting of an innkeeper who disappeared from Hampstead, Lord Lucan-style, about ten years ago. 'Clive's out here,' he writes. 'I've seen him, trust me. He's running a cock fighting and Russian Roulette parlour in Laos. Mrs Clive's knocking out scampi 'n' chips downstairs, and Portia's changed her name to Tut-Tut ... Felicitations, your friend and comrade, Lt. John Rambo.'

People like the Baron are too busy squeezing the very pips of existence to ever pick up a phone or lick a postage stamp or learn how to upload content to a web site. The typo-riddled emails are the only record. The money will go and the music will finally stop and no one, not even the Baron himself, knows where he'll be at that point. But what the hell? The important thing is where he journeyed.

Byte 9 – Pitch Perfect

Incoming Email:

> To: <BritWriter>
> From: <Bubble>
> Subject: Strange Movie Ideas
>
> Found these movie projects online. Some are quite old but all are listed as still being in development.
>
> Fatalis
> Sabre-toothed tigers spring to life due to the effects of El Niño and invade Los Angeles. Stallone attached to star.
>
> Jesus Twice
> A wacky scientist clones Jesus Christ using DNA from the Turin shroud.
>
> My Cat is a Serial Killer
> A pet cat is suspected of committing a series of grisly murders. Comedy.
>
> My Slut Mom
> A 17 year-old girl makes up with her promiscuous mother.
>
> Leaving Las Vegas 2
> Nicholas Cage as a drunk ghost?

And this one is still listed as being in development with Jim Womack and New Line. Shouldn't that read Development Hell? The Female Full Monty
The judge of a small town beauty contest confesses on his deathbed that the result of a contest 30 years earlier was fixed when he slept with the mother of one of the contestants. The contest organisers decide to re-stage the event and the original beauty contestants, now in their 40's and 50's, some overweight or riddled with cellulite, have to squeeze into their swimsuits one more time to find the real beauty queen. Meg Ryan to star.

'The next idea, capable of generating hundreds of millions of dollars, could come from anyone,' producer Jim Womack tells me the first time I meet him. 'Everybody who sees movies says to themselves at one time, I've got an idea that's as good as that.'

Jim Womack is a producer at Warner Bros who develops films based on ideas from people outside the Hollywood system – waiters, housewives, policemen, construction workers. I'm interviewing him for a magazine article about pitching ideas in Hollywood and meet up with him at his office on the Warner's lot.

'Have you been drinking?' is the first thing he says to me. It's lunchtime and I've been in the pub all morning to avoid spending the day with Roxy and the Baby Eater.

'Err, yes,' I say. And leave it at that.

He narrows his eyes warily, trying to sum me up. Then breaks out in a broad smile and suggests we do the interview at a bar a few blocks from the studio.

He sucks down an elaborate-looking cocktail adorned with a poison-red cherry and paper umbrella. I stick to beer.

'I needed that,' he says, draining the glass. Then orders another.

He's in his late forties, dressed Hollywood casual: designer pants, white T under a grey V-neck to highlight the tan, immaculate hair. Even after half a dozen cocktails, he's still sharply eloquent, brimming with enthusiasm; an effortless salesman. He tells me about the launch of his web site where aspiring creatives can submit pitches to him. If he finds one he likes, he has a way of making things happen very quickly. Within twenty-four hours of emailing his idea to Jim, one penniless hopeful had a cheque for $125,000 in his hand. Two studios bid on his idea and Julia Roberts was attached to star.

'That tells you just how good an idea can be,' he says, draining another cocktail. 'Let's go somewhere else.'

I take him to a bar in Sherman Oaks, decorated in a Brazilian rainforest theme. We find seats at the end of the bar and order more drinks. I opt for a water as well.

'Shouldn't you be taking notes or something?' Jim asks.

'No,' I say. 'I'll just make it all up anyway.'

He laughs. 'What kind of journalism is that?'

'The honest kind. I'm not after the facts, just the truth.'

The barmaid recognises him. 'Aren't you that producer?' she says. 'You made that Bruce Willis movie last year, right? Listen,' she leans forward so no one else can hear, 'I've got this amazing idea for a movie if you wanna hear it.'

'Sure,' Jim says. 'Fire away.'

This is not an unusual scenario for him. He has people pitching him ideas in bars, post offices, taxi-cabs, even once while he was taking a leak in a restaurant bathroom. Of the hundreds of ideas he hears a week, though, he'll like only find one or two good enough to pitch to the studios. About ten per cent of those pitches will result in sales and a handful will eventually become movies. Unfortunately, the barmaid's idea isn't one of them. It's about a drug bust that goes wrong, a variation of an idea Jim's heard a thousand times before. But he manages to reject her idea in such a diplomatic way that she couldn't have been happier if he'd written her a cheque for it there and then. The next round is on her, she says.

My head is feeling a little woozy at this point, but Jim is still as eloquent and enthusiastic as ever, if maybe a little louder than at the start. With dollar signs and the promise of overnight success flashing in my head, I ask if I can pitch him a couple of ideas. We start with a story Chattering John, a columnist at the magazine, came up with as a joke. Called *Blackjack*, he wrote it with Tom Hanks and George Clooney in mind as 'a couple of French-Canadian canned tuna salesmen. Hanks is the brains of the outfit while Clooney is the street-wise hustler with a weak bladder. Hanks doesn't speak English and Clooney doesn't speak French so all the jokes are visual. When they walk into a seven-eleven to sell a case of Chunk White Albacore, an armed robber bursts in and Clooney takes a bullet in the back of the head from Kate Hudson disguised as a Filipino hooker. Clooney makes a final wisecrack about never having to stand in line for the bathroom again, then croaks in the fruit and veg aisle. His ghost reappears to Hanks whenever he opens a can of tuna and together they track down the evil Kate Hudson. It's a dolphin-friendly version of *Ghost*. With a message.'

Jim laughs, partly because my slurred delivery makes the idea sound even more absurd than it really is.

'Very funny,' he says. 'But no one's going to pay $20 million to have Hanks speak French.'

Instead of pitching him another of Chattering John's ideas I try one that Bubble and I came up with. I rattle off two sentences. He looks stunned.

'That's a good idea,' he says. 'I'm serious. I'm shocked that you actually have an idea that I like.'

Roxy picks me up in the van, on her way home from the Baby Eater's house. I jump in, giddy with excitement and alcohol. I lean over and kiss her on the cheek. She scowls. I know instantly she's in a bad mood.

'How was the B – How was your mum?' I ask.

'You know,' she says. 'Same as always.'

'What did you do?'

'We watched TV. And ordered pizza.'

'Oh.'

The Friday evening traffic along Ventura moves at a crawl. The traffic on the 405 looks even heavier.

'Try Sepulveda,' I say. She pulls onto the freeway instead and tells me I smell like a brewery. 'I know. Jim likes a drink. It would've been rude of me not to join him.'

'Did you pitch him your alien movie?'

'No, it's not really high concept enough.'

'What about a movie about The Krays?' she says.

'It's been done.'

'Yeah, but it wasn't very good. Not as good as the book.' I shake my head and go to speak but she cuts me off. 'Fuck you, then. I'm only trying to help.'

I close my eyes. I'm in too good a mood to fight with her. We sit in silence for a moment then Roxy nudges me awake.

'What did you pitch him?' she says.

'The beauty contest idea Bubble and I came up with,' I say. 'You know, the sort of female Full Monty.'

The following Monday Jim calls me up to say that even sober he still thinks it's a good idea. I email him a few pages of notes to flesh-out the story. By the end of the week he calls to say that Meg Ryan is attached to the project and New Line wants to make us an offer to write the script.

Bubble and I go out to celebrate.

Of course, it takes me years to achieve an overnight success in Hollywood, years of projects dying vile and painful deaths somewhere on the lonely roadside of Development. The action screenplay I sold to the producer in the bar is never made and I quickly regret signing a two-year contract with the agent. He doesn't sell my screenplay for hundreds of thousands of dollars. In fact he doesn't sell it for anything. Presumably Jodie isn't interested in playing the wife of an alien serial killer. Undeterred, I quickly write another, a complex crime thriller, a sort of sci-fi version of *LA Confidential*. The agent reads it, but doesn't 'get the alien'. He invites me round for dinner to discuss some other ideas.

I walk into his house in Woodland Hills. It's bathed in candlelight and insipid rock is playing somewhere in the background – Michael Bolton, I think, complaining about another woman leaving him. I find the agent in the living room, scooping lines of coke off the coffee table, something he's been doing with increasing frequency in the office during the day. He tells me his wife and kids are away for the evening, so we have the house to ourselves. I shift uncomfortably.

'You can take your shirt off if you like,' he says. I tell him I'm OK with my shirt on, thanks all the same.

'You look tense,' he says. 'How about a massage before dinner . . . Or a blow job?'

The drive home is a quick one. From then on, I'm the only struggling screenwriter in Hollywood who doesn't return his *agent's* calls.

Eventually, I drop by his office one Tuesday morning to see if he'll release me from the contract. There's a new guy answering the phones in reception: another fresh-faced, hopeful young writer. I wonder if I should warn him about accepting dinner invitations to the agent's house but before I can say anything he tells me the agent has asked not to be disturbed.

'For how long?' I say.

'Err,' the boy stutters. I know he's lying so walk through to the office.

The agent is lying passed out on the couch while his secretary cuts up lines of coke on the photocopier for him. A line of drool seeps from the side of his mouth as he snores. My Hollywood agent. I feel a pang of sympathy for the sexual misfit stretched out on the couch in front of me drooling saliva into the fabric and awaiting a nose full of coke just so he can face the day. I figure he and his agency will expire long before our contract ever does. I walk out and resolve to give up on agents and represent myself instead. I just need to come up with a creative 'in'.

I download a list of producers from the Net and fake some letters of recommendation on BBC-headed paper and start telling outrageous lies to receptionists. The letters claim I worked as everything from writer, director and producer to tea lady and set decorator on fictitious BBC films. A dozen or so producers are impressed enough by the letter that they agree to read the script and I'm convinced I've finally cracked Hollywood.

But I'm wrong.

The phone rings at just after four o'clock one morning. Roxy leans over and grabs it and grunts something unintelligible. She throws the receiver at me.

'It's the Baron,' she says. 'Pretending to be from the BBC. Tell him he's not funny.'

I fumble for the phone in the folds of the duvet and eventually hold it up to my face. 'Mate, you know what time it is?' I say.

'I'm calling from the BBC in London,' the posh English voice on the phone says.

'Who is this?'

'I'm the assistant to the Head of BBC Films,' the voice says. 'We've received a very puzzling letter from a production company in Los Angeles.'

I sit bolt upright. This isn't the Baron jerking around. It really is the BBC. One of the producers I'd given a script to sent it back to the BBC in London rather than the LA address I included in the letter. The posh voice sounds angry. It wants to know what the hell is going on.

'We don't even know who you are. You sent us an

alien script two years ago from a London address and we returned it explaining the material wasn't suitable for us. Now this producer is under the impression you worked here.'

'Mmmmm,' I say. 'Oh.'

'Well?' The posh voice is getting angrier. 'Do you know who might have sent this letter? Do you have an agent who might have done it?'

The chance to blame everything on Agent Bisexual is tempting, but I decide it's better to own up. It's the subtle difference between being a cheeky hustler and a flagrant con artist.

'No,' I say. 'It was me.'

The posh voice explodes. It wants to know which production companies I've given the letter to.

'Just a few,' I lie and rattle off the names of two other companies. There is no way I can admit to handing the letter out to half of Hollywood. The posh voice tells me the BBC will bring legal action against me if I ever try anything like this again.

I hang up the phone and jump in the shower. It's going to be a busy day. I need to go back to all the other production companies I've given the letter and script to and ask for them back before anyone else makes contact with the Beeb. It may sound like a simple mission, but if there's one thing harder than getting someone in Hollywood to look at your script, it's getting them to return it unread. As soon as I ask for it back they immediately assume someone is interested, so they suddenly want to read it. The whole scene is absurd. Producers reject struggling writers, not the other way around. Last week I was begging them to read it, now I'm begging them not to.

*

A day or so later I receive an email from one of the production companies I'd named to the BBC. 'I spoke with a representative from the BBC,' the email reads, 'who informed me that the letter you sent to us from them was indeed a forgery.

'Although I understand how difficult it is to get your material considered, and breaking into the business in general, dishonest business methods are never the answer. Unfortunately, I am keeping this letter on file as a reminder to us of this incident. I do wish you luck on all your future endeavors, I hope that if our paths ever cross again it will be a more positive experience.'

That's about as much of a chastisement as it's possible to receive in Hollywood. He isn't sure whether to condemn me for lying or admire my nerve for trying. He certainly doesn't want to run the risk that I might become the next hot writer and he'd admonished me excessively. Still, I probably need to keep a low profile for a while. Or maybe adopt a name change.

Sometime later, I'm introduced to a producer who back in the 80s made a Disney kids' film and a Stallone comedy that was notable only for having a less plausible premise than *Blackjack*. I pitch him an idea for a romantic comedy and he pays me to write it. Another script with no alien monsters.

An executive at Paramount describes it as a romantic *Fawlty Towers* and wants to option it. The producer turns the deal down and says we'll get a better offer if I 'pump up the ending.' He offers me a few extra bucks to rewrite the third act. The idea of paying rent on time for the second consecutive month is too irresistible so I add a gunfight at the end of the romantic comedy. The producer likes it and offers me even more to change the first and the second acts as well. I add two more gunfights. He seems pleased. Unfortunately, the exec at Paramount is less so. He describes the rewrite as a romantic *Reservoir Dogs* and passes on the project completely. New Line considers it for a while. And then also passes. The following month I'm back to paying rent a week late and writing another alien script on spec.

Then one weekend Bubble gets drunk at Bar Marmont on Sunset and wakes up in bed next to an actor from one of the *Star Trek* TV shows. She claims she didn't recognise him without the alien prosthetics.

'He said he can get us in to pitch for the show,' she says.

'I've only ever seen the one with Captain Kirk in it,' I say.

Bubble and I had been planning to write something together for a while but I'm not convinced an episode of *Star Trek: Deep Space Voyager: the New Generation* or whatever it's called is the ideal first project.

'Well watch it tonight and see if it sparks any great ideas,' she says. 'It could be a good "in" for us. God knows, he wasn't a good "in" for me.'

I watch five minutes of one episode and am so bored/tired/irritated that I'm forced to seek respite in a crate of ale. The following night I rent a *Star Trek* movie. Five days later, twenty-five minutes into the film, I give up and take it back to Blockbuster.

'Unwatchable,' I tell Bubble as I slide into the booth opposite her.

It's 4.30 on a Wednesday afternoon and we're in Norm's Diner on La Cienega for the early bird special, just as we are every Wednesday at 4.30. We bill it as our weekly creative meeting but it's really an excuse to eat cheap comfort food with the only person either of us knows who isn't appalled at the thought of eating meatloaf or chicken pot pie in the middle of the afternoon surrounded by the cast of *Cocoon* just to save a few bucks.

'Well, the pitch meeting's next week, do you want to go or not?' she says.

'Of course,' I say. 'I've got some ideas.'

'You want to pitch some ideas for a show you've never seen?'

'I don't have a choice. I can't watch that crap.'

She shakes her head in disbelief. 'So what are the ideas then?'

'The first one's called Dreamcatcher. Captain Kirk and his crew beam down to a planet where the population is being abducted in their dreams by some mysterious alien force. Sort of *Nightmare on Elm Street*. One of the crew falls asleep and is abducted and the others have to stay awake or they'll be next. It's down to Spock to save them because Vulcans have some special ability whereby they don't need as much sleep or something.'

'Actually,' she says. 'That's not bad.'

'Really? I thought it was bollocks.'

'Yeah, but they all are. Just one thing, though. There's no Kirk and no Spock anymore. It's Pickard or Janeway, depending on–'

'OK, so you change the names. I don't need to watch the thing. How many different ideas do we need?'

'Four or five maybe.'

'OK. I've got another one. Err, you done with your mash?'

*

The pitch meeting is at the Paramount offices of *Star Trek* and goes surprisingly well. I feign enough interest in the crap that I'm talking to get through the first pitch and only have to stifle a laugh when Bubble uses the term 'space time anomaly' for about the tenth time. The producers like a couple of the ideas – including Dreamcatcher – and ask us if we'd like to pitch to another sci-fi show of theirs. It's moving from Fox to the Sci-Fi Channel, the TV equivalent of being relegated from the Premier League to the Conference in one season. I haven't seen the show of course, and have no intention of doing so, but nod my head vigorously all the same.

Bubble explains the premise of the show and gives me a brief description of some of the characters. I drink three mugs of Norm's coffee but still feel my eyelids grow heavy.

'OK, Bubble.' I say at last. 'That's enough of that.'

Trying to explain crap TV to me is like trying to explain the theory of relativity to a piece of toast or rudimentary geography to George W. Bush: nothing is ever going to stick.

We come up with some more nonsense about worm holes and time warps or time holes and worm warps and drive back to Paramount for another pitch meeting. Unfortunately my van breaks down on Melrose and we have to run to the studio in the hot sun. We're both sweating by the time we get there.

'Would you like something to drink?' the receptionist asks.

'Water,' we both gasp at once.

She raises an eyebrow and fetches us a bottle of Evian each. We drink them down in one and she shows us into the producer's office. His assistant greets us and I decide immediately that he must be the campest man in the world – Priscilla, Queen of the Paramount Lot. Then the producer enters. He's wearing nail varnish and walks with a pronounced wiggle, holding his hands up by his shoulders. I was wrong. *This* is the campest man in the world. I feel like I've wandered into Madame Jo-Jo's cabaret by mistake. They make small talk about the show and 'our new home at the Sci-Fi Channel'.

'I really loved the first series,' says Bubble. 'Great characterisation as well as a really interesting premise.'

'Mmm. Me too.' I say, then immediately regret it. I sound like such a muppet.

'I haven't seen the show but it sounds crap,' is what I really want to say. 'And we're only here because we need a writing credit, any kind of credit, to get our foot in the door of that giant night club called Hollywood.' But I don't. I pitch a stupid idea instead. Madame Jo-Jo and Priscilla coo and gurgle and flutter their eyelids, which I take to be signs of approval. At the end of the meeting, they say they'll be in touch in a day or so. I'm not sure whether I should shake their hands or curtsey.

The next afternoon I get a call from Priscilla. They want to make a deal. We sign the contracts, cash the cheques and spend the next two months writing bad television and paying rent on time. We hand the completed script in. Priscilla and Madame Jo-Jo love it.

It's scheduled for production and we're about to have a credit. On a crap TV show. 'At least it's better than *Star Trek*,' Bubble keeps telling me. But the Head of Programming at the Sci-Fi Channel apparently disagrees. The viewing figures are disappointing so he cancels the show before our episode is produced. Something I've never been able to get truly upset about.

Then I'm assigned the interview with Jim Womack and I'm back to flirting with TV's much more attractive older sister, the motion picture. Unfortunately, the story doesn't end in true Hollywood fashion with me strolling down the red carpet with Meg Ryan at the premiere. Like so many ideas and scripts that are bought, only a tiny fraction ever makes it to the big screen. We write the script and bid a tearful farewell to it at the onramp of Development, which is where the little fella is still loitering to this day.

The sale does, however, generate enough heat that Bubble and I are able to pitch to several other companies and sell four more scripts. But there is still little sign of anything actually being produced.

As Jim says, all you need is a great idea or the rights to a true story along with a little luck. Luck I can't budget for, but finding that one killer movie concept is easier to strive for. If I can find it, then maybe everything else will slot into place and my thirty day quest will be more fruitful.

Before I turn back to the Internet and start my search for inspiration, I order food: meatballs with fettuccine and a Cobb salad for dinner tonight; ham sandwiches and a bucket of fried chicken for tomorrow; vodka and aspirin for sporadic emergency use. I pin three dollar bills onto the front door but the delivery guy still rings the bell. I peer out at him as he pulls the hamster whiskers away from his face and scratches his nose. He rings again, but half-heartedly this time, then walks off.

Unbelievable. Merlot, NyQuil and more laxatives instead of vodka and aspirin; ravioli instead of meatballs and tuna sandwiches instead of ham. And no fried chicken. I'd email him to take it back but I'm just too damn hungry.

Byte 10 – To Live and Die Online

The street suddenly explodes with excited, morbid crowds. Hysterical women surge forward in a frenzy, screeching in almost sexual ecstasy, scratching and fighting the police and paramedics in their attempts to reach the body. One fat-breasted woman with stringy yellow hair breaks through the tape and dips her handkerchief in the blood, clutches it to her sweaty chest and runs off down the street.

That's how John Dillinger died. While I like the idea of grief-crazed women flocking to my corpse, it's certainly not how I imagined I'd go. Not gunned down in the street by a dope fiend at three o'clock in the morning. But then who said I was ever going to get to choose?

Roxy and I are held up at gun point in Venice Beach one night walking home from a party. A car pulls up in front of us and two guys, their faces covered with bandanas, Jesse-James-style, jump out and point silver handguns at us. They only want cash and become very angry when Roxy can produce only a single dollar bill from her purse. I suddenly think about the German tourist who was recently shot and killed by muggers in a nearby but much busier and better-lit neighbourhood. I look around. The street is empty. It's foggy. If they decide to shoot us, it will be hours before anyone, let alone grief-crazed women, find our bodies. Thankfully, the $83 in my wallet is enough to appease them and the guns go back into their waistbands.

'Imagine if I'd been on my own,' Roxy says as we reach the relative safety of home. 'I'd be dead, right?'

'With just a dollar bill?' I say. 'Yeah, I think you would.'

'Fuck, at least you know the price of human life now,' she says. 'Forty-two dollars a head.'

Police Warn of Dangers of Meeting Someone Online

Anyone You Want Me to Be: A True Story of Sex and Death on the Internet

Has the Internet Helped Serial Killings?
Reuters.com headlines

The violence of everyday life seems to be seeping into the virtual world. I begin the day listening to an archived interview with John Lennon and somehow end up on an NRA supporter's web site reading about the death of John Dillinger and the need for every God-fearing American to install a rocket launcher on his patio. Only is this possible on the Internet. It's a microcosm of my time in cyberspace. An innocent search for information on the death of a pop icon ends with me being confronted by fat white men using the language of Christianity to justify random violence.

The link I follow from there inadvertently leads me

into a mire of bizarre porn. I'm bumped over to a site dedicated to hermaphrodite prostitutes and then a cheery gallery of farmyard animals engaged in various sexual acts with people. It's the Six Degrees of Separation rule: online, you're never more than half-a-dozen links away from pig fuckers or pop-up ads. A few more clicks and I'm back on the subject of death, wandering through undertakers' web pages and memorial sites. From death to dumb-asses to sore assess to death again.

I pause at the following anonymous eulogy to a recently deceased girl posted on Legacy.com:

Petra, you died cheaply in the glare of strangers.
And you left us nothing but questions and shadows
and this, the darkest of places, to remember you.

I'm intrigued. All love stories begin with a crime, someone wise once said, and all great mysteries begin with a death. 'You died cheaply in the glare of strangers ... left us nothing but questions and shadows ...' What the hell does that mean?

Hollywood loves a true story so that's what I'm going to uncover. I fuel my search with cupfuls of red wine and NyQuil. By the early evening I have heart palpitations and severely bloodshot eyes and a craving for fried chicken but I have also pieced together a story that took place a couple of months ago just a few miles from where I'm sitting.

The police emergency switchboard lights up like a Christmas tree. Not unusual for the early hours of a Saturday in West Los Angeles, but the content of the calls are anything but usual. Twenty-three people living as many as eleven miles apart phone to report a crime they've all witnessed simultaneously – the brutal slaying of a young girl in her home by a masked intruder.

Petra Lader is a freshman student at UCLA who moved into a campus house share with four other students. Encouraged by the popularity of reality-based TV shows such as *The Real World* and *Big Brother* and the renowned Jennicam site, her roommates wire the house with web cams. One room at first, then other rooms until every angle of their lives is on view twenty-four seven to anyone who cares to log on to the Geocities site.

The six eat, sleep, study, fight, drink, shower and shag live on camera. This is unscripted drama in its rawest form; grainy black-and-white images crackle and flicker as student lives stream through processors and cables to the watching world. 'You wanna live in front of these cameras?' one of the roommates asks Petra the day she moves in. 'Then ask yourself what sort of person you are. No, scratch that. Ask yourself what sort of person you *should* be. Funny and smart? Arrogant and aloof? A stoner? Because let me tell you, you don't get to decide. They do. It's up to them who you are. The audience decides. There's no narrative story for them to follow so they just observe and draw their own conclusions about who we are as people.'

The whole venture is part social experiment – two of them are studying 'The Nature of Communication in the Internet Age' – part shameless exhibitionism, and part greed – Jennicam reportedly earns hundreds of thousands of dollars a year from subscribers.

Of course, there are unforeseen problems. Too many people refreshing the same web cam image all at once – which happens frequently during drunken parties and sexual encounters – causes the server to crash, as does the synchronised use in the house of a hairdryer and vacuum cleaner. There is also a much darker problem. The hundreds, sometimes thousands, of visitors to the site know the layout of the house intimately. They know the students' habits, their routines. They know when they're home, when they're out and when they're alone.

There are nearly two hundred viewers logged on to the site early Saturday morning. Most are fellow UCLA students – the site hasn't been publicised much beyond the confines of the campus – a handful live as far east as Colorado and one is a teenager in Reykjavik, Iceland. They see the masked intruder enter the house and attack Petra. Titillated by the scent of death, they barrage the server with refresh commands, causing it to crash and leaving them all staring at eerily blank screens. Twenty-three viewers call the cops. The others, when questioned later, either claim they weren't sure if what they'd seen was real or just assumed the police would somehow already know about it.

By the time the LAPD reaches the house and by the time Petra's roommates return home, there is nothing but a massive pool of fresh blood on the carpet and streaks of crimson where the killer has dragged the body to the window and disappeared into the night.

When the server comes back online it brings with it thousands of new viewers, anonymous ghouls eager to see 'the house where that girl was murdered live on camera'. Photos and online eulogies for Petra appear on Internet memorial sites. The place where Petra lived is now where she is to be mourned. Students and regular visitors post their thoughts and tributes to a lost life, a fallen comrade. But what unfolds next is the stuff of urban legend, an investigation that plays out like the juiciest dime novel or Hollywood thriller. *Ten Little Indians* at broadband speed.

Detectives, still missing a body, quickly discover that Petra has no social security number. At least none under the name Petra Lader. She has no rap sheet, no driver's licence, no next of kin, no medical or dental records and no bank account. Her roommates have only known her for a few weeks. She pays rent and, as far they can tell, everything else in cash. And there is also no record of her enrolment at UCLA. Or at any other college for that matter. Ultimately, beyond the web cams in the house, Petra Lader simply doesn't exist.

Perhaps the really surprising thing about this story is that it doesn't receive more coverage in the media. The story just seems to end at this point, the last snippet posted on a bulletin board over a week ago, dubbing the perpetrator of this crime the first Internet murderer. He's not though. I stumble across a report from the Internet Crimes Division of the Secret Service alerting police agencies to the threat of online serial killers. It's dated February 1994 and estimates 'there may be as many as a dozen killers presently at work on the Internet.' One, dubbed SlaveMaster, lured women from chat rooms and bludgeoned at least five to death in Kansas. He was caught. But that still leaves eleven.

I'm scared. This is where I live; this is my home, my playground. I'm being pursued by the violence from the outside. Every spam, every foray into a chat room, every cookie collected on my hard drive is a threat. Or a clue. Maybe they're on to me already;

maybe they're in here waiting for me. Maybe they know that I know.

Petra Lader. I know that name. I heard it a long time ago.

Outgoing Email:

> To: <Cellophane Girl>
> From: <BritWriter>
> Subject: Remember me?
>
> Hey. I know it's been a long time since we spoke but I'm trying to get in touch with your old friend Cleo. Don't worry, I'm not still sore about the camper van. Do you have an email address for her?
> Hope everything's going well with you.

Incoming Email:

> To: <BritWriter>
> From: <Cellophane Girl>
> Subject: Re: Remember me?
>
> Holy crap! You're still here? How the hell did you manage that?
> Cleo's email address is CleoPetraMail@aol.com. We were talking about you only the other night. Cleo agreed that I owe you an apology. I've made a lot of changes in my life – I'm engaged! – and I feel much more centered now, much more in touch with myself. I know you didn't mean to but you hurt me badly at the time. And I accept that you were just pushing the label

on my skirt down – I shouldn't have done what I did, I apologise.
I read in *Variety* that you sold a few scripts. Well done, I always knew you'd make it. I haven't heard from Roxy in a long time.
How was jail?

Outgoing Email:

> To: <Cellophane Girl>
> From: <BritWriter>
> Subject: Re: Remember me?

Congratulations on the engagement, I'm glad you're happy. There are no hard feelings on my part. To be honest, I rarely think about jail or any of that stuff. It all seems such a long time ago, it happened to a different person. I didn't mean to hurt you though. Things worked out for both of us, so let's leave it at that.
All the best.

Outgoing Email:

> To: <Cleo>
> From: <BritWriter>
> Subject: Who is Petra Lader?

Drunk, romantic Englishman wakes up in the City of Angels for the first time, woozy from jet lag and vodka shots. Discovers he's purchased a VW bus from an aspiring web entrepreneur for 75 times its value.
Much to his surprise, the van lasts several years

before being cruelly towed away. Like a sentimental fool, he keeps the pink slip in a shoebox of memories. This pink slip lists the last registered owner as one Petra Lader who was recently murdered live on web cam at a house in Westwood. For the sake of karmic retribution and to make the $7500 I spent on the van look like a decent deal, please fill in the blanks: I know who. I can guess why. But I have no idea how.

Incoming Email:

> To: <BritWriter>
> From: <J2>
> Subject: Voice Message
>
> You have one new voice message.
> Click to download.

The voice message is from Cleo. She says she won't email the story to me; she wants to be able to deny it all later if she has to.

'OK, Mr Smartypants, I can't believe you figured this out,' she says. 'I forgot about the pink slip. What are the chances a little thing like that would come back to haunt me?'

She takes a deep breath and tells me the rest of the story. And it's a beautiful one. Sometimes uncovering great stories is all about being in the right place at the right time and smuggling out an 'exclusive'. It's the little luck Jim Womack talked about. The right time for me is now, the right place the Internet. I stay online all night researching the background to her story, verifying the details, chugging more red wine and NyQuil. By the early hours I have the full story and the reasons why it evaded most of the mainstream media.

The real tip off came to the police, when, in the true spirit of American commerce, an Internet company invested in the suddenly very popular web cam site. Cleo refuses the name the company, for obvious reasons. It didn't need Miss Marple to figure out the entire murder was staged as a morbid publicity stunt to generate hits for the site. That's the 'why'. The 'who' I figured out from the pink slip and the fact that the demure, blonde Cleo and the raucous brunette Petra were never seen together in the same room.

Cleo switched personas under the cover of darkness or in a well-choreographed bathroom manoeuvre, out of view of the web cams. The transformation simply required her to pull on a dark wig, hide her face under dark, gothic makeup and adopt the personality of a Rottweiller. Viewing over grainy webcam images, none of the viewers were ever able to spot anything unusual.

To hide the embarrassment of those unwittingly involved, the site was quickly dissolved along with media interest in the story. Cleo's family is well connected enough in LA circles to help hush up the whole affair. But Petra and her message remain unique entries in the murky annals of Internet lore.

She was one who truly lived and died online.

Outgoing Email:

> To: <Cleo>
> From: <BritWriter>
> Subject: Re: Who is Petra Lader?

One last question, Cleo. There have to be easier ways of making money, why choose a scheme like this?

Incoming Email:

> To: <BritWriter>
> From: <Cleo>
> Subject: Re: Who is Petra Lader?
>
> *What drives people is not power or money but conspicuousness*
>
> George Bernard Shaw.
>
> This is the Internet Age, my friend. All our dreams lie online. For conspicuousness, for instant celebrity: just add web cams.

It's after 3 am when I email the whole web cam story – tentatively titled *To Live and Die Online* – to Jim Womack. Sure, there are no aliens, but I'm still convinced it will make a great movie.

Outgoing Email:

> To: <Jim Womack, Warner Bros.>
> From: <BritWriter>
> Subject: Outline: To Live & Die Online
>
> Jim,
> Attached is a Word doc with another outline, this time for a cyber thriller. Let me know if it interests you.
> Hope all is well. How about a few drinks soon?

I click send then throw up. Too much NyQuil perhaps. I turn on the ceiling fan and the air conditioner in the bedroom and strip naked and fall asleep in the icy cold room. Today was a good day I think. It feels like I'm finally getting somewhere. I have the American Dream firmly in my sights.

I sleep fitfully and dream. I dream of that bus; I dream of places and events that were so long ago they seemed to have happened to someone else ...

Byte 11 – Felony Blues

According to dumblaws.com, in Alabama it is illegal to spit on the sidewalk after 4 pm; in Kentucky, it is illegal to carry ice cream in your back pocket or to marry your wife's grandmother; in Texas it is illegal to have sex with a fish; in Florida it is illegal to get a fish drunk; and in North Carolina it is illegal to have sex with a drunk fish. And nowhere in the US is it legal to send a building through the mail. Hell, it's a brave man that visits the beach in Santa Monica without his attorney present. A sign at the edge of the sand details twenty-six ordinances outlawing such heinous crimes as: walking dogs, consuming beer, playing the drums, and undressing. Is it any wonder that even the most law-abiding Brits who move to America occasionally find themselves staring at the wrong side of a jail cell door? 'Arrive on vacation, leave on probation,' fat little judges are fond of saying. And the buggers are right.

I awake this morning to an urgent voice message from Nervous Bob. He's talking machinegun-fast, peppering words into the mouthpiece like a crow spitting corn.

'Man, where are you? I need your help. Really. I need you to call your attorney. Find out if he can recommend an attorney here in Louisville. I've been arrested, mate.' The words don't sound real to him. 'Can you believe it? Same shit that happened to you. Call me, mate. It's the Louisville Sheriff's Department. Find the number. Can't fucking believe this. Jesus Christ. I keep trying the British Consulate but there's no answer. Get a number for me. As soon as you get this message. Shit, mate, I wish you'd pick up . . .'

He repeats the message over and over rather than hang up the phone. There's some comfort talking to a friendly voicemail service. He's scared. I can hear it. I play the message again, pacing the room. I know that fear. I recognise it well and it sends a cold stream of dread rinsing over me. It isn't seven o'clock yet. I email Howard, my attorney, asking him to call or email me back as soon as possible with the name of a good criminal attorney in Kentucky. If I haven't heard from him by nine, I'll have to phone. To hell with the assignment, I think.

Howard calls back within the hour and leaves me a message with a Louisville attorney's phone number and email address. I instant message him with details of where Nervous is being held. He IMs me back saying he'll go down there and speak to him.

I log on to the Kentucky Offender Online Lookup System. I want to call, but it's a desire founded solely on ghoulish interest. I know they're unlikely to let him come to the phone and I know there's nothing I can do even if they did. He isn't listed on the web site yet. But he will be. Kentucky posts details of every inmate in its jails and prisons so that anyone can find out who's behind bars, what they're charged with and what they look like.

I flick through the photos of Kentucky's inmates – most look like the 'before' pictures on cosmetic dentistry ads. Could these unfortunates be any further from their American Dreams?

'Same shit that happened to you,' he said. 'Same shit that happened to you.'

I IM the Louisville attorney again and ask him to get in touch as soon as he has some news, any news. And then I sit back. There is nothing else I can do. He has a well-recommended attorney. Whatever will happen now will happen slowly, of that much I'm certain.

I pull out the ragged, broken beach shoes and stained workout top that I keep at the back of my cupboard and stare at them and wonder why I've kept them all these years. Perhaps as a permanent reminder of the consequences of a bad decision? I meant to hold a sacrificial burning of them in the hope that it would finally banish the monkey that's clung to my back all these years. But I haven't. Something's always stopped me. So they remain there, in the darkness of the closet, keeping the monkey company.

They smell of that bus. I look at the calendar pinned above my desk and realise that it was six years ago today that I sat on that bus. Six years later and now my friend is experiencing something similar.

In Alabama, it is illegal to wear a fake moustache that causes laughter in church.

The knock at the front door came at 3.39 am on a Saturday. I remember it exactly. I roll over and look at the clock on Roxy's side of the bed. 3.39: bright red numbers slicing through the darkness. No good can ever follow a knock on the door at that hour. I expect it to be Roxy, having lost her keys. I returned home without her. It's a dance we've done a dozen times before. She's drunk and wants to cause a scene in the middle of Santa Monica. I search for her then give up and drive back to Venice. She would get a cab and hopefully use the time to cool off. We've been living together for less than three months but I am already fully reacquainted with her temper.

I hurry out of bed adjusting my boxer shorts and pull open the door. Two Venice police officers peer back at me.

'Step outside please, sir,' says the first, a gaunt, bald Sergeant in his late forties.

He pushes my face against the wall and cuffs my hands behind my back. The sharp stucco pinches my cheek.

'What's this about?' I shiver, partly from shock, partly from the cold.

He pushes me hard against the stucco again while his colleague – younger, Aryan-blond with a weightlifter's physique – enters the apartment behind me. I strain my head to watch him. I've seen enough cop movies to know he needs a warrant or something to search the apartment. But I decide not to say anything. If the bald one presses me against the wall any harder I'm likely to lose a tooth.

The Aryan steps back outside and they grab an arm each and start to lead me off.

'What's going on?' I ask again.

'We're taking you in,' says the bald one.

'What? Why? What've I done?' They ignore me.

'At least let me put some clothes on. I'm freezing.'

The Aryan pushes open the door and grabs the jeans hanging over the arm of the couch. He removes the belt and throws it to one side. My hands are still cuffed behind my back so he helps me step into them. I slip on a really old, battered pair of beach shoes and the Aryan hands me an already soiled, sweaty workout top hanging from the laundry basket, then pushes me out again.

They drive me to the Santa Monica police station. A sign on the wall reads: 'No Firearms in Booking Area'. I'm not sure if that's supposed to be comforting or threatening. The desk sergeant, a statuesque woman with Hollywood cheekbones and surprisingly bright lipstick (even the cops in LA look like movie stars) asks me questions from a form. I answer them all, shivering again from a cocktail of cold and shock.

'What am I being charged with?' I say at last.

'You live with,' she checks her notes, 'Miss Hepburn ... Roxy Hepburn, right?' I nod. 'One count of two seventy-three point five,' she says. 'PC Felony. Inflicting corporal injury on spouse or cohabitant.'

My mouth drops. Inflicting corporal injury? I can't begin to imagine what Roxy has told them. It doesn't really matter, though. I know Roxy. She'll tell them the truth as soon as she sobers up. She'll be repentant and I'll be out of here. My look of astonishment must have registered with the desk sergeant. She tells me she'll look up the level of bail.

Another cop uncuffs my hands and puts me in a small holding cell with a circular grate in the floor. I pull on the sweaty workout top to stave off the cold and eye the vagrant curled up asleep in the corner. A steady stream of piss seeps from his body and tracks its way across the cell floor and disappears down the grate in the middle. I sit as far away from him as possible and breathe through my mouth to avoid the smell.

I hear the desk sergeant ask another cop whether the bail is 'twenty-five or fifty'. Thank God, I think to myself, no more than fifty bucks, I'll be out of here straightaway. She looks over at me peering at her from behind the bars.

'Your bail,' she says, 'is fifty thousand dollars.'

I smile – she's joking, right? She stares back at me, her expression rigid. She isn't joking. Panic hits, swiftly and without warning. My chest instantly feels rubber band-tight. I can't breathe. I can't think. I can just smell piss. Old man piss, drunk's piss, acrid, violent-smelling piss. Piss trickling across the floor, piss trickling under my feet. Piss, piss, piss.

Fifty thousand dollars! I don't have that kind of money. I rest my head against the bars to stave off the mounting sense of claustrophobia. I tell the desk sergeant I need to speak to someone, clear this whole mess up.

'There's no detective on duty at the moment,' she says.

'When will there be?'

'They don't work the weekends,' she says. 'And Monday's a holiday. So I guess it'll be Tuesday.'

Another wave of panic pounds into me, knocking the air from my lungs. I struggle to breathe again. Fifty grand or at least three days in jail. I can't believe this is happening. Roxy's gone too far this time. It isn't funny.

*

'I know my rights,' I call out to the sergeant. 'I'm entitled to a phone call. I want to make my call.'

She stares at me again, then suddenly breaks out into a huge grin. 'You've been watching too many movies,' she says. 'Yeah, you can make your phone call.' She unlocks the cell door and leads me towards the phone.

'And I haven't been read my Miranda Rights,' I say.

'The arresting officers read them to you.'

'Did they?' They may have done. I was probably too shocked to remember.

'Yes they did,' she says, still smiling. 'Pick up that phone there and I'll dial the number behind the desk.'

She finds the number for the British Consulate in LA and puts me through. I hover next to the phone as it rings and rings, willing for someone to pick up. It's a machine. The desk sergeant suggests I try a bail bondsman. I'm not exactly sure how a bail bondsman works, but agree anyway. All that matters is that I am out of that cell and away from the vagrant and his river of piss.

A man's voice, as gruff as charcoal, answers. I tell him what's happened.

'Do you own any property?' he asks. No, I don't, I tell him. 'What about friends? Any of them own a house they'd be willing to put up as collateral?' No, most of my friends in LA are struggling writers and actors. 'The only other thing you can do,' he says, 'is raise fifty grand on a credit card.'

I hang up. And ask the desk sergeant if I can make another call.

'You've had two already,' she says. It's just after 5 am. 'Why don't you wait until later. It'll be easier to get hold of people then.'

She tells me I need to have my prints and photo taken anyway. A small Hispanic man with a massive Zapata moustache that makes him look like the cartoon character Yosemite Sam leads me through to a side room.

Finger, ink, pad. Finger, ink, pad. Hold this number up under your chin. Snap. Turn to the side. Snap. And all I can think of is the Hugh Grant mug shot plastered all over the tabloids the day after he was arrested for shagging a hooker off Sunset. Even that wouldn't be so bad. There's still something glamorous about being arrested for having an uncontrollable libido and indiscriminate taste in sexual partners. And he could afford bail, of course. Being arrested for that would be OK. But assault? On a woman?

Yosemite Sam leads me up a flight of stairs to a row of cells. He pauses by a steel closet. He pushes a blanket into my arms and I hear the pissing drunk wail in the darkness. Yosemite Sam touches the nightstick hanging from his belt and yells at him to shut up.

'You want something to read?' he says, turning back to me.

I nod. He hands me a book and a magazine from the closet and opens a cell door. There are bunk beds on one side, a stainless steel toilet and sink on the other. I step inside. The door clangs behind me and the lock turns. I hesitate a moment. At least I don't have to share with the pissing drunk. I haul myself up onto the top bunk. The drunk wails again and I hear Yosemite Sam rap his nightstick across the bars and whisper something violent. I'm exhausted and sleep comes surprisingly quickly.

In Devon, Connecticut, it is unlawful to walk backwards after sunset.

Waking up is much harder. Morning doesn't come easy to a place like the Santa Monica jailhouse. The inmates don't leap out of bed eager to start the bright new day. For a split second after I open my eyes I'm at home, stretched out under the soft feather quilt, ready to go for a morning run along the beach or a coffee at the café overlooking the ocean. Then I hear the drunk wailing again (has he been doing that all night?) and I feel sick.

Yosemite Sam offers me a tray of food, airplane-style. I have no appetite so just take a paper cup full of an unidentified orange liquid. It tastes thick and sugary, two parts orange cordial to one part water. I pour it out and fill the cup with lukewarm tap water. I ask to make another phone call. No. *Please.* No.

A long December and there's reason to believe ... Snippets of songs play in my head, an incongruous soundtrack for my prison movie. *Maybe this year will be better than the last* ... I try sleeping again but it's too noisy and I'm too cold. I have no socks on and the workout top is thin and short-sleeved and the blanket isn't long enough to stretch from my shoulders to my feet. I pick up the reading material, a six-month-old copy of *Popular Mechanics* and a book of short stories from a British author I've never heard of. I read the first story. It's set in a provincial English town in the 1930s. The narrator goes to visit his grandmother for high tea. He describes the parlour furniture for three pages. I still feel sick.

And it's one more day up in the canyons ... I stare at the frosted windows opposite my cell. One is cracked open, shielded by steel bars, and I can just make out the freeway onramp beyond. Morning commuters file onto Interstate 10 heading east towards Downtown. Sunlight glints off each car, diffused by a cloud of smog and exhaust fumes.

Morning passes (slowly) into afternoon. The traffic grows thinner. Yosemite Sam comes by with a lunch tray (is he on duty *all* the time?). Lunch is the same as breakfast: burger patty, refried beans, something yellow-white, and the orange liquid to drink. Can I *please* make a call? No. *Please*. No, ask again and you won't get any dinner. Dinner is the same as lunch: burger patty, refried beans, something yellow-white (what the hell *is* it?), more orange liquid. What about that call? OK. *Yeah?* Yeah, but just one.

Bubble answers on the second ring. I start to blurt everything out. She stops me, she already knows. I ask her to call the British Consulate and–

'Calm down,' she says, 'it's already being taken care of.'

Nervous has called my father in England. He's sorting out an attorney. Bubble has been trying to call me all day but they wouldn't put her through.

'Whatever you do, don't give a statement,' she says.

'What?'

'Just don't. Not without an attorney. Trust me.'

'What about Roxy?' I say. 'Have you heard from her?'

'She said she's sorry. She didn't mean for it to go this far.'

'So can she tell the cops that,' I say, 'get me the fuck out of here?'

'She has,' says Bubble. 'It doesn't matter, though.

They won't drop the charges, no matter what she says.'

She's right. I have been accused and in post-OJ Los Angeles that is enough. The District Attorney's office has a policy of never dropping domestic abuse cases and prosecutes with or without co-operation from the alleged victim.

'There's one more thing,' says Bubble.

'Yeah?'

She hesitates. 'She went back to her husband last night. He has connections at the DA's office. I don't think he likes you very much.'

I slump against the wall. My whole world is caving in around me.

'You still there?' Bubble sounds worried. 'Hey?'

'Yeah, I'm still here.'

'Listen, buddy, just hang in there. Nervous spoke to her this morning as well. She told him that you didn't touch her; she made it up. So whatever they come up with, you've got plenty of people on your side.'

'Thanks, Bubble.'

'I'll call tomorrow and see if they'll let us come see you.'

I nod and hang up.

The cell grows smaller as day turns into night. Car lights in the distance sweep across the frosted glass. Commuters returning home, white lights becoming red as traffic slips down and round and onto the freeway. *And it's one more night in Hollywood ...* The drunk is wailing again. It's the sound of night at the Santa Monica jailhouse. Wailing, screaming, a dull booming. The feelings come in waves. Boredom, frustration, disbelief. Frustration, disbelief, boredom.

Cellophane Girl would have been proud of me, acknowledging my feelings like this. And none that begin with the letter h.

I tune the Counting Crows out of my head and replace them with a rousing rendition of 'Jerusalem' to lift my spirits. *And did those feet in ancient times, walk upon England's mountains green* ... That's what I need. *And was the hol-y lamb of God on England's pleasant pastures seen?* Something, something *And was Jerusalem build-ed here, among these dark Satanic Mills* ... I wish I could remember the rest of the words. *Bring me my bow of burning gold, bring me my* something, something. *Bring me my Char-i-ot of Fire* ... Repeat until spirits raised or sleep ensues.

I doze, read, shiver, sing 'Jerusalem' in my head. I'll be out of here soon, I tell myself. Tuesday or Wednesday at the latest.

In Florida, it is illegal to sing in a public place while wearing a swimsuit.

I sleep fitfully. More wailing and shouting punctuates the night. A trio of fresh drunks join the pissing man, all screaming gibberish, like a chorus of dogs barking at the moon. I try to pull the blanket over my head but that leaves my feet uncovered. I shiver and curl up into a ball. Who knew LA could ever be so cold?

Morning arrives as hard as before, still no one bounding up to greet the sun. Breakfast: burger patty, refried beans, and more of the yellow-white stuff. All congealed together in a lukewarm blob.

I read the *Popular Mechanics* magazine again. Still don't understand what an alternator is. Struggle through another short story. This time the narrator visits his tailor and somebody called Violet Simmons. He has tea with both. In a tea shop this time, one he dedicates another three full pages to describing in excruciating detail. Quite frankly, I couldn't care less what the paper doilies look like or how many cream cakes the Violet Simmons character manages to devour. The drunks are wailing again and the yellow-white stuff has given me violent diarrhoea and there's no soap to wash my hands and Yosemite Sam has finally gone off duty. And all Violet bloody Simmons can do is stuff her face with chocolate eclairs and talk about the narrator's new suit.

I don't hear anything from the attorney. In fact I don't hear anything from anyone. *Any chance of making a call?* You've got to be kidding. No way. *What about some soap then? Just a small bar. I'll give it back when I'm done.* Lunch: burger patty, refried beans, and yellow-white stuff (don't touch that again). I'd swap it all for an apple or some toothpaste. The orange liquid has left my teeth covered in a strange fur and I'm convinced the front incisors are coming loose.

I finally get some soap. It comes in with a thin black guy sporting glazed eyes and a pair of expensive-looking Nikes. He hands me the soap without saying a word, drops onto the bunk below me and almost immediately starts snoring.

He sleeps all the way through to Tuesday morning. He wakes up when Yosemite Sam (back on duty) wheels around breakfast. He sucks down the burger and refried beans and even the yellow-white stuff without stopping for breath. I ask him what he thinks the yellow-white stuff is. He doesn't know, but he hasn't eaten for three days. I offer him mine. He siphons it straight down then introduces himself as Joey. He's been arrested for possession. Marijuana. He'll do three months jail time at the most, he says. Only bad thing is he'll have to do it at County.

'You think the food's bad here,' he says. 'You should have it at County. Man, that fucking place, you wouldn't believe it ...'

He asks what I'm in for. I tell him. 'You got an attorney or PD?' he says. I think my dad is sorting out an attorney. 'Ah, you'll be OK then,' he says. 'Ain't no way a white boy with an attorney is gonna get sent down to County on some bullshit charge. Are you gonna get back with her when you get out?'

I haven't even thought about that. Bubble said she was back with her husband. 'No, mate,' I say, 'not after all this.'

Joey nods and pulls his pants down and squats over the toilet. He lets out a loud fart and I hear liquid rattle against the stainless steel. I roll over on my bunk and try to block out the smell.

'Sorry, man,' he says. 'Fucking breakfast's gone straight through me.'

He does this twice more then decides we should play a game of Sorry. He uses the rest of the soap to mark out a board on the stone floor in front of the toilet then tears up pages from *Popular Mechanics* to make counters and dice. We sit cross-legged on the floor and play for hours, revising the rules, adding more counters as we go. It's the lamest, saddest game I've ever been a party to, but it silences the choruses of 'Jerusalem' and beats the hell out of high tea with Violet Simmons.

In California, it is illegal for women to drive in a housecoat.

Tuesday afternoon is arraignment time. Yosemite Sam opens the cell door and shackles my hands and feet to Joey and we shuffle along the corridor and down the stairs. The desk sergeant and her bright lipstick are back on duty. She glances at me as we bobble past like a geriatric conga and I hear her whisper to a colleague.

'Poor guy. They're taking him to County. How long's he gonna last in there?'

I strain my head to make eye contact with her but Yosemite Sam is intent on getting everyone out of the door and into the back of the waiting van as quickly as possible. The American legal system is nothing if not a well-oiled machine. Like a meat grinder.

The van bucks and jolts, throwing me alternately against Joey and the pissing man. He reeks of urine and regret, sober now. And quiet.

The van screeches to a halt and the back doors fly open. Sheriff's deputies, all regulation muscle and military buzz cuts, unload us like cattle at a slaughterhouse. I feel the sunlight hit my face and let my eyes close to savour the moment. When all else disappoints in Los Angeles, there's always the sunshine. I feel a shove in the back and nearly trip on the leg chains. I open my eyes and am already inside the holding cells behind the courtrooms.

A buzz cut unshackles the chains and cuffs and pushes us two at a time into a cell. Joey slumps onto the wooden bench and I pace the room, hovering near the door, panic mounting. Where is my attorney?

'What happens now?' I ask Joey again and again.

'Then what? And? Then what happens? I heard her say I was going to County – can that be right?'

He answers me each time with the patient tone of a parent answering a curious child. He's done this a dozen times before. I am a rookie. A 'fish'.

The door beyond the cell opens and a lean, bookish man clutching a battered briefcase strolls over to the cell. He looks like he's about to announce the budget. He smiles.

'Your father hired me,' he says pulling out a notepad from the briefcase. 'My name's Howard Roos. Here's my card. A friend of your dad's in London recommended me. You know Bill Moore, right?'

I do – he's a magistrate in Barnet – but that isn't what I want to talk about. He's trying to make polite conversation, chat about London and mutual friends and screenwriting, trying to put me at ease with his cell-side manner. But all I want to know is what the fuck is going on and how quickly can he get me the fuck out of here?

He senses my unease and instantly changes tack. 'So tell me what happened?' he says.

I press my face hard against the door and whisper through the steel bars. Add a tearoom scene, I think, and a Violet Simmons character and it would make a great short story. Howard makes notes on his pad as I talk, interrupting only occasionally for me to clarify a point or spell a name. By the time I'm done I'm exhausted. I've waited three days to tell someone all that.

He pats me on the arm and tells me they'll be taking me upstairs to appear before a judge in a moment but we'll have the opportunity to talk more afterwards.

*

I stand in the area normally reserved for the jury, cuffed again and chained to four other defendants, leg irons pulling tight on my ankles. A buzz-cut deputy tells us to sit. We sit.

The first guy is charged with marijuana possession and trafficking. His bail is reduced to $25,000. The second guy is on an attempted homicide rap. Bail is set at $25,000. The next guy is facing charges of first degree murder, heroin possession, illegal use of firearms, illegal possession of firearms, possession of stolen property, resisting arrest and driving under the influence of alcohol and narcotics. Bail is $50,000. I'm next. A tall District Attorney with pale, tight features and a mustard trouser suit addresses the fat little judge. She says I brutally attacked my girlfriend and have a history of abuse in England.

'That's not true!' I yell out.

Howard spins round and signals for me to be quiet. The DA continues. I am also an illegal alien, she says, therefore a flight risk. Howard explains to the judge that I'm a decent, law-abiding young man (apart from immigration laws, granted), and a judge in England will vouch for my good character, how about reducing the bail to $10,000?

The fat little judge considers it for half a second. 'Bail remains at fifty thousand,' he says and raps his gavel. 'Next!'

Bail is fifty grand, the same as if I'd been accused of killing someone, so I'm on the bus chained to a tattooed gangster and on my way to the Los Angeles County Jail.

*

Incoming Email:

> To: <BritWriter>
> From: <J2>
> Subject: Voice Message
>
> You have one new voice message.
> Click to download.

The message is from the Louisville attorney. He's been down to the jail and seen Nervous. He's taking his case and will be in touch with me tomorrow. I check out the Kentucky Offenders' web site again. This time Nervous's photo is up. He has a startled expression on his face, like a jowly priest who's been caught with his hands down a choirboy's pants. The charges are listed next to the photo. They're the same charges I faced. Inflicting corporal injury on a spouse or co-habitant, a little more serious than getting a salmon drunk or carrying a tub of lemon sorbet in his back pocket.

Byte 12 – Bottoming Out

I am at this all night. At some point Day 11 turns into Day 12, I'm just not exactly sure when. I surf the web for hours, looking up court documents at the LA Superior Court site, reading accounts from County Jail, reliving the events again. And writing it all down, the whole story. The words won't stop, they keep spewing out of me like lies from a politician. I need to tell this story. It's somehow tied up with my search for the American Dream. Someone once told me that you can never be sure what your real goals are in life until you've bottomed out.

I remember walking out of a club on Sunset early one morning and seeing a man in his early thirties lying on the sidewalk, his body wrapped around a tree. Puke seeped out the side of his mouth, his pants were round his knees and he was masturbating furiously. A week earlier he was probably another wide-eyed hopeful in search of Hollywood's version of the American Dream: an actor, perhaps, who'd been passed over one too many times; or a producer whose pilot had just been cancelled; or a writer whose screenplay option had just expired. Who knows? All

I can say for certain is that lying in the middle of the Sunset Strip wanking and puking had to be his moment of bottoming out. Didn't it? Surely there is no further anyone can fall . . .

The last words Roxy speaks to me that night still ring in my ears. 'I'm gonna have you arrested,' she spits. 'I'm gonna get you deported.'

Her vitriolic eulogy comes at the end of another wretched evening. She is horribly drunk and complaining bitterly about my oppressive, controlling personality. Maybe she has a point. I had refused to let her start a brawl in a nightclub and I was now doing my utmost to stop her wandering around the back streets of Santa Monica at three in the morning.

The evening began with a trip to the Baby Eater's house. Roxy's mother lives in a huge place in the hills above Encino overlooking Ventura Boulevard, the main artery pumping traffic and smog through the San Fernando Valley. The house, like its owner, has an ugliness that seeps deep below the aesthetics. The whitewashed boards fronting the house are weathered and beaten, deep termite tracks stream across the wooden deck like exhaust plumes from an aircraft, and inside, the air hangs thick and muggy.

We enter through the rear porch. The smell is sharp and overpowering: rotting meat. The Baby Eater sits in the armchair in front of the TV, watching *Cops* and eating chicken wings. I watch as she drops the tiny bones into a Styrofoam box next to her chair then licks the grease from her fingers. *Preschool Triplets Missing in Encino*, tomorrow's LA Times headline might read. *Bones Stripped of Flesh*.

I stare at the back of her head, the tight fresh perm

doing little to disguise the thinning hair. Her left arm moves rhythmically from lap to mouth to bone dump. Only the blue eyes are Roxy's, but less fiery now.

There's a loud *ping-ping* from the other side of the house. 'It's Hud,' the Baby Eater says, eyes not moving from the TV screen, 'playing pinball again.'

Hud is the Baby Eater's male companion. He's been around ever since Roxy's dad hit the bottom of the ravine (maybe even before that, Roxy isn't sure). Either way, he's been in and out of the house for the last twenty-five years. Roxy says they don't sleep in the same room – Hud has a room of his own in the basement – but she remembers as a kid hearing them doing it in the bathroom one time. Just the thought makes me feel nauseous.

Hud is old-time Hollywood. He produced a few B movies back in the day and claims to have been a lounge singer in Vegas. A few years ago he ran a public access TV show, broadcast live from the Baby Eater's basement. He'd fold away his sofa bed and dress up in a tux or top hat and tails and viewers would call in with requests for him to sing show tunes or old jazz standards.

'You sound just like Sinatra,' one caller told him.

'Better,' he said.

The noise disturbed the Baby Eater's TV viewing so she made him quit. Or maybe she just hated the idea that someone she knew was still chasing a dream. Now Hud spends all day dressed in a bathrobe, smoking cigars and playing pinball.

Roxy pulls out the videotape of her McDonald's TV commercial and goes to put it on. 'I'm watching this,' says the Baby Eater, indicating the TV.

'But it's the commercials,' says Roxy.

The Baby Eater sighs. 'But I don't wanna miss it when it comes back on.'

'It's like fifteen seconds long.'

The Baby Eater rolls her eyes. 'Fifteen seconds? I don't know why you're making such a fuss. I know what McDonald's looks like and I know what you look like. Why don't you do a TV show, a good one like Melrose or Roseanne? There's good money in TV. Ask Hud.'

'I don't need to ask Hud, mom. Do you wanna watch it or not?'

'At the end. When my show's over. Put it in then. But be quick. There's another one on after. They're showing back-to-back *Cops*.'

So we sit in silence for another twelve minutes as white policemen chase black criminals along miserable-looking streets. I stare at the back of the Baby Eater's head and say nothing. The programme ends. And the familiar theme song about *bad boys*, *bad boys* rings out.

'Mmm.' I say, like I'm savouring a fine wine. 'Great show.'

The Baby Eater mutes the volume and glances up at me. There's no love lost between us. I'm not successful enough or rich enough or handsome enough to even warrant her acknowledgement under normal circumstances. But the sarcasm in my voice is too much even for her to resist.

'You could do worse than write for that show,' she says. 'At least it pays.'

'He hates TV,' says Roxy. 'Don't you?'

I nod. 'There's not much on *Cops* that needs writing anyway.'

The Baby Eater snorts her derision again. 'Put the

tape in, Rox,' I say, 'while the commercials are still on.'

The *ping-ping* of Hud's pinball again. The tape plays. Baby Eater glances at her watch.

'He's been playing pinball for two hours,' she says. 'Two hours.'

Ping-ping. Roxy's eyes are fixed on the TV, watching herself on screen in a bikini, smiling, diving on the sand to spike a volleyball. Then she and a group of other fit, hopeful-looking young people eat fries and slurp on milkshakes. Cue the golden arches. End of commercial. Roxy looks across at her mother. She's still muttering about pinball and looking at her watch.

'Quick, quick,' she says, 'if I miss the beginning I won't know what city it's in.'

Roxy pulls out the tape. 'So what d'you think?' she says at last.

'Very short,' says the Baby Eater, biting down on the last chicken/child bone. 'You could hardly tell it was you.'

Ping-ping. Roxy decides it's time for us to leave. Baby Eater doesn't look up from the TV as we walk out. Twenty minutes of silence on the 405 and we reach Santa Monica and The Bar With No Name, a New York-style nightclub with exposed brick walls and huge velvet couches.

Roxy orders a beer and sucks down a couple of shots of whiskey. I say nothing and look around for Nervous. He's in town for a job interview and a blind date with a girl he met on the Internet. He wants Roxy and me nearby just in case she turns out to be too ugly even for him. I find him at the far end of the bar, looking very smart and very, well, very nervous.

Roxy joins us, sucking down another whiskey. Nervous congratulates her on the commercial. She shrugs and feigns modesty and recounts the details of how many takes it took for her to nail the volleyball spike. Nervous glances around trying to spot his date. Roxy is at the point where she criticises the director and the lighting guy for being 'unprofessional' when Nervous' jaw abruptly drops. I look over my shoulder to see a tall, thin, endlessly attractive girl approach.

'Bob?' she says. Nervous nods, jaw still resting on his chest. 'I'm Janelle.'

She looks like a catwalk model, designer threads emphasising the curve of her hips as she sashays closer to shake his hand. She smiles, all white teeth and sun-kissed skin. After all those years of going ugly early, Nervous has very suddenly and very definitely gone 'lovely late'.

Roxy says hello, tries to make conversation with her, two American girls united in their amusement of Englishmen, but she's already downed so much whiskey she isn't making a whole lot of sense. Janelle smiles and nods politely and casually sips beer from the bottle in her two thousand dollar outfit. She cracks jokes about meeting people on the Internet and recounts tales of modelling in Europe. Nervous stares at her, laughing in all the wrong places, unable to manage anything like coherent conversation. And Roxy glares at her. With *that* look. I can sense the change coming over her, the metamorphosis from girl-I-travelled-across-the-globe-for to rabid-homicidal-maniac. Janelle's appearance has not only subdued the world's most enormous personality it has also ignited the world's most volatile. I can see it in

Roxy's eyes. This girl is taller, thinner, younger, prettier, richer, better dressed. And happier.

I kiss Roxy on the cheek and whisper in her ear, 'You want a glass of water?'

She glares at me. 'Fuck you.' And downs another whiskey.

She stumbles onto the dance floor, which is really just the area furthest from the bar and the couches, and starts swinging her hips. A couple of guys immediately join her, like steel shavings drawn to a magnet. She smiles and whoops and shoots a quick glance back to the bar to make sure we're all watching. She has to wrest the limelight from Janelle somehow. She's the actress, the singer, the dancer. So she dances. As provocatively as she can until the whole bar is staring at her.

The music fades and the lights rise. One of the steel shavings approaches me, flushed and sweaty from dancing.

'That your girlfriend?' he says.

I nod. He gives me a conspiratorial nudge and says, 'I bet she's a great fuck.'

He turns and heads back towards the dance floor. I watch him walk off, not sure whether I'm supposed to find that funny or annoying.

Roxy shakes me by the arm. 'What did that guy say to you?'

'What?'

She's caked in sweat, hair stuck to her face, makeup streaking down her cheeks. 'What did that fucking guy say?'

'It doesn't matter,' I say.

If I even hinted at what he said, she'd scamper across the bar after him, swinging her fists like a rotary scythe. I'm an illegal alien, the last thing I want is to be involved in a bar fight.

'Let's just go.'

'Tell me!'

'It doesn't matter.'

'It was something about me, wasn't it?'

'No.'

'Then tell me what the fuck he said!'

'Rox, please don't start. My friend's in town, can we please just get along.'

'Fuck you,' she says, picking up a beer bottle by the neck. 'I'll make him tell me.'

I grab her hand. 'For God's sake, what are you doing?'

Damn, I should have let her hit him. Then maybe she would have found herself sitting on that bus instead of me. It's a mistake, but then even great men make mistakes. Napoleon made a mistake at Blucher, Churchill at Goschen and I've just made my first.

'Tell me what he fucking said!'

Nervous and Janelle walk over. 'I'm walking Janelle back to her car,' he says, eyes down like a scolded puppy. I know that look. It isn't working out with her. Poor Nervous. 'I'll call you tomorrow, huh.'

I nod and watch them walk off. I turn back to Roxy. 'This place is done, you ready to go?'

She starts to follow me outside, then pulls away from me. 'So what did he say?'

'He didn't say anything.'

She picks up a glass by the entrance. 'I'll smash this in his fucking face.'

I wrestle the glass from her and put it back on the bar and somehow manage to get her outside. It's like trying to have a romantic evening with a Millwall supporter. Mistake number two: I repeat my first mistake.

I walk back to the van. Roxy dallies a few yards behind me like a petulant toddler, spitting abuse. I am controlling, a control freak, a fucking uptight control freak, passive-aggressive English motherfucker. 'Tell me what he fucking said!' She yells over and over. I just want to get to the van, get home and get her sobered up. Mistake number three: I only realise at this moment, at this fag end of yet another pitiful evening, that I'm not having fun anymore.

We reach the parking lot on the corner of Second and Colorado. It's quiet and dark and reeks of petrol fumes. I look around uneasily. Roxy's voice echoes in the darkness. I open the passenger door.

'Here, get in,' I say.

'No.'

I take a deep breath. 'Look,' I say, as calmly as I can manage. 'You've had a few drinks, let me drive you home. I'll sleep on the couch and we'll talk about this in the morning.'

'Fuck you! Tell me what that cunt said. Tell me what he fucking said, you jerkoff Limey motherfucker!'

'Look, darling,' I say. 'I'm getting mixed signals here. If you're in any way displeased with me, I think you should say so.' An attempt at humour to lighten the situation. It sometimes works.

'Fuck you!' Not this time, apparently.

I unlock the driver's door and pull up the house brick handbrake. I start the engine, flick on the radio and sit back. *Star 98.7 FM, bad pop all day, every day.* The only channel I can pick up clearly. '*If you think that you might come to California ... I think you should ...'* sing The Counting Crows.

I can't leave Roxy there. Not at three in the morning. Eventually, I figure, she'll grow tired of the game and get in the car. At least she might stop screaming obscenities. I've had four beers over the course of the evening, not enough to put me over the limit, but enough to perhaps prompt a passing cop to start asking questions, questions like where's your driver's licence or, worse still, where's the stamp in your passport?

Sting is singing *I'm So Happy That I Can't Stop Crying* by the time Roxy walks up to the passenger door. Mistake number four, the granddaddy of all mistakes, the mistake that will forever haunt me, forever change my perspective on relationships, LA and the power of a crazy woman: I make her get in the van.

She slumps onto the seat next to me and pulls the door closed. I force the van into reverse and pull out. She's staring at me, her face that dangerous puce colour again. She snatches at the radio dial and changes the station.

'Your taste in music sucks,' she says, still pushing for a fight.

I say nothing. I turn right out of the parking lot onto Second Street and immediately realise I should have turned left. I pull into the left turn lane at the junction of Broadway. The lights are red.

A flash of pain suddenly explodes in my cheek. Instinctively I cover my face with my hand. She punches me again. Not a playful, catty punch but a screwed-up fist pulled back and weightily launched into my cheek.

'For God's sake!' I scream. 'Not while I'm driving!'

The lights turn from red to green. Mistake number five: I carry on driving. I catch my breath and turn left and then take another left into the late night traffic on Ocean.

'I'm gonna have you arrested,' she spits. 'I'm gonna get you deported.'

She punches me again, in the eye this time and everything suddenly goes blurry and rushes towards me in a series of rapid cuts like an MTV music video ...

I hold up one hand to shield myself and steer with the other. White lights of the cars behind flare in the side mirror. Roxy's teeth sink into my arm. Fuck! I pull it back and shake her off. Her face: puce and pale at the same time, fury, hatred. Launches another punch towards me. I bat it away and scan the street for somewhere to pull over. Nothing. Mirror, lights. Don't make any erratic manoeuvres, don't do anything that might attract the attention of any cops – another punch ... and another in quick succession, a left and a right maybe. Steering wheel slips, van skids across two lanes. Christ alive, am I being beaten up by a girl? A horn blares, a car swerves around me. Shit, fuck. Please no cops, please no cops. Another punch. Veering again, in front of oncoming traffic this time. I pull on the wheel, hold my arm out to keep her fist away. Straighten the van. Phew ... She screams and pushes open the door. Somewhere to stop, please, somewhere to stop. Where, where? White lights in the mirrors. Still traffic behind. Her seatbelt undone. What's she – Jesus, she's going to jump!

I hit the brakes and reach for her. Brakes lock. Old

tires on new pavement. Lights in the mirror, moving, swerving. Car horns. I grab the strap of her bag but – snap! She launches herself out of the van. Rubber tracks on the street. Brakes catch. Van skids to a halt.

The whole thing lasts ten seconds, maybe fifteen. The last I see of her she's jumping out into the night. The van stops forty or fifty yards further up the road. I spin round to scan the street behind me. Shake my head to clear the blurry vision. No Roxy. I turn back and spot an empty meter further on. I pull over and jump out of the van and run back along the street. I scan the park that runs alongside, separating Ocean from the sheer drop down to PCH and the beach. Homeless people in soiled blankets and sleeping bags, curled up on benches, under trees but no Roxy. I run along the side streets and back streets. No Roxy. I can't find her. I walk back to the van, cheek stinging, a sharp pain in my forearm. Blood seeps from the teeth marks. Did she bite me? She must have. I tell myself she must be OK, she probably got a taxi back to the apartment. If she hurt herself in the fall, she couldn't have run off so fast, right?

I drive back to the apartment, but she isn't there. Where can she be? At a friend's house? She doesn't have any. At her mother's? Maybe. Fuck it, I lie down on the bed, but keep my watch on, a simple act that's usually enough to keep me from falling in to a deep sleep. She'll be home any minute and I want to be awake when she walks in. I don't know it then, of course, but I'm about to embark on an eleven-month journey that I could never have envisioned. And the glittering prize at the end of it promises to be a felony conviction, two years in a state penitentiary and ignoble deportation.

Five mistakes or just one, one huge one? If there was somewhere for me to pull over, what then? Would the same thing have happened anyway, later or on a different night? Or would that have been warning enough for me to get away from her? Was I trying to avoid the cops at precisely the time I should have been trying to find them? How many mistakes did Nervous make, I wonder, one big one or lots of little ones, or both?

Nervous's attorney leaves a message on my voice-mail. The arraignment is scheduled for this afternoon. He'll contact me afterwards with news of whether he's been granted bail. Whatever happens, it seems likely that Nervous will spend at least one night in the County lockup.

Outgoing Email:

> To: <Ralph>
> From: <BritWriter>
> Subject: Money
>
> I need bail money. Or rather, one of my degenerate friends does. Any chance of getting an advance on the rest of the columns? Wouldn't ask if it wasn't important.

Receive another message from the attorney. Nervous' bail is $25,000, half that of mine. He has a green card, a job, and an apartment with furniture in it. Evidently that makes him less of a flight risk.

Byte 13 – Number 460702

Incoming Email:

> To: <BritWriter>
> From: <Ralph>
> Subject: Re: Bail Money
>
> Not sure about the wisdom of advancing you money. Is it really such a big deal if he has to spend a night or two in jail? How bad can it be?

Los Angeles is often described as the planet's richest third-world city. At the Downtown Men's Central Jail I finally understand why.

The bus pulls up at County some time after dusk. We file off one at a time, legs and arms in chains linking us together. I look up to see the Twin Towers Correctional Facility looming overhead. It's destined to be the world's largest jail facility, I find out later, with enough space to house 4,200 inmates. But right now it's empty. Political wrangling, the details of which I can't remember, means that more than 7,000 inmates are squeezed into Men's Central, the crumbling structure next door that's designed to house less than a third of that number.

As I step through the entrance and stare at the windowless interior, I think I've found my moment of bottoming out. But I'm not even close. The chains and cuffs come off and I shuffle into a stark room with a hundred others, the solitary white face among a sea of black and brown. Another huge buzz cut deputy orders everyone to empty their pockets and turn to face the wall. I pull out a tissue and a crossword puzzle I tore from the *Practical Engineering* magazine and drop them on the floor. I stare at the wall. It was obviously whitewashed once, but most of the paint has long since peeled away from the grey-brown cement. I run my fingers against it. It's moist with damp. 'Hands by your sides!' the buzz cut barks. 'Turn around!'

I shuffle around. The tissue and crossword puzzle have been swept away. The buzz cut stands in front of me and shakes his head. Evidently, I look even more out of place than I realise.

'What the fuck are *you* doing in here?' he says. It's a rhetorical question. He stares at me trying to figure it out. 'What are you charged with?'

'Assault,' I say.

'What, hit your boyfriend did you?' He thinks this is hilarious. I hold his gaze as long as I dare. He snorts, pleased to have had the last word, and moves on.

The next room is similar to the first – damp cement and rusty bars – save for a few wooden benches in the middle and a thick glass window, like a ticket counter, set into the far wall. There are already a hundred or so inmates in there, crushed together on the benches, spread-eagled on the stone floor, one is even asleep against the latrine. I find a space against a dank wall and slump to the floor and the painfully slow process of admission begins.

A female deputy behind the thick glass calls out names one by one. And I wait, shivering with cold, tired beyond belief but too scared and too uncomfortable to fall asleep. A fight breaks out every now and then. I shift along the wall, trying to keep out of the way. One savage-looking Hispanic, his face and neck covered in homemade tattoos, pummels a smaller man's face against the stone floor. He has three black tears tattooed under the corner of his left eye, one for each 'kill'. He wants the other guy's shoes. By the time a deputy strolls in, his victim is laying semiconscious on the floor, blood seeping out from his mouth and forehead. As the deputy drags him out by his bare feet, I catch a glimpse of what looks like a front tooth lying next to his ear.

Joey speaks to me once or twice but he knows he shouldn't. He's black, I'm white, and this is County. We're at the sharp end of a racially divisive city. Every cell, every room is divided in two: blacks on one side, Hispanics on the other. They sit on different benches, eat at different tables, piss at different latrines. The few Caucasians in there – most white boys have attorneys and can afford bail – hover nervously somewhere in between. They can sit on the Hispanic side, but only on the floor, not on a bench. They can use the Hispanic toilet but only if no Mexican is waiting. And they can't so much as talk to any black. 'Nigger lovers' are dealt with swiftly. Joey nods at me. I understand.

*

I hear my name called. The deputy behind the glass – a different one now – straps a numbered armband to my wrist. I'm number 460702. I ask her what time it is. So many hours have passed in that windowless room, it's impossible to even guess the time.

'Ten thirty,' she says. I stare at her. 'In the morning,' she adds.

I've been sitting against the wall for sixteen hours.

I'm herded into yet another packed, windowless room and ordered to strip. Most of the men in there look like Chicano versions of the Guy Pierce character from *Memento*: arms, torsos, legs covered in random black lettering, huge crucifixes, images of the Virgin Mary, smoking guns, black tears. They have black teeth, gold teeth, missing teeth. Bald heads, long moustaches that curl like pieces of black felt from top lip to mid-throat and even longer yellow-white scars across the face, from temple to cheek or ear to shoulder blade, knife wounds, broken bottle wounds, bullet wounds.

I drop my jeans, boxers and workout top in a plastic bag and sit naked, legs straddling a long wooden bench, staring at the back of a Mexican's head. I'm only allowed to keep my shoes – the battered beach shoes. A trustee – a convicted inmate on work duty, discernible by his bright orange jumpsuit – hands out regulation uniforms: undershorts yellowed with bleach stains, blue trousers that end mid calf on me and a baggy blue top, like a short-sleeved fisherman's smock, with 'LA County Jail' daubed in white letters on the back.

I dress then sit back on the bench and wait, staring at the shaved head in front of me. A black tattoo wrapped around his neck reads Eighteenth Street, a

Downtown gang notorious for drive-by shootings. Another trustee hands out breakfast, or lunch maybe, I can't be sure how much more time has passed. Either way, it consists of a bologna sandwich and a carton of sugary drink. More time passes staring at the tattoo, swaying back every time he moves, making sure we never actually touch, in case the propensity for extreme violence passes like a virulent disease through the skin. I just want to sleep. A trustee drops a blanket in my lap. We stand. We file out and line up along a corridor wall. The once-white walls stretch as far as I can see, dotted intermittently with steel doors. The floor is marked out in different coloured lines – red, yellow, blue – like psychedelic highway lane dividers. Every sound echoes, amplified as it rumbles along the corridor.

   I'm next to Joey again. He whispers something but I don't hear what so I nod and try to look like this is just another day at the office for me. The line starts to move along the yellow marks. I enter what looks like a canteen at a homeless shelter following a riot. It's a day room that's been hurriedly converted to a cell. There are half a dozen shiny metal picnic tables fixed to the floor. Only people aren't eating at them, they're lying on them, huddled under blankets. A broken TV, a clock and naked light bulbs sit behind steel mesh covers. Benches snake around three sides of the room and a few bare bunk beds stand in rows, like deckchairs on a winter beach. A torn sheet hangs over the far corner, partly shielding a sink and two toilets, one of which is overflowing with piss and excrement. I glance down at the floor. Sewage gathers in yellow-brown pools around my feet and the islands of trash that rise up like shifting rocks in the surf.

I move through them, displacing sandwich crusts, empty drinks cartons and used toilet rolls.

I follow Joey towards the adjoining room. A hand pulls me back. I spin round and come face to face with a Hell's Angel, with a shaved head, long ginger goatee and alarmingly vacant eyes.

'Only niggers in there,' he says. 'Woods in here.'

I nod. I knew that really.

I quickly realise the name of the game is musical chairs. In a room meant to house thirty inmates, there are nearer sixty or seventy fighting for a piece of space. The music stops when the last inmate is in and the door closes. The losers sleep on the floor with all the piss and shit and garbage. The beds and tables are all taken so I dart for a spot on the bench behind a row of bunks. It's just wide enough to lie on my side without falling off. I wrap myself up in the blanket and look up at the clock. It's 5.30. PM I think. There are no windows in the room – there are no windows anywhere in the jail – and the naked lights shine constantly. I've already been in County Jail for twenty-three hours. I pull the blanket over my head and try to sleep. Is this it, I wonder, the moment that I finally bottom out?

Day turns into night and turns into day again. It makes little difference. Night isn't much quieter than the day. A sudden movement wakes me up in the early hours. A swarm of Hispanic gangsters brush past me and use chair legs to beat the guy asleep in the cot by my feet. The deputies either don't hear or don't care. I lie still with my eyes closed, pretending to be asleep, listening to the sickening sounds of metal on bone. The guy eventually struggles to the door, drenched in his own blood, and calls for help. His attackers slink back to their cots, cockroaches disappearing into the shadows. A deputy opens the door and he staggers out. I curl myself into a tight ball and try my hardest to fall back to sleep.

Breakfast and lunch are served through the hatch in the door. Trustees throw bologna sandwiches and sugary drinks in to us. Fights break out in the rush for food. Dinner is served in the food hall, a five-minute march along the *blue* line on the corridor floor. The routine is simple: grab a tray of food-like substance, sit at a long picnic table, eat until a deputy shouts move, then clear your tray and leave. And don't even think about trying to take any food with you. The whole process takes less than three minutes. My chest burns with indigestion as I march back to the cell along the *red* line. It will take me weeks after getting out to learn how to eat slowly again. Anyway, the latrines are overflowing, there's no soap and no toilet paper. It's better not to eat too much; it reduces the frequency I have to add to the sewage.

A heavy-set, acne-scarred man in the bunk by my head turns to me.

'I'm fucked,' he says by way of introduction.

He's caught in the Three Strikes Law, he says. He was arrested for possession of marijuana, but it was his third offence, so he's facing a minimum sentence of twenty-five years. Twenty-five years for possession of a single joint seems excessive, even for Los Angeles. I eye the swastikas tattooed on his enormous forearms. He says he used to be a racist but has now found God. He pulls out a bible and reads a passage to me. I nod politely and pretend to be interested.

'I can just see you on the outside,' he says, laughing to himself. 'Anyone fucked with you yet?'

'No,' I say.

'You better eat, just the same. Keep your strength up.'

He squeezes some of his toothpaste out on my finger so I can rub it over my teeth. He also gives me a pencil and a tiny notepad. I make notes for a screenplay about an alien creature that devours inmates in the County Jail.

There's a payphone in the corner that accepts collect calls. I wait for the Mexicans to finish using it then call Bubble and Nervous and my attorney. Howard tells me that my dad has wired him the bail money. He still can't get me out, though. As soon as he posts bail, Immigration will arrest me and take me to one of their jails. I'll have to be processed, appear before a judge and post a second bail. That will all take time and I might miss a court date on the criminal trial.

'If you miss a court date,' says Howard, 'even if it's because you're in INS custody, they'll issue a bench warrant for your arrest and your father will lose his bail money.'

'So how long do I have to stay in here?' I ask, not looking forward to the answer.

'At least until the bail hearing next week,' he says. 'We'll try to get you out then.' His voice changes, suddenly dropping to a whisper. 'How is it in there?'

'Mmm,' I say. 'Delightful.'

'Anyone ... messing with you?'

Why does everyone keep asking me that? I look around, not sure quite what I should be expecting. 'No,' I say.

'Just keep your head down. I'll be down tomorrow to see you. Call anytime you want.'

I hang up. A couple of Mexicans sidle over to me. They look like all the other Hispanic gangsters: short, shaved heads, aggressive facial hair, tattoos.

'Over here, homes,' one says, nodding his head towards the far side of the room.

'What?'

'The Man wants to see you, homie,' the other one says.

Oh, shit, I think. Maybe this is it. I follow them over. The Hell's Angel with the ginger goatee and wild, empty eyes signals for me to sit down on the bunk in front of him. The Hispanic gangsters huddled round him make space for me. This is The Man.

'Where you from, homes?' The Man speaks like a Mexican. 'Whatchoo doin' in here?'

He assesses my case in about thirty seconds, a jailhouse Johnny Cochran on speed. He tells me I'm fucked, the best I can hope for is a suspended sentence. I tell him I'm not guilty.

He snorts. 'No one in here is, ess-sai.'

He tells me to stay away from the niggers and if I need anything I should come to him. And that's it; I can go. The little gangsters look disappointed. I walk back to my space on the bench before he changes his mind.

Four or five days pass, maybe more. I'm so bored I swap my blanket for an airport paperback about a second Korean War. I ration my daily dose so the book will last longer. Fifty pages a day, sixty at most, read slowly, twice if necessary, anything to make it last. My mouth is dry; I desperately want to clean my teeth. The incisors seem to be getting looser.

I'm moved to another cell. Inmates in County Jail

seem to be in perpetual motion, shuffled from one cell to the next for no discernible reason other than there simply isn't enough space to house everyone. I spend twenty of the next twenty-four hours lined up in another dark windowless corridor, shivering with cold. The floor is covered in huge puddles of liquid (urine?) and mounds of discarded food. It reeks of piss and vomit.

More bologna sandwiches for lunch. I sit on my haunches against the wall, ankle deep in trash, arms tucked under the fisherman's smock, hugging myself to get warm. It's far from being the usual balmy seventy degrees in here. I wish I still had that blanket.

Eventually, I'm moved to a two-bunk cell that already contains six people, wrestling for space on the floor to lie down. The only room left is next to the toilet. I lay down with my head just inches from the filthy bowl and use the paperback as a pillow. I'm still shivering. The guy on the floor nearest the front stuffs blankets under the door. I ask him if I can have one of them.

'No way, homes,' he says. 'Gotta to stop the rats gettin' in.'

The next morning I'm moved again, this time not just to a different cell but an entirely different facility. The Sheriff's Department receives money each time an inmate is checked into a new facility, so they keep them moving from one place to the next as often as possible. The Wayside jail is situated near the Magic Mountain theme park, an hour's drive north of LA. It's a much newer lock up than Men's Central, the sanitary equivalent of George Michael: outwardly neat and tidy but still likely to effect something unpleasant. Of the varying security levels, I'm placed not in minimum security or even maximum security, but *super maximum* security. There is no Fletcher or Godber or Mr Barrowclough to exchange witty banter with. I'm with the bad boys: the drive-by shooters, the rapists, the gang-bangers.

Inside, deputies remove the chains and handcuffs and what is to become a degrading daily ritual begins. Surrounded by three-dozen hardcore felons, all stripped naked, I'm ordered to bend forward, spread my butt cheeks and cough. A deputy then shines a flashlight up my arse looking for contraband.

That has to be the moment, the equivalent of lying on a busy sidewalk, trousers round my knees and puke dribbling from my mouth, while I masturbate for England. When I came to LA I had nothing on my mind except writing movies and falling in love. Now a barrel-chested law enforcement officer is peering up my arse. It's official. I've plummeted as far as I can. And everything becomes as clear as it ever has. What do I want most? To get out, sure, but then what? A dozen thoughts rush through my head but they all slowly dissolve into to a single image: the beach at Santa Monica. LA's my home. I know that now for certain. And I don't want to leave.

The cells at Wayside are a similar dormitory-style to those in Men's Central, although much cleaner and with enough bunks (and mattresses) for every inmate. There are showers in the room, too, and I'm finally able to purchase a 'fish kit', a toiletry bag with toothbrush, toothpaste and shampoo.

I call my attorney and tell him I've been moved to Wayside. 'They moved you *where*?' his voice is filled with disbelief.

'Wayside,' I repeat.

'Dear God,' he says.

A couple of weeks ago, there had been a major riot, a massive altercation between blacks and Mexicans. Officers in riot gear stormed the cells firing tear gas and rubber bullets. Several inmates were killed, a dozen or so seriously injured.

'I can't believe they put you there,' Howard says. Neither can I. 'Just stay alive,' he says.

I sit on my bunk and sing 'Jerusalem' in my head again and read my carefully rationed fifty pages of pulp fiction. A piercing alarm rips me from *England's green and pleasant land*. Red lights flash and the pounding of military-issue boots echoes along the corridor. It's a lock-down. Deputies in kevlar body armour, guns at the ready, storm into the cell, screaming at everyone to lay face down on their bunks. Anyone who moves will be shot, they yell. They toss the place, ripping up mattresses, sifting through fish kits, searching for weapons and other contraband. I lay face down, barely daring to breathe. Someone screams. I don't look up. I'm not here, I'm somewhere else. *And was Jerusalem built here, Among these dark Satanic Mills?* The screaming continues. Real pain. I hear the deputies back out, dragging someone with them. But still I don't look up. The room slowly comes back to life. Hushed chatter; someone curses. I remain frozen on the bunk, eyes closed.

I call Bubble that evening.

'I saw Roxy,' she says. 'She's changed her story again. She's going to testify against you.'

'And say what, for God's sake?'

'That you pushed her out of the van.'

I want to laugh. I should laugh. But it just won't come out. 'Why?' I say. 'Why is she doing this?'

'She wanted to know if you'd asked after her,' Bubble says. 'If you were worried about her.'

'What did you tell her?'

'I didn't really think about it. I just told her I thought you had a lot of other stuff on your mind.'

'And?'

'She was pissed. Said you didn't care about anyone but yourself.' Bubble takes a deep breath. 'She now says she broke her nose when she hit the ground.'

'Did she?'

'No, of course not.'

'Did her husband put her up to this or something?'

'I don't think so. That might be the problem. I don't think he wants anything to do with her. She's blaming you for that as well.'

'For breaking up her marriage?'

'She's crazy, she really is. What were you thinking, buddy?'

'I know, I know, I'm an idiot.'

She gives me the chin-up talk and says she'll see me in court. 'See you in court. Always wanted to say that.'

I sit in the jury box again. This is a hearing to show cause, Howard tells me. I want to testify, to finally tell my side of the story. He says that isn't protocol. It's better to hold my testimony for the trial.

He's spoken to the DA prosecuting my case. She's convinced that I pushed Roxy out of the van. It's so absurd I want to laugh again. But all that comes out is a sort of chuckle-come-grunt. Howard frowns.

'Are you OK?'

'Jack the Hat,' I say. Howard doesn't get it. 'Have you ever seen a British movie called *The Krays*?'

He shakes his head. 'Well Roxy has. She was a big fan of the book it was based on.'

I tell him about the letters she wrote to Reggie Kray and how Jack 'The Hat' McVitie threw his wife out of a moving car. 'It's quite a well-known story in England,' I say. 'The Kray twins ended up killing him.'

'Because he threw his wife out of a car?'

'Partly.'

Howard shakes his head in disbelief. 'Is that going to help us?' I say.

'I doubt it. Unless we screen the movie in court.'

The DA won't offer a plea bargain of any kind. She wants to hit me with the maximum possible charges. 'I'm going to put him away,' she tells Howard.

The next court appearance is set for ten days' time. It's the window of time we've been looking for. I have ten days to get discharged from County, transferred to the custody of the INS, make an appearance in immigration court, post bail there and get released. Ten days, not a moment more or I'll officially be a fugitive.

A deputy turns to lead me out of the court but the judge stops him. He looks me in the eye. 'This isn't the crime of the century,' he says. 'So don't make it worse by jumping on a plane and going back to England.'

Incoming Email:

> To: <BritWriter>
> From: <Ralph>
> Subject: Re: Bail Money
>
> OK, point made. We'll advance you the rest of the month's payment. Get your friend out of there.

Byte 14 – Dreaming of Mondays

The Ferris wheel shifts in the distance. The sand is warm between my toes. I'm on the beach at Santa Monica, watching the surf chase up the shore, listening to 'A Long December' again: *It's been so long since I've seen the ocean ... I guess I should ...* The sun pecks at my shoulders. I close my eyes and shift my weight in the sand. Someone calls my name from across the beach. I'm too relaxed to even look up. My name again, louder this time. I come to with a start. An INS officer is barking at me from the door.

The movie running through my head spools to a halt. I'm in another holding cell, but one that feels more like a Latino street market – filled with the aroma of fried onions and Mexicans pacing up and down, yacking away to each other in Spanish. I've swapped Men's Central with an INS holding pen and the blue two-piece for my street clothes: the workout top and beach shoes again. But my underwear has gone. What the hell happened to that, I wonder? Is there some illicit trade in used underwear from county jail inmates? I make a mental note to search on eBay when I get out, keywords: inmate undies. The INS officer barks at me again. I shuffle over, my balls rubbing against the rough denim of my jeans.

The officer raises his eyebrows. 'Not disturbing you are we?'

He's a short, stocky man wearing a cheap shirt dotted with coffee stains. The buttons strain against his round paunch and look as if they might pop at any moment. He reeks of stale tobacco.

'I was on the beach,' I say. And smile.

His eyes are cold. 'You won't be seeing the beach for a long time, Englishman.' He hisses through his nose as he speaks. 'Not in this country.'

I follow him into a square room with beige walls and a single table in the centre. He drops the file of papers he was carrying with a thud then kicks a chair out like the cops do in the movies. All his movements seem exaggerated for dramatic effect. He indicates for me to take a seat.

'So when did you enter the United States?' he hisses.

'July ninth,' I say.

'So you've been here well over a year.'

'Yeah.'

He pulls out my passport from his folder. 'Always makes it so much easier when you've got the passport.' He grins, revealing a set of crooked teeth and a couple of missing molars. 'Ms Hepburn gave it to us.'

I shrug.

'You threw her out of a moving car,' he says.

'That's not true.' I say.

'Yes it is true. You're a woman abuser and you're gonna spend the next two years behind bars.' I study his face, trying to figure him out.

'State penitentiary,' he says. 'You know what the niggers and the wet backs do to people like you in there?'

There isn't much to figure out, I decide. He's just another fat, buzz-cut racist. And he's long overdue a visit to the dentist.

'You know what they do, huh?' The gaps in his teeth grin back at me.

'What's this got to do with immigration?' I say.

'Everything. You pushed her out of a car.'

'Look, I didn't. And anyway, it's being dealt with in the criminal court.'

'She said you pushed her out.'

'She's lying.'

'No she's not,' he says, shaking his head like he's dealing with a difficult child. '*You're* lying.' I hate those cold eyes. You can't reason with eyes like that. I just have to let him bully me. I shift in my seat.

'You overstayed your visa.' It isn't a question.

'I know,' I say. 'I've admitted that.'

'Did you work?'

'Yes.'

'Who did you work for?'

I sigh. The last thing I want to do is get anyone else in trouble. 'We'll find out anyway,' he says.

'I worked for myself. Before that for the Job Connection.' I give him the name of the guy that owns the Job Connection web site. 'He had no idea I was illegal.'

The fat racist looks pleased. 'You'll do time for tax evasion as well.'

'I paid taxes.' I say. When I first got here I applied for a social security number. I received a card with a number that was stamped 'not eligible for employment'. I bought a forged one outside a McDonald's in Koreatown with the same number but no stamp. The Job Connection site deducted taxes at source.

He seems disappointed. 'Look mate,' I say, trying to disguise the fear and anger pissing through my veins. 'All I've done wrong is overstay my visa and work illegally. And I've admitted to both.'

His disappointment turns to anger like a switch being flicked. 'You beat your girlfriend up.' He's on his feet, leaning over me now, screaming. 'You're a fucking woman abuser.' His fleshy ears have turned pink and his spittle peppers my face as he yells. 'You fucking beat her up and you're going to prison and then you're going to get deported!'

I lean back and chew nervously on the inside of my mouth. There's crazy in those eyes and I don't want to provoke him any further. He slowly sits down.

'Is my lawyer here yet?' I say.

'What lawyer? You're not getting a fucking lawyer!' He's out of his seat again. He slams his fist down on the open folder – another gesture straight out of the movies – and his ears flush pink again. 'You're mine, you fucker!'

I know the script. This is the moment where I get the shit kicked out of me. They find me lying in a bloody heap on the floor. He'll have to take early retirement but I'll lose my front teeth and a lung and a few ribs or something. This guy is nuts.

The door opens and another officer peers in. 'His attorney's here,' he says.

I breathe a sigh of relief and the fat racist slumps back into his chair. I watch the pink drain from his ears like the level on a thermometer on a cold night.

He nods his head at me. 'Get him outta here.'

Incoming Email:

> To: <BritWriter>
> From: <Abby>
> Subject: Byte 14
>
> I see where you're going with this. Are you sure you should be telling this story?

Outgoing Email:

> To: <Abby>
> From: <BritWriter>
> Subject: Re: Byte 14
>
> No, I'm not sure, but I've started, it would be weird to stop now. I'm on the trail of the American Dream and I've picked up my first clue. I found it in the torchlight of a contraband search in super maximum security. And this is where it's leading me.

My attorney is leaning against the wall chatting easily with an INS officer when I enter the visiting room, relieved to be away from crazy, pink-ears.

'Hi, man.' Carl Grbac looks like a beat poet, an ex-California hippie who's never quite shaken off his roots. He has raw, pockmarked skin, a short ponytail partially hidden by the collar of his shirt and a hint of blond stubble on his chin. I look round for Scooby-Doo.

'So,' he says, adjusting the lie of his jacket. 'How's it going?'

Howard told me he comes highly recommended.

He's a little unorthodox but is very tight with the immigration judges. I figure he probably dropped acid with them or led them on civil rights marches in the 60s. He sits me down and goes over my case, umming and ahhh-ing occasionally then adjusting his jacket. He seems uncomfortable in the confines of a grey linen suit. He'd probably look more at ease in a tie-dyed T-shirt and an enormous reefer hanging from the corner of his mouth.

'Well,' he says leaning back in his chair. 'We shouldn't have a problem. All we're asking the judge to do is let you stay in the country long enough to have the criminal charges dismissed. Then you'll leave voluntarily.' I nod. 'You just won't be allowed to work while you're here,' he says.

I ask him how I'm supposed to live. 'We'll tell the judge your father's going to support you.' My father doesn't have that kind of money. And even if he did, I can't expect him to pay for me to spend months sitting in the sun.

Carl smiles. 'Don't worry, man,' he says. 'They have no way of checking up. If you need to work, work. Pay taxes, keep outta trouble and everything'll be cool. Just don't tell the judge I said that.'

He smiles and adjusts his jacket again. Great, I think. I've got Jack Kerouac as an attorney.

Back in the holding cell, a small South American guy in expensive trousers barks at the guards. He claims he was mistakenly arrested at the airport. He has a green card, he says. He threatens all kinds of legal action and seems adamant that his captors will never work again. He wants to speak to his attorney, the head of the Justice Department and someone from the UN. A group of Mexicans laugh at him and eye his clothes.

I just want him to be quiet but don't think it wise to say as much. The last thing I need is another lawsuit against me, so I just float off to a different place, somewhere between the beach and a smoke-filled coffee shop listening to the soothing tones of a Carl Grbac/Jack Kerouac-character reading poetry.

The sound of crying snaps me back. A black kid, about sixteen or seventeen, curled up on the bench next to me fights back tears. I ask him if he's OK. He doesn't say anything at first, so I close my eyes and try to float back to the beach or the coffee shop. Then he starts talking. The words tumble out. He's close to having a full-on panic attack. He was born in Jamaica, he tells me, and came to the States when he was an infant. He has a green card but never became a citizen. He was arrested for marijuana possession and the INS is going to deport him back to Jamaica, even though he has no family there and hasn't been there since he was a babe in arms. 'You should have become a citizen,' the judge told him.

'I never thought about it,' the kid says between sniffles. 'My green card was one of the old ones, you know, without an expiration date.'

What an end to his American adventure, I think, cast off to a strange country. At least I am only faced with going back to England. *Arrive on vacation, leave on probation*. No shit. The group of Mexicans have turned their attention away from the expensive trousers and are now taking turns to punch and kick a little Japanese guy. With blood pouring from his nose, he finally hands over his Nike sneakers. The biggest Mexican swaps them for his battered sandals.

I ask the Jamaican kid why the Mexicans are so keen on upgrading their footwear. As soon as they're sent back to Mexico, he tells me, they just turn around and run straight back across the US border. Being pursued through the desert by Border Patrol works best in new sneakers. I look at my own footwear. I have one more reason to be grateful for the battered beach shoes.

I want to make a phone call, speak to a friendly voice. Bubble or Nervous, maybe. I walk over to the bank of phones on the far wall. They're regular payphones, rather than the ones in County that only handle collect calls. I have my phone card number memorised so I call my home voicemail. Roxy hasn't changed the access code.

There's a message from Karina, the Iranian lady of letters. 'English, I get message from lady say you in jail, arrested, English. She name herself Rocky. She say you beat ladies and hit them and, English, I mean I say I know you not beat ladies, English. I say you need help you call me, English. And I mean I have letters to write. To the President, English. It's very important. Please, English, I mean you call, let me know if what is going on.'

So. Roxy is calling up my clients and telling them I am a wife beater. Maybe I should save her the bother and just add it to my résumé. Under 'Hobbies and Interests'. Violent drunk, wife batterer, habitual criminal. Or maybe I'll just put 'Idiot boy, small brain located at the end of his penis.'

The next message really takes me by surprise. It's for Roxy. 'Yeah it's Tony,' the message begins. I recognise the voice instantly. I can almost hear spittle hitting the phone receiver as he speaks. 'We have him here,' he says. 'I'm taking care of him. He denied everything, like you said he would, then his attorney showed up, which kinda screwed things up. But I'll get another chance to work on him. I think I at least scared him. You can call me here but don't leave your name and don't mention money.'

Wow, that's some plot twist. The romantic comedy I have been living has already taken a sharp turn into dark exploitation piece and now has abruptly segued into a conspiratorial thriller. I'm living *Three Days of the Condor*. Roxy and that fat, buzz-cut racist, Mr Pink Ears, are trying to fit me up. I change the pass code so Roxy can't access or erase the message.

I phone Carl and give him the pass code. He tells me to call him back in five minutes after he's had a chance to listen to it. I pace up and down the holding cell, counting down the seconds.

'Unbelievable,' he says when I call him back. 'I can hardly believe it. Outrageous. Really.' He sounds much more excited than a beat poet has the right to. 'You think she's fucking him?'

I don't know and frankly don't care. It's clear there's at least money involved. 'Did you tape it?' I say.

'Yeah, man, you bet I did.' He suggests we keep it in reserve rather than immediately file a complaint with his superiors. 'Leave it to me,' he says. 'You won't have any more trouble with him. I guarantee it.'

Incoming Email:

> To: <BritWriter>
> From: <Nervous>
> Subject: I'm Out

Holy mother of Vishnu, I'm out. Made bail this morning. Thanks for the money, mate. I'll get it back to you ASAP. I'm due back in court tomorrow. I'll contact you then, let you know what happens. Right now I'm going to take a long hot bath and sleep. How the fuck did you survive all that time inside? I thought I was going to end up as a bad man's boyfriend. What a nightmare.
Yours in peace, love and unfettered buttocks,
Nervous

The INS Jail is situated down in San Pedro, a port near Long Beach, some twenty-odd miles south of LA and the holding pen and Mr Pink Ears. I see him just once as I shuffle in leg chains to the bus. He stares at me then quickly looks away like a frightened kitten. Cool, Carl, I think. Very cool, my man.

The positive feeling ends soon after I reach the processing room of San Pedro Jail. I'm naked again and even have to relinquish the beach shoes. A trustee replaces them with flip-flops and a jumpsuit, bright yellow this time. All I have left is the paperback, gripped tightly in my hand.

The cell is another large dorm, but infinitely cleaner than those at Men's Central and infinitely safer than those at Wayside. I grab a top bunk. The guy below introduces himself. He's a huge, handsome Italian called Franco, who's been transferred from Federal jail after the FBI caught him on videotape selling steroids. It's a felony offence and, like me, he has no visa or green card so is facing prison then deportation. The first thing he wants to do is phone his girlfriend.

'I'm going to ask her to marry me,' he says. 'It's

the only way out. I'm not going back to Italy. You know how much money I make over here?'

I guess it's a lot. 'You bet it is,' he says. 'I have my own business, live in Beverly Hills and drive a Porsche.'

I point out that, in the eyes of the FBI at least, he's a drug dealer.

'It's so stupid,' he says. 'The steroids I sell are legal in Europe.'

'Really?'

'Yeah, they're only illegal over here. And everyone's using them anyway.' He works as a personal trainer and says his clients are always asking him what they can take to *increase muscle mass*. 'That's why there's so much money in it,' he says.

I offer him my calling card number. 'Thanks,' he says and goes to call his girlfriend.

Fifteen minutes later he slumps back on his bunk. I lean over the side. 'What did she say?'

'She said no.'

'Oh.'

'Said she didn't want to get married for the wrong reasons. Shit, we've been living together for three years,' he says and rolls his eyes. 'Ahhh, you know what Californian women are like.'

Indeed I do. 'So what now?'

'I spoke to my landlady. She said she'd do it.'

'Your landlady?' She's about 30 years older than him and he isn't sure whether the INS will ever buy it as a real marriage. 'But what the hell?' he says. 'I want to stay.'

My immigration court appearance is late Monday afternoon. If all goes well I can post bail immediately and be processed for release in time to appear at the next criminal court hearing the following morning. If all goes well.

I sit in the small courtroom cutting a dashing figure in bright yellow offset by sparkling silver cuffs. Carl hands the judge a fistful of character references from friends and clients (not Karina, though, for obvious reasons). The judge seems impressed and retires to his chambers to read through them all.

'Things look good,' Carl says, smiling. Then his expression suddenly sinks. 'Uh-oh.'

I follow his gaze to the back of the court. Two slim, well-dressed women enter, hand-in-hand. I feel a stirring in the undercarriage of my yellow jumpsuit, the first twitch of life in that area for weeks. Then I recognise the couple and everything slinks back to floppy.

Roxy is dressed in her best suit, the one she always wears to lunch meetings with casting directors or producers, a sexy, smart Chanel number in cream. She stares at me, her face cold, barely recognisable under all the makeup. Her friend is taller, fuller in the chest and much fuller in the mouth. Last time I saw her, I was holding Roxy back from killing her. Now they are holding hands.

Carl looks at me. 'Who's the other one?' he asks. I tell him. 'What the hell do you do to these women to make them hate you?'

'I don't write down my feelings,' I say.

'What?'

I shrug. 'I don't know,' I say. 'I really don't.'

'What's she going to say?' says Carl.

'I don't know. There's nothing she can say.'

'Is she gonna say you pushed her out of a car as well?'

'God, I hope not.'

'He has a sexually aggressive personality,' Cellophane says, leaning back in the witness stand.

Someone at the back of the courtroom giggles. Carl looks at me. I shrug. I have no idea what she's talking about.

'What does that mean?' Says the judge. 'Did he ever hit you or throw you out of a car?'

'No,' she says.

'Did he ever threaten to hit you?'

'No,' she says.

'Did you ever see him hit anyone else?'

'No.'

The judge raises an eyebrow. 'So what exactly do you mean by a "sexually aggressive personality"?'

'He once tried to undress me in front of another woman.' There's more giggling at the back of the courtroom. My mouth drops open. I shrug and shake my head at Carl. I still don't know what the hell she's talking about.

The judge frowns. 'In front of another woman . . .?'

'It was Ms Hepburn,' Cellophane adds, indicating Roxy. 'He just lunged at me, trying to pull my skirt off.'

More snickering. The judge shoots a black look towards the gallery. I roll my eyes at Carl. At least I know what she's talking about now. The night Roxy and I returned from the Crypt, we ran into Cellophane on Bubble and Squeak's doorstep and I tried to tuck her label into her skirt. Dear God, does she really think I was trying to sexually assault her?

Thankfully the judge seems to be having a lot of trouble buying her story as well. 'Did he hurt you?'

'No,' she says.

'And he's never hit you or thrown you out of a car,' he says, 'or threatened to hit you or anyone else?'

'No,' she says reluctantly.

'So this lunge or whatever it was, was a one-off?'

'Yes,' she says.

The judge shakes his head in disbelief. 'This is not a criminal hearing,' he says. 'It's an immigration hearing to establish whether the defendant broke any immigration laws. He's admitted to overstaying his visa and working without authorisation. Bail is granted.'

Carl pats me on the back. The judge looks over at me with a wry smile. 'I will say one thing to you, though,' he says. 'Maybe you should choose your girlfriends a little more carefully in the future.'

Byte 15 – Stepping Out

It's almost dawn the morning after the Immigration hearing and I can still hear the judge's words running through my head. 'Maybe you should choose your girlfriends a little more carefully.' I pace up and down the cell as the hours before I'm due in criminal court tick away. Eventually, a guard opens the door and calls my name. It's 7.20. I have to be in Santa Monica, a 45-minute drive away, by nine.

The guard leads me to a holding cell downstairs. Back in the workout top and beach shoes. Waiting, waiting. So close now I can taste it. 7.30. 7.45. Eight o'clock. Another INS officer walks in.

'Your people are here,' he says.

He gives me my possessions back: my watch, the paperback and the notepad containing a rough draft of my alien-in-a-jail-cell script. He unlocks the door and leads me out. Through another steel door. I can see the moody grey sky outside now. No sunshine to greet me, just cold, damp air. The officer opens the steel gate and I step out, ending two months of incarceration. I want to pause, to savour the moment but there isn't time. Squeak gives me a hug and drags me to her car. Inside she quickly winds down the windows.

'It's the workout top,' I say. 'It was smelly two months ago when I put it on. God knows what it must smell like now.'

'Really bad,' she says and winds the window down further as we approach the freeway onramp. The cold air beats against my face. Onto the 405, over the bridge, into heavy traffic. Squeak indicates the clean clothes and deodorant she brought for me and suggests I change before appearing in court.

'Use all the deodorant,' she says. 'Really.'

As I change she tells me what's been going on while I've been away. I listen, saying little. Her voice is comforting, the familiarity soothing. I could have curled up and gone to sleep in the rich, velvety tones. If it wasn't for this damn court appearance. 8.20. 8.30. Stuck in traffic. I'm out but it could all be for nothing. Who knew the whole stupid case would ultimately hinge on the flow of LA traffic? Could there be a worse variable to have your liberty pinned upon?

Squeak drives like a lunatic: mounts the hard shoulder, weaves in and out of traffic, jumping red lights, making illegal turns. It's like the car chase scenes from *Bullitt* and *The French Connection* rolled into one. But performed in a VW Beetle by a twenty-something nurse. By the time she pulls up outside the courthouse we're both caked in sweat. She screeches to a halt and drops her head on to the steering wheel, tears of relief rolling down her cheeks.

'Holy fucking shit,' she gasps. 'I don't think I've ever been so scared.'

'No kidding,' I mutter. 'And you were driving.'

I jump out and run for the courtroom. 9.05.

Howard is pacing outside the door. He breathes a sigh of relief as I hurtle along the corridor. 'OK, I told the judge you were already here but he's taken another case first. You've got two minutes to make a decision,' he says. 'The DA wants to make a deal.'

He rattles off details of their conversation earlier that morning. She has completely changed her opinion from the first time I was in court. She wants to drop the charges against me, but can't. California law dictates that once she's filed felony abuse charges, she can't later drop them. She knows Roxy is lying; she knows I didn't hit her or throw her out of the van. She's never lost an abuse case, she told Howard, but she knows she'll lose this one.

'She offered a plea bargain,' Howard says. 'Reduced misdemeanour charge, no jail time–'

'No way,' I interrupt immediately. 'I didn't do anything wrong, I'm not pleading guilty to–!'

'Wo, wo, easy, sport. That's exactly what I told her. She completely understands.' She told him that Roxy is a nightmare to deal with; she keeps changing her story. The whole case stinks. It's going to blight her record. So she worked out a better offer, but one she'll need the judge to approve. She'll file additional, albeit lesser, charges against me. I'll have to agree to take weekly anger management counselling for twelve months. At the end of the year she can then recommend that all the charges against me are dropped. Howard likes the scheme.

'You get to stay in the country for a year and at the end of it, you're free and clear, with no criminal record whatsoever.'

I'm not convinced. 'I didn't do anything wrong, why should I have to have counselling?'

'I understand how you feel,' he says. 'Listen, we can go to trial. And I'm pretty sure I'll win. But either way, I'm going home to dinner with my wife and kids at the end of it all. But you might not be. You're one bad judge or one bad jury away from two years in the state pen.'

I let his words sink in. Going to trial will cost my dad at least fifteen grand. And at the end of it, I might get a hung jury or a mistrial and have to do it all over again. For another fifteen thousand.

'This way,' says Howard, 'you don't have to admit to doing anything wrong but you're certain of getting the charges dropped at the end. And who knows, maybe you'll sell a screenplay in the next year.'

He stares at me for a moment. Then glances at his watch. I'm out of time. 'Think what it was like in County Jail,' he says. 'And state prison is even worse.'

The fat little judge raises his eyebrows at the DA. He knows what she's doing.

'I sat up all last night considering these motions,' he says. 'I wish someone had run this by me first.' He's pissed. He agrees to the DA's motion, though. Then adds, 'A lot of this testimony seems to be set in bars and nightclubs. How about we add AA classes to this and a stipulation that he's not allowed to drink in public?'

The DA looks at Howard. He nods. What? Wait a minute. I didn't agree to this. No bars, no pubs for twelve months?

'You can still have a beer at home,' Howard says as we walk out of the courtroom. 'It's probably a good idea anyway. The last thing you want is to bump into Roxy in a bar and not be sober enough to make a quick escape.'

That's it. I'll have the occasional court appearance in the meantime just to check I'm complying with all the terms, but I am ostensibly a free man again.

Squeak is waiting for me in the car. 'Everything OK?' she says as I get in.

'Yeah,' I nod.

'Good, I can open this then.'

She holds up a bottle of champagne and pops the cork. We take a couple of chugs each then she drives me to the church hall and my first AA meeting.

Byte 16 – The Trouble with Drunks

Outgoing Email:

> To: <Nervous>
> From: <BritWriter>
> Subject: Re: I'm Out
>
> Good luck in court today. Sorry I can't phone you but this experiment is paying for your freedom at the moment. Let me know what happens. If you get AA or anger management classes, see if you can do them online. Trust me, they're too brutal to do in the real world.

The church hall is in Venice and I'm already feeling a little light-headed from Squeak's champagne by the time I arrive. I vaguely recognise the meeting leader – he's an actor who played a recurring character on a short-lived, painfully unfunny TV sitcom. Three-dozen of his clergy gather on foldout chairs in front of him and smoke hundreds of cigarettes and recount tales of pious sobriety and recite pseudo-religious mantras in unison. I feel like a Jew at Nuremberg, a heretic trapped in the Bible belt.

Reformed drunks have to be the most self-absorbed, self-pitying, self-righteous bunch of moral fundamentalists I've ever staggered into. Put them together in a room for two hours and the nausea builds as thick and fast as the cigarette smoke. I drank four beers over the course of six hours that night in the Bar With No Name. Hardly the stuff of alcohol addiction. Except in AA, maybe. The organisation unites problem drinkers in worship of the 'Higher Power' that supposedly governs the Twelve Steps to recovery from alcoholism. Step One: Admit you are powerless over alcohol. Step Two: Believe that a Higher Power can help you. Step Three: Decide to turn your will and your life over to God, as you understand Him. In other words, admit you're a loser, blame it all on the booze and turn to some hokey religion for redemption. How or why AA has developed into part of the state-sponsored recovery and punishment programmes is beyond me. One meeting is enough to leave the most virtuous teetotaller screaming at the shadows and swigging raw ether.

At the end of the two hours, everyone links arms and chants some facile rubbish about 'it works if you work it', then I have the meeting leader/sitcom actor sign my attendance sheet. Two meetings a week for twelve months, the judge said. But I know there's no way I can sit through eighty plus hours of sophomoric proselytising amid industrial clouds of cigarette smoke. So I decide to look for alternatives online. The judge would understand; surely Twelve-Step meetings violate my right to religious freedom? Besides, it seems unfair to the regulars who derive some benefit from these meetings to have such a vehement objector in their midst.

*

I walk back to Nervous' apartment after the meeting. He got the job in LA and moved to a huge ground floor rental right on the beach. I push open the back door and Nervous immediately offers me a beer.

'How was AA, you drunk bastard?' he says. I look at him and his chubby face creases into a huge grin. 'You must be dying for this.'

I chug the beer down in one. He hands me another. I take it to the shower with me. Wash away the jail smell, the stench of incarceration, court and AA. Scrub my fingernails. Clip them. Shave.

Nervous picked up my stuff from Roxy so I have clean clothes to wear. No more jumpsuits or the workout top/beach shoes combo. Nervous makes a bed up for me in the spare room. I ask what happened to my van.

'Impounded, mate. I tried to get it out but couldn't prove it was mine. They auctioned it off last weekend.' I shrug. No car.

'What about my furniture? My desk, my books?' I ask.

It's Nervous' turn to shrug. 'I got everything she'd let me take,' he says. 'I can call and ask about the rest.'

'Naa,' I say. 'Fuck it. Doesn't matter. I won't be able to take it all on the plane back to England anyway.'

I look at what I have left. One bag of clothes and a laptop. Apartment, van, furniture, TV, stereo, all gone. No money, no job, no home. I'm back where I started. A few more clothes maybe and a lot more crushed dreams.

*

Incoming Email:

> To: <BritWriter>
> From: <Nervous>
> Subject: Today's Court Appearance
>
> OK, just got back from court. No AA classes but I have to attend anger management classes. And I am allowed to do them online. First class is tomorrow night. I'll keep you posted, let you know how it goes.
> Cheers mate,
> Nervous

'I'm Cliff,' says the thin man in the yellow trousers and matching tie. He bounces the clipboard on his knees. 'You're all here because you are unable to manage your anger. I'm here to teach you how to manage that anger, how to behave in appropriate ways and how to break the cycle of abuse. Let's start by going round the group and introducing ourselves. Who'd like to start?'

Everyone shifts uncomfortably in their seats. 'OK,' Cliff says. 'I'll start. I'm Cliff. Hi. I used to use drugs and alcohol and abuse my wife. Then I found God and turned my life around. Now I'm going to do the same for each of you.'

I shift in my seat again, anticipating more tales of pious sobriety. The guy to Cliff's left introduces himself. He's a stocky, pale man in skin-tight faded blue jeans and a combat jacket.

'I'm Jay,' he says and launches into a detailed account of how he broke his wife's arm and pelvis when he kicked her down the stairs. He runs his hand through the lank hair at the back of his mullet. 'But I'm sober now,' he says. 'And I've been reading the Bible.'

Cliff bounces the clipboard on his knees again. He seems pleased. I feel nauseous. 'The first step is admitting you have an anger problem,' he tells Jay. 'What were you using?'

'Crack mainly,' says Jay. 'Sometimes just speed.'

'Mmmm,' says Cliff, approving his choice of narcotic. 'I did a lot of crack.' He nods at Jay. 'Good, good.' Then he turns his attention to the next man in the circle.

'My name's Vez,' he says. 'I shot my woman in the leg.'

There are a dozen of us crammed into a tiny room for Domestic Violence Diversion in The Therapy Center, hidden behind a Ralph's supermarket in Torrance. It's Friday evening and we're seated in what Cliff refers to as 'a circle of sharing'. I sit in my own private circle of stunned silence as I listen to these guys' stories. One beat his pregnant wife repeatedly with a broom handle. Another left his girlfriend in the hospital for three weeks. Another beat his children as well. These guys are hardcore. They all had brutal, deprived childhoods and have matured into dysfunctional monsters.

Cliff looks at me. I explain my story as briefly as possible. I am here because it is cheaper than going to trial. I'm supposed to have thrown my girlfriend out of a moving 1969 camper van – with custom bumper and house brick handbrake. Cliff seems unimpressed, by either my story or my choice of ride.

'It says here you were drinking,' he says, referring to his clipboard.

'I had four beers,' I say.

He nods, eyes fixed on me. 'I think there's still some denial here,' he says. 'What about your father, did he ever abuse your mother?'

I laugh. I can't imagine the man with the world's loudest golfing trousers raising so much as his voice at my mother. Cliff, on the other hand, clearly could.

'Maybe this is a good time for a cigarette break,' he says, then turns back to me. 'And you can think about your answer a little more.'

The others file outside after him to spark up and chat with each other. I sit on my own, away from the smoke, and make notes for another screenplay. This time an alien monster attacks a counselling group in Torrance.

Cliff takes my reluctance to turn his weekly class into a networking event as a personal slight. I turn up to every class on time, pay my fee and politely answer his questions. During most classes Cliff launches into a diatribe on the goodness of the Lord and the wickedness of alcohol. According to his definition, if you've ever had more than two drinks in a single evening, then you're an alcoholic. I wonder what he'd make of the UK at Christmas. The entire country should be pulled out of the pub and crammed into a circle of sharing to grumble about the wickedness of a pint of mild. What about cigarettes? These guys are all on two hundred a day but I'm the dysfunctional freak because I enjoy the odd tipple. Smokers are waging a war on drinkers; the rest of the country is waging a war on smokers. Isn't it about time someone gave counsellors and aerobic instructors a damn good thrashing?

The session ends at 8 pm. I drive back to Nervous's apartment and crack open a can of beer to wash away all the sycophantic gibberish I've been beaten with for the past two hours.

Angry, me? The only things that make me angry are anger management classes. And computers. Well, anything electrical really, especially air conditioning units that don't work. Reformed drunks, computers, consumer durable goods and anger management classes. Oh, and online food delivery services. They make me angry.

Technically, the purple hamster boy gets tonight's dinner order right. I wanted meatballs and fettuccine again but thought I'd try a double bluff and order ravioli and garlic bread in the hope he'd get the order wrong again. He doesn't. Or maybe he knew I was bluffing all along. He finally managers to deliver vodka as well. But instead of one bottle of Absolut and a six pack of beers, he leaves me half a dozen litres of the hard stuff and a single can of Heineken. I add it to the others in the cooler and email a violent complaint to his boss, one that even Karina may have been reluctant to send.

Byte 17 – Beer and Therapy

It's 3.30 am and I can't sleep. It's hot. Swelteringly hot. The ceiling fan buzzes overhead with little effect and I can feel the beads of sweat trickle down my spine. Jesus creeping shit, it must be a hundred degrees in here. I finally sit up, let my eyes adjust to the darkness then unleash my frustration on that idle swine of an air conditioner. It burps and gurgles and finally dies. Dammit! I mean it has one single function in life – to cool my bedroom so I can get a few hours sleep so I won't feel like some strung-out vampire junkie all day tomorrow – but do you think that bastard machine can handle that one simple task?

My head hurts. I stumble through to the kitchen and pull up a chair and sit with my head resting in the icebox and my eyes fixed on a chilled bottle of Absolut. What the hell is wrong with me? Is it the solitude? Or all that crazy talk of jails and judges? I can't see why, it was a long time ago. The past, over, done with. I did eat late. Maybe it's a belly full of half-digested spinach ravioli that's causing my unease. Or maybe it really is the heat? But, damn it, it's often this hot in LA, I should be used to it by now.

I log on. Run a search for 'testicular cancer'. It's the middle of the night and my neuroses are running rampant. I need to rule out insomnia and a pounding behind the eyes as early symptoms of some rare malignancy downstairs. OnTumor.com says I'm OK. I also rule out melanoma and gum disease but decide to floss anyway then email a desperate message to my dentist's office asking for someone to please get in touch with me please with the earliest possible appointment for a check up please. I click send before I realise just how weird that sounds. When insomnia struck in the pre-Internet days I used to run out to the amusement arcade at Kings Cross and feed fifty pence pieces into one of those machines that you slip your middle finger into and its neon display tells you how healthy or sexy or fat you are ... No, not really, but it's a thought.

Nowadays insomniacs and other late-night malcontents like me have the option of e-therapy, counselling sites that link us directly to mental health professionals. An anonymous and sympathetic ear is only a click and $15 away, which could be a godsend, since the British especially still see a real stigma attached to traditional therapy. We tend to subscribe to the notion that there's no problem that can't be resolved by chatting with some mates down the pub over a few beers. That may be true, but I'm in California, it's four in the morning and all the pubs are shut.

I find a self-help site that promotes positive thinking and carries a celebrity endorsement from that epitome of mental good health, David Duchovny. I take the free trial.

'When things go wrong,' the site tells me, 'or you are feeling blue, just remember that you are a neat person.' Nonsense, you degenerate swines! What kind of piffle is this? It's never going to get me off to sleep. I'd be better off watching one of Duchovny's movies.

My head is pounding like the bass line at a summer rave. The pharmacy aisle of E-Deliveries offers the usual name-brand painkillers, but this is a proper headache, gentleman's size. I need a prescription strength solution, or even something stronger that will maybe knock me out for the rest of the month. I surf onto a site proclaiming to be 'the world's largest entheogenic library and community'. In other words, it's home to a bunch of stoners. Perfect. Hard drugs and alcohol: the trusted answer to most maladies.

After reading some enlightening info on the home manufacture of synthetic drugs, I find an intriguing page containing the recipe for methylamine, a primary ingredient in the production of amphetamines. Now, I might not be any great whiz in the kitchen but I'm certainly capable of following a simple recipe, and as the site says, 'If you have half a clue and some reasonable grasp of chemistry fundamentals, you can make a good chunk of methylamine in an afternoon.' Instant gratification, I like it. My headache is easing already.

The webmaster of this site is quick to point out that methylamine is a poisonous, noxious and highly inflammable gas with a strong ammonia/rotting fish-like odour. It's also a felony offence in the US to possess it without a permit, so kids: don't try this at home. Like all the best recipes, this one comes with a handy itemised ingredients list and explains what each chemical does, which companies supply them and what kind of lies I need to tell in order to get my hands on them.

Unfortunately, confidence in my own ability to follow a simple chemical equation diminishes substantially as I read through some of the recipes. Or more exactly, as I read through the highlighted caution notes. 'CAUTION: This compound is EXTREMELY EXPLOSIVE and HIGHLY TOXIC! I am not exaggerating! Do not, under ANY circumstances, allow the acid to heat above room temperature. CAUTION: The lower nitroalkanes form shock and/or temperature-sensitive EXPLOSIVE compounds with amines and hydroxides. BE CAREFUL, DAMN IT! You have been warned.'

Mmmm. Maybe this isn't such a good idea after all. I've resigned myself to gently toasting my sanity this month, I don't want to end up nuking the apartment as well. For the first time I almost regret playing hooky from chemistry classes. I consider investing in a home chemistry start-up kit, then reject it out of sight. Who am I kidding? I don't know my reagents from my analogues, let alone the principals of chemical synthesis. So I start wondering: if the Net is truly the place to see and buy everything, is there a site out there that is insane enough to sell ready-made illicit drugs?

Yes. Well, almost. HyperReal has a compilation of narcotic prices in just about every city on the planet, with helpful pointers on availability. For example, hash is readily available outside the Safeway in Congleton for £15 an eighth or from the Uni Halls of Residence in Southampton or at the amusement arcade in the centre of Southport. Marijuana is on offer at the Disneyland Hotel in Anaheim, California or the Arcata Plaza between 3pm and 7pm; and the Quickie Mart in Camarillo, California apparently does a nice line in magic mushrooms, priced to sell at $20 for one-sixteenth of an ounce.

The site offers price and availability for every conceivable narcotic in every conceivable destination. There's cocaine in Montevideo, marijuana in Belgrade, speed in Moscow and LSD in Afghanistan. Everything the weary traveller could wish for. Although if you do find yourself in Afghanistan, maybe a shortage of hallucinogenics shouldn't be your primary concern.

I run more searches: on 'anger' then 'mental health' and finally plain old 'insanity' and end up on a counselling site which attests that psychological dysfunction is a completely logical result of a violent, oppressive society. Dark things have always gone on 'out there' in the big bad world. But it doesn't just happen 'out there' anymore. It happens in your living room, in your bedroom, wherever that evil grey box is housed. I've spent sixteen days trawling a Kafka-esque world of darkness and depravity. The fact that I am feeling sick to my stomach is somehow reassuring. I'm not totally immune to the vileness that lurks on the Internet and have not been desensitised by overexposure to it. Just amazed and a little alarmed.

I find my way to a list of e-therapists but by now the first rays of morning sunlight are streaking through the window. I step outside onto the deck and watch the sun climb above the palm trees. The lights are already on in an apartment across the street and the first of the early morning commuters pulls onto Montana Avenue. I download an MP3. I don't care what anyone says, there's nothing as likely to soothe the psyche as the Style Council's *Long Hot Summer*. I see Bessy sitting on the sunlounger, last night's beer still in front of her. What the hell is she doing up this early?

'I'm still on UK time,' she says without moving her lips.

I nod perfunctorily and continue staring into the distance. She hesitates a moment then picks up two cans of Heineken from the cooler. She pops one and hands me the other.

'So,' she says, 'what's up with you then?'

I take a long swig of cold beer. And begin ...

Incoming Email:

> To: <BritWriter>
> From: <Nervous>
> Subject: Anger Management Tips
>
> Mate, I have some anger tips for you, ones I picked up in my online class.
> There are few 'always' in therapy, but here's one: anger is always based upon unfulfilled expectations. If you can let go of your expectations, you will not feel angry. If your anger keeps coming back, that is a clear indication that the issue has not been resolved. Your anger is skewed, neurotic, off-target and/or you are expressing the wrong emotion. Anger difficulties most often have their roots in repressed 'trauma knots' that you do not want to face. The part of these trauma knots most often avoided is hatred, hatred from the past.
> Until you are willing to feel the hatred from your past, you will continue to have difficulties with anger, my friend.

Outgoing Email:

> To: < Nervous >
> From: < BritWriter >
> Subject: Re: Anger Management Tips
>
> Piss off, Nervous. I think I preferred it when you were addicted to horoscopes.

Incoming Email:

> To: < BritWriter >
> From: < Nervous >
> Subject: Re: Anger Management Tips
>
> That's it, mate, let it out. Don't you feel better now?

Byte 18 – Who is Bessy?

Incoming Email:

> To: <BritWriter>
> From: <Ralph>
> Subject: Byte 17
>
> I have only one problem with yesterday's column: WHO THE HELL IS BESSY? You're supposed to be living on your OWN on the Internet! No girlfriends, roommates, neighbours or landladies.

Incoming Email:

> To: <BritWriter>
> From: <Ralph>
> Subject: Copy?
>
> Hey, deadline time, still haven't received any copy. Everything OK?

Incoming Email:

> To: <BritWriter>
> From: <Ralph>
> Subject: Copy?
>
> It's the end of the day. I'm about to leave. You OK?

Incoming Email:

> To: <BritWriter>
> From: <Ralph>
> Subject: Urgent – Copy?
> Hellooooo?

Byte 19 – Dddddddddddddddddddd

The dddddd key on my keyboardddddddd appears to be
                       jammedddd
                      dddddd
                             d
                                d
                                   d
                                    dd
                                       ddddd
                                             d.

Byte 20 – Disconnected

–What's wrong with your ear?
–My what?
–Your ear. You keep slapping your ear.
–There's a fly in my ear.
–A fly?
–Yeah. There are always so many flies out here.
–Really?
–Yeah.
–I've never noticed. I sit out here most days. And I've never noticed the flies.
–When do you sit out here?
–On the deck? Most afternoons. About four o'clock. I skip rope to keep fit.
–Don't you work?
–Yeah, I work. I write from eight til four then I come out here and go skipping then go back to writing.
–You write?
–Yeah.
–What do you write?
–I write lots of stuff. At the moment I'm living on the Internet and writing a daily column about it for a magazine web site.

–Wow.
–Mmmm.
–So what's wrong?
–What's wrong? It's not writer's block if that's what you mean.
–No?
–No. My computer crashed. I can't log on.
–Log on?
–You know, get on to the Internet.
–Ahhh. Does that matter?
–Of course it matters. It matters a lot. I'm supposed to be living on the Net.
–You can't work?
–I can't work. I can't do anything. My whole life has stopped.
–Sounds bad.
–It is. I can't even email the editor to tell him I'm going to be late with the copy.
–Oh.
–My life was on that computer. My whole life. Everything.
–Your life?
–Everything, I'm telling you. I'm lost. I don't know what to do with myself. Everything I've ever written was on that hard drive. And like an arse I never backed it up.
–Arse is a bad word. But I know how you feel.
–What did you say?
–I know how you feel.
–How the hell do you know how I feel? I mean, what, you spend your life on this bench. Sitting here. Have you ever had a computer?
–A computer? No.
–No. Exactly. Your whole life is spent here. Sitting

on this bench on my deck. Looking at the view.
–It's nice. You don't like it?
–Yeah, I like it. Of course I like it.
–I know stuff.
–You know stuff?
–Yeah.
–What stuff do you know?
–I know what the street looks like at 5 am. I know what time that crow starts squawking and singing and flapping his wings. I know what the deck feels like when it's been raining. I know the Purple Hamster keeps switching your orders.
–You know all that, huh?
–Yeah.
–But nothing about computers or the Internet?
–Nope.
–See this.
–Cool.
–Yeah, you like it?
–Yeah. What is it?
–It's a Blackberry. A PDA. Personal Digital Assistant. Every address of everyone I know is on here. I can email them from anywhere. And I can log on to the Internet and check the football scores and read my email. It's brilliant.
–Wow.
–You betchya wow.
–Betchya wow.
–Trouble is the service has been cut off.
–No good?
–No good. Very no good. I reviewed it for another magazine and gave it a really good review so they let me keep it. And the service was free. Now it's stopped. I guess the review wasn't that good.

–Oh.
–So now I can't log on to the Net with this either. I'm screwed.
–You betchya.
–Yep. I'm screwed all right. Can't log on, can't work, can't do anything.
–You can sit on the deck.
–Yeah. Yeah, I can sit on the deck.
–You can see the crows in the morning. The big one flaps his wings and sings when the sun hits the roof. I have to be quiet now. You gonna be out here later?
–Yeah, maybe. I'm rebooting the computer. Not sure how long it's going to take. Everything takes so long.
–I have to be quiet now.
–Maybe I'll sit here for a while longer.
–OK, just don't talk to me anymore. In case someone hears.
–Who's going to hear?
–You know, sometimes the neighbours come up here. They've seen me. They think you're strange.
–You're right. Don't talk anymore.
–OK. Maybe we'll talk later if you need to.
–Maybe. It'll be fixed soon. I'm reloading the software.
–Are you feeling OK?
–I'm talking to you, how good can I be?
–Not just me. You've been talking to Brian, too, I've heard you.
–Yeah, you and Brian.

Byte 21 – Lou 'Cherry Nose' Brown

Ten Things I Miss Being Online: View of the mountains.

Feel of the sun and the sand. The taste of fresh oranges.
And fresh pasta.   Background noise in a bar. Watching the sun set over the ocean.

Or rise over the mountains. How many is that?

I miss people. Some people.   A few. Some more than

others.   Abby maybe.   Abby.

I think I can hear the ocean in my pillow when I lay my head down at night. Something in me died in a red double-decker bus with the Young Ones.

Ten Things I Wish I'd Written: "The Young Ones".'

Alien. The movie.   *Aliens*. The movie. Every short story by Raymond Carver. Every single one. I don't think the guy wrote a bad line let alone a bad story.

Every novel by George Orwell. Especially *Keep the Aspidistra Flying* and *Nineteen Eighty-four*. *Arthur*. The movie.

Hunter Thompson's introduction to *Generation of Swine* where he describes Hell as a 'viciously overcrowded version of Phoenix.'

The most ferocious three pages of writing ever published. Ever.

Santa Accused of Slapping Child

Robber Holds Up Bus his Mum is Travelling On

Hundreds Hurt During Annual Stone-throwing Festival
– Reuters.com headlines

Who is Lou 'Cherry Nose' Brown? And why is his name written a hundred times on my bedroom wall?
Lou 'Cherry Nose' Brown
Lou 'Cherry Nose' Brown
Lou 'Cherry Nose' Brown

Did I do that? I've never read the "Ballad of Reading Gaol." Maybe I should. Do I have enough health insurance? Maybe I need some vitamins. What's good for memory? Gingko Biloba, right? I think so. But I'm not sure I agree with the vitamin culture. How much self-medication does anyone need? Lots. I suppose.

Yeah.

I am a collection of bad decisions. So many decisions, so many bad ones. I'm not making any more decisions. Time to go with the flow. Proactive no more. Why do I miss Abby?

Bessy has stopped talking to me.

The solitude is melting my EARS.

Byte 22 – Stress-Free Companionship

Incoming Email:

> To: <BritWriter>
> From <Ralph>
> Subject: Who is Bessy?
>
> What is this madness? No more blank days! I ask again, you degenerate, WHO THE HELL IS BESSY? You're supposed to be living on your OWN on the Internet! No girlfriends, roommates, neighbours or landladies.

Bessy, Bessy, Bessy ...
My friends introduce me to her at my eighteenth birthday party. They arrange dinner in the back room of the White Swan and pass her down to me under the table. She's brown-skinned with perfectly spherical breasts, a Tintin-like swirl of hair on her forehead and a permanently astounded look on her face. I dress her in lacy undies and a charity store frock and strap her in the passenger seat of my Mini and drive her to college every day. In the summer, I take snaps of her in a photo booth and make her a fake passport so she

can accompany me on a jolly boys' holiday to Ibiza. I still have the photo of her being pushed from a sixth floor hotel room balcony into the swimming pool below. She sustains such serious injuries that we have the hotel manager rush in an emergency puncture repair kit. One friend even claims he was intimate with her at a party once but I doubt it. Bessy is a lot of things but she isn't erotic in any way. Even to a group of sexually indiscriminate teenage boys she's always just an inflatable toy, about as raunchy as a rubber dinghy.

After years apart, Bessy and I were reunited a couple of days ago. For two months she travelled on a boat from England to LA, folded amongst a stack of old books and records in a crate from my parents' attic. She'll like it here. There's too much discrimination against plastic people in the UK. Southern California is much more conducive to the lifestyle of the fake and inflatable. People keep mannequins or rubber dolls in their cars so they can use the car pool lanes and enjoy the last meaningful conversation of the day during the lonely commute to work. Women driving alone at night use male dolls to ward off any would-be car-jackers as well as the growing realisation that Mr Right may have a moulded silicone smile and glue-on moustache. And no one raises an eyebrow at the sexual deviants and barefoot mystics and self-promotion junkies who curl up every night in the arms of eternally shocked-looking rubber women and cry themselves to sleep.

Life in Los Angeles can be a solitary experience.

Tami: body type three; face type two; a leggy five feet seven inches; thirty-eight DD; blonde, red or brunette; stain-resistant; odourless, flavourless and guaranteed non-toxic. Leah: body type two; face type four; five feet one inch; a svelte seventy pounds; sexy and pleasurable; the poise and relaxed state of a sleeping girl.

'Maybe you should choose your girlfriends more carefully in future,' the judge told me. I wonder if this is what he had in mind?

The anatomically correct dolls of RealDoll.com are made of silicone rubber over a flexible metal skeleton with (all) their parts moulded from life casts. Customers select a head and body type from the online catalogue, the colour of the doll's hair and eyes and even the style of her makeup and nail varnish. A fully-loaded Real Doll comes equipped with an electronic motor to thrust her hips and sensors on her intimate areas to trigger audio samplings via Ethernet like 'Ooooh, baby. Yes, yes, yes.'

Next to the voluptuous Tami or the Victoria Principal look-a-like Stephanie, poor Bessy is but a cheap female caricature. With prices starting at over $6,000, though, I can't see my friends chipping in to get me a Real Doll for my next birthday. Clearly, these latex lovelies are too expensive for most teenage boys. Instead, they're likely to find themselves in the hands of the lonely hordes constantly clamouring for attention and a wet mouth or the beaten-down hearts condemned to walk the nights in search of stress-free companionship.

'Maybe you should choose your girlfriends more carefully.' For the best part of a year I do just that. 'Maybe you should choose your girlfriends more carefully.' I repeat the judge's words like a mantra every Saturday night when the loneliness bites.

'Maybe you should choose your girlfriends more carefully. Maybe you should choose your girlfriends more carefully.'

I choose them carefully.

I attend anger management classes and AA sessions and lose myself in violent tales of aliens and bloody murders where everyone is a suspect and no one can be trusted. In the evenings I walk past bars and clubs and coffee shops, bask unseen in the warm neon outside, then slip back into the shadows and scamper home like a rat returning to the sewer to lick its poisoned wounds.

I choose them carefully.

'What happens now?' I ask.

She shrugs. 'Convulsions, probably.'

'Convulsions?' I can hear the sound of dry heaving echoing somewhere deep within the bowels of the ER.

'That's how it usually goes,' she says. 'Profuse vomiting and incoherence followed by convulsions. Her arms and legs will flail around and her head'll bob up and down like a crazy person. Then she'll slip into a semi-conscious state, maybe even a coma for a bit. Her breathing'll become extremely shallow and hard to detect. They'll have to clear her lungs of vomit. Then in about four hours she'll regain full consciousness. And in another two or three she'll be ready to walk home. She's got no insurance so she'll have a huge hospital bill and an almighty hangover that'll leave her introspective for days. *Painfully* introspective, you know what I mean?'

I nod. I think I can relate.

'She'll apologise to me,' she says, 'maybe you as well if you're dumb enough to stick around, and she'll be sober for a while. Maybe even for a few months. Then, eventually, she'll do it all over again. She always does. That's just Julie.'

I meet Julie while I'm hovering outside a bar on Washington, wondering if it's safe to venture inside. Body type one, face type three, brunette, fair complexion. She mistakes me for the doorman and hands me her ID. I smile and chat to her for a while then tell her she's too young and too beautiful for me to let her in. She realises I'm not the doorman and shakes her head in mock disgust.
'Does that line usually work?' she says.
'No.' I say.
She hesitates, expecting me to say more. I don't.
'You coming in for a drink?' she asks.
'No,' I say again. 'I have to go.' I turn to walk off but a thought hits me and I call back to her. 'I saw the address on your licence.'
She smiles. 'You did? Then pick me up tomorrow. Eight-ish.'
I nod and watch her disappear inside.
The next day I turn up on her doorstep, a ground floor apartment just off Abbott Kinney in Venice. Her sister opens the door in a wild panic and asks me where I'm parked.
'Just on the corner,' I say, indicating Nervous' Mercedes I borrowed for the evening. 'Where's Julie?'
'She's fucking OD'd! Can you drive us to the ER?'

Julie complains about the bees as we drive. They're coming out of her nose and swarming around her head, she says. The bees. Then she says her lungs feel itchy and throws up on the back seat. Nervous won't thank me for that. I drive faster.

'Where's the music coming from?' she says. The radio's off. I wonder what she can hear. 'Whitney Houston? Where's it coming from?' she yells. Then vomits again.

She's still throwing up and muttering gibberish about Whitney and bees as we pull into the ER.

I sit in the waiting room with her sister, quietly sipping weak coffee.

'So what did she take?' I ask at last.

'GHB, acid, alcohol,' she says. 'Helluva cocktail.'

She ordered GHB from the Net, her sister tells me. It's shipped to her in kit form: two bottles and a one-page disclaimer. One bottle contains Kalium Hydroxide, small white crystal pellets, the other is filled with a clear liquid, Gamma Butyrolactone. The disclaimer spares the web site from responsibility for any 'misuse' of the product. The contents of the bottles are not themselves illicit, since one crucial ingredient is missing: water. Once mixed together with H_2O, the two legal chemicals become the illegal substance GHB.

For vomiting, incoherence and convulsions, just add water.

I nod and we sit in silence again. As first dates go, this is an interesting one. I look around nervously, half expecting to see the judge spying on me, seething with outrage at how spectacularly I've failed to heed his words. But there are only two other people in the waiting room: a vagrant slouched across a row of chairs, half asleep, and an old Middle Eastern man muttering what sounds like a prayer into his cell phone.

The sister touches my leg and I jerk back. 'Look,' she says. 'I really appreciate you giving us a ride here. A lot of people in your position would have just run a mile. You're a stand up guy. But you don't have to stay. You don't owe her anything.'

'What about getting home?'

'Like I said, by morning she'll be fine to walk.'

'You sure?'

'If they call the cops, you'll get dragged into all this.'

I picture myself standing before the judge trying to explain just how a guy with such a tenuous hold on his liberty came to be driving a semi-comatose GHB addict in a car full of puke to the hospital.

I wish her sister well and head for the door, ushered out by the sounds of bees and *The Greatest Love of All* and my date dry-heaving. The old me would've stayed, would've witnessed this tale play out in full. But not now. Too much has changed. I'm no longer the male lead in this movie, the one that I'm no longer writing inside my head, but rather the quirky, damaged sidekick who gets a few laughs and a couple of interesting lines along the way but never the girl, unless she's plastic or a dope fiend or a freak.

I choose them carefully.

Missy Townsend – body type two, face type five – has steely blue eyes and hair so blond it is almost white in places. She has a smile that lasts into tomorrow and sings in a band called Crash something. I meet her when I finally venture into the bar. She's playing darts with her mother who packs a snub nose .45 and a World War Two-issue Luger in her handbag and lives somewhere in the Valley in a house that used to belong to one of the Marx brothers. We go back there when the bar closes and drink eighty year-old whiskey from crystal wine glasses. The house is like an armoury. The walls of every room are lined with weapons, everything from eighteenth-century muskets to Bren guns to M16s. Her mother is crazy. But I like Missy.

She develops a habit of dropping by Nervous's apartment unannounced at three in the morning and crawling through my bedroom window. I wake up to find her pale, naked body squirming beside me. She once modelled for a porn magazine and believes the spirit of her dead father lives in a cookie jar in her kitchen. And she has a whole cupboard filled with handcuffs and chains and whips. She's a wild one, even for California.

Then she catches me reading her journal. It's just sitting there and I only read a couple of pages and they contain nothing more intimate than a to-do list and this is a woman who has bared much more than her soul to the subscribers of *Hustler* magazine. It's still wrong and she erupts in anger. Not a violent anger, not the sudden, bone-trembling rage of Roxy, but a woman screaming at me is still enough to chill me to the core. She apologises minutes later but it's too late, the damage is done. Nervous and I move into a new apartment soon after, one on the third floor that she would need a fireman's ladder to reach the bedroom window of, and I never see her again.

I choose them carefully. I choose them so carefully I feel like I'm about to burst.

Outgoing Email:

> To: <Ralph>
> From: <BritWriter>
> Subject: Re: Who is Bessy?
>
> I know what the rules of this assignment are. My best friend was arrested and thrown in jail and I'm still adhering to them. Bessy and Brian are my only companions.

Incoming Email:

> To: <BritWriter>
> From: <Ralph>
> Subject: Re: Who is Bessy?
>
> Brian? Who is Brian?

Outgoing Email:

> To: <Ralph>
> From: <BritWriter>
> Subject: Re: Who is Bessy?
>
> A plant.

Incoming Email:

> To: <BritWriter>
> From: <Bubble>
> Subject: Perfect
>
> Once upon a time, a perfect man and a perfect

woman met. After a perfect courtship they had a perfect wedding. Their life together was, of course, perfect. One snowy, stormy Christmas Eve, this perfect couple was driving their perfect car along a winding road when they noticed someone up ahead in distress. Being the perfect couple, they stopped to help. There stood Santa Claus with a huge bundle of toys. Not wanting to disappoint children on the eve of Christmas, the perfect couple loaded Santa and his toys into their car. Soon they were driving along delivering toys. Unfortunately, driving conditions deteriorated and the perfect couple and Santa were in a terrible accident. Only one of the three survived.
Who was the survivor?

Outgoing Email:

> To: <Bubble>
> From: <BritWriter>
> Subject: Re: Perfect
>
> Let me guess – the woman?

Incoming Email:

> To: <BritWriter>
> From: <Bubble>
> Subject: Perfect
>
> CORRECT!
> The perfect woman survived. She's the only one who really existed in the first place. Everyone

knows there is no Santa Claus and there is no such thing as a perfect man.

Outgoing Email:

> To: <Bubble>
> From: <BritWriter>
> Subject: Re: Perfect

So, if there is no perfect man and no Santa Claus, the perfect woman must have been driving. Which explains why there was an accident in the first place ...

Byte 23 – Cleaning the Net

Incoming Email:

> To: <BritWriter>
> From: <E-Deliveries>
> Subject: Your Food & Beverage Orders
>
> Dear Sir,
> Thank you for bringing this matter to my attention. While I am not familiar with all of the expressions used in your email, I understand that you are less than satisfied at the level of service you've received from E-Deliveries. For this I offer my sincerest apologies. Your business is very important to us and we value you highly as a loyal and frequent customer. Please allow me a few days to investigate this matter fully and I will make sure any errors that may have occurred with your orders are rectified without further delay. I will also ensure your account is credited with an extra $25 as a token of our apreciation for your understanding.
> Sincerely yours,

Hamed Tulif
Head of Customer Service
P.S. Yes, sir, six bottles of vodka is indeed a large quantity of liquor, especially for a single gentleman living, as you put it, 'all on his bloody lonesome,' and while I appreciate your pledge to consume 'every last sopping drop' I would urge you to practice restraint and enjoy your E-Deliveries order responsibly. I would also like to point out that E-Deliveries cannot be held liable should you choose to fulfill your pledge.

Incoming Email:

To: <BritWriter>
From: <Ralph>
Subject: Are you OK?

Your copy's late again today; you're talking to plastic women and house plants. Is everything OK? Are you going to be able to continue?

Outgoing Email:

To: <Ralph>
From: <BritWriter>
Subject: Fwd: Cleaning the Net

PLEASE PASS THIS NOTICE ON TO OTHER USERS!

As many of you know, each year the Internet must be shut down for 24 hours in order to allow us to clean it. The cleaning process, which eliminates dead e-mail and inactive ftp, www and gopher sites, allows for a better-working and faster Internet.

This year, the cleaning process will take place from 12:01 am tomorrow until 12:01 am GMT the day after. During that 24-hour period, five very powerful Japanese built multilingual Internet-crawling robots (Toshiba ML-2274) situated around the world will search the Internet and delete any data that they find.

In order to protect your valuable data from deletion we ask that you do the following:

1. Disconnect all terminals and local area networks from their Internet connections.
2. Shut down all Internet servers, or disconnect them from the Internet.
3. Disconnect all disks and hard drives from any connections to the Net.
4. Refrain from connecting any computer to the Internet in any way.
5. Avoid placing operating microwave ovens or toaster/toaster ovens near your computer modem.
6. Avoid wearing nylon (or other dielectric fibre) undergarments because of the possibility of electrical discharge.

We understand the inconvenience that this may cause some Internet users, and we apologise. However, we are certain that any inconvenience will be more than made up for by the increased speed and efficiency of the Internet, once it has been cleared of electronic flotsam and jetsam.

Sysops and others: Since the last Internet cleaning, the number of Internet users has grown dramatically. Please assist us in alerting the public of the upcoming Internet cleaning by posting this message where your users will be able to read it. Please pass this message on to other sysops and Internet users as well. Thank you.

Byte 24 – Netlore

Incoming Email:

> To: <BritWriter>
> From: <Ralph>
> Subject: Re: Internet Closed for Cleaning

For the love of Jehovah, what are you talking about? Have you finally toasted your last semblance of sanity? We're not insured for this, you know ... We've paid you for a month in advance, we can't fork out for the cost of your mental breakdown as well.
Get a grip, man. Pull yourself together. There's copy to be written, a story to be told. KEEP IT TOGETHER.

Outgoing Email:

> To: <Ralph>
> From: <BritWriter>
> Subject: Re: Internet Closed for Cleaning

I'm back. Everything's still a little fuzzy at the edges, but I'm back.

Incoming Email:

> To: <BritWriter>
> From: <Ralph>
> Subject: Re: Internet Closed for Cleaning

Where have you been?

Outgoing Email:

> To: <Ralph>
> From: <BritWriter>
> Subject: Re: Internet Closed for Cleaning

It's difficult to say with any certainty. I've been here in the apartment, if that's what you mean. On my own. Fuck, definitely on my own. So don't hassle me about that. I haven't broken any of the rules and I don't need some bloodsucking editor barking electronic obscenities at me like some short, French, angry person.

Things got a little weird, that's all. Everything went dark. There's no alcohol left in the fridge, just a lot of empty vodka bottles. That may have something to do with it. Or it could have been the homemade methylamine. I'm not sure I cooked it for long enough. Again, it's all very hazy. I may have just slept for a couple of days. Besides, the Internet cleaning story is true. Every last word of it. I know because I read it in an email.

*

For months after my release from jail, I long to be somewhere else, somewhere I don't have to attend AA meetings or anger management classes, somewhere I don't have to choose carefully anymore. I develop an almost weekly habit of packing my few remaining possessions into a bag and making the trip to the airport with the sole intention of getting on a plane back to England. Forever. But each time something stops me.

The first time, I make it as far as the line at the Virgin ticket counter that snakes around the Departures area. The couple waiting behind me are so sunburned it looks painful. They can't wait to get back to Manchester, they tell me, so they can get a decent cup of tea. I smile and nod like I somehow understand. The line inches forward and I push my bag with my foot. Then I hear a familiar voice call out.

'English, why you no answer phone, I mean not answer it?'

'Hello Karina, how are you?' I step out of the line and let the sunburned couple take my place. They stare at me sympathetically like I've been abducted by an embarrassing aunt.

'I email because I call then after I call, I mean and you no answer, English. I have letter to go to Governor, English. I very upset. I mean, I fly and they hate Iranian lady. I ask extra pillow, English, but I no get. Who what they expect for me to sleep? I need you to write letter, English.'

'I'm leaving, Karina,' I say, indicating the line at the ticket counter. 'Going back to England.'

'Going back to England? No. Why?'

'I'm just ... I dunno. I just need to go back.'

She stares at me like I've completely lost my mind.

Then digs through her purse. 'Look, English, see.' She withdraws an envelope embossed with the Seal of the President of the United States and carefully pulls out a letter. 'Remember, English? Letter we write to President about Denny's the diner and I mean waitress who be rude to Iranian lady? I mean he write to me back, English.'

I look from her beaming expression to the letter, and read. The most powerful man on the planet assures her that he condemns any and all aspects of discrimination and promises to forward her letter to the Denny's Board of Directors. That'll teach them to screw up her order, I think. The letter closes with the President saying how proud he is that the United States is a nation of immigrants.

'Give me your tired, your poor, your huddled masses ...' I say as the line at the ticket counter bumps past me.

She frowns. 'Who?'

'It's a very nice letter, Karina.'

'Only happen here, English. America. Why you want go somewhere else?'

The Manchester couple wave at me as they pass, tickets in hand, red faces pulsing like warning lights. Less than twelve hours from a scalding cup of PG Tips.

'I need you to write best letter, English, like only you can write. To President. I mean, you want that I call or email to you?'

I smile and pick up my bag. 'Email me,' I say.

'Yes, phone.'

A week later, my immigrant ideal of the wretched, the homeless and the tempest-tossed breathing free has faded and I'm back at LAX. This time I make it as far as the gate and the standby list for a flight to Heathrow. With two hours until departure I stop at the bar for a beer and one last pretzel. CNN plays on the TV overhead. The guy next to me nudges my arm and indicates the news coverage of yet another school shooting.

'This country represents the best and the worst of everything,' he says, slurring his words slightly. 'We have the freedom to behave like that.'

Not that I'm in the habit of gleaning life lessons from every deranged alcoholic that corners me in a bar, but I think he has a point. I tell myself that as long as the good continues to outweigh the bad, I'll never be able to give up this city and everything that comes with it.

Twenty minutes later I'm back in Nervous's spare room staring at the Pacific Ocean, steeling myself for another evening with Cliff, the reformed crack addict.

The third time, I'm not even sure how serious I am about leaving. Nervous has been in Kentucky for a job interview and I'm supposed to pick him up from the airport. I don't have time to clean the GHB addict's puke out of his car so I call for a cab and instinctively pick up my bag and passport, just in case.

'LAX?' the cabby says as I slip into the back.

'Yeah, downstairs at arrivals, though. We're picking someone up.' He pulls off and I ask him which route he's going to take.

'You want me to take the freeway?'

'No, Lincoln's much quicker.'

He nods and peers at the rear view mirror. He's a

heavy-set Latino. 'Where you from anyways, Australia?'

'England,' I say.

'England,' he repeats. 'I was close. I knew someone from England once. Tall guy, brown hair.'

'Oh, yeah?'

'Yeah. What was his name?' he says, scratching his head. 'Chris I think. Yeah. Chris something. From England. Nice guy.'

He looks at me again. My mouth is hanging open and I'm staring at the slither of his reflection in the rear view mirror. I switch my gaze to his license fixed on the dash. I don't recognize the name. It should say 'Fat, laughing, junkie cab driver.'

'You're a writer?' I say.

'Yeah!' he yelps. 'I drive you before?'

'Long time ago.' I smile and put my passport away and ask him what he's working on now. He leans forward to open the glove box and pulls out another huge manuscript.

'My book,' he says. 'I started it two years ago. 'Bout halfway through.'

'Two years?' He's getting quicker at least. 'What's this one about?'

'It's about American folklore,' he says. 'I've had to rewrite a lot of it because of the Internet.'

We're on Lincoln now and the traffic's heavy. Maybe we should have taken the freeway. The cabby hardly seems to notice. He's more interested in talking about his book.

'See, the Internet is like this breeding ground for folklore,' he says. 'Folklore, myths, hoaxes. People forward all these crazy virus warnings in emails because they don't trust technology. You know?' I nod. 'People don't understand the Internet or computers so they turn to superstition and myth to explain it.'

It sounds a lot more plausible than his nuclear fusion theories.

'See, cab driving is just a sideline for me. 'Till I finish the book.'

'It's your American Dream.'

'Say what?'

'You got to have an American Dream, right?' I say, throwing his own words back at him.

He snorts and shakes his head. 'Tttssssh. American Dream . . . I tell you, buddy, biggest myth out there? The American Dream. Greatest. Myth. Ever.' He holds a business card out to me over his shoulder. 'You should check out my web site,' he says.

'Sure,' I say, taking the card. 'I'll give it a look.'

I don't, of course. Not until today, anyway.

I find the cab driver's card in the back of the same cupboard as the beach shoes and workout top and the pink slip from the camper van. I plug in the web site address listed on his card and it loads quickly. The first thing that surprises me is that all these years later the site is still up at all. But then again, he probably still hasn't finished writing the book yet. The second thing is how surprisingly coherent his theories are. He must have given up the junk.

There are two mythical components to the American Dream, he argues on the site. Firstly, the lone cowboy myth – that made famous by John Wayne, Clint Eastwood's nameless stranger in the Sergio Leone westerns, even Sigourney Weaver in the *Alien* movies. 'These movie characters teach us that it's admirable to function as a lonely but self-reliant individual,' he writes. 'The second mythical component to the American Dream is the drive for change and our relentless desire for the new and the unexplored. Americans led the race into space and God knows how many of us regularly self-medicate boredom with a new gadget or a new outfit.'

The Internet reinforces both myths. 'Loneliness and change have undoubtedly shaped the way Americans relate to computers and the Internet.' As I've discovered, the Internet is the ultimate isolationist medium, with each experience online inherently unique to the user and to the moment. And of course the Internet is also new and ever changing. It's inevitable that the unfamiliar will eventually become familiar – TV's TV, the phone: so what – but the Internet is growing and evolving at such a rate that it's always possible to uncover something new, something you haven't seen before. It just takes a little more effort each time, a little more junk to fuel the rush as the cabby might say, a little more surfing to find the next looking glass to step through.

Loneliness and change.

So ... this is it. I've found the American Dream. In fact I found it twenty-four days ago when I first Logged On. Or was it eight years ago, at the London ad agency with Nervous, when I *first* Logged On and saw the girl rollerblading atop the Hollywood sign? I'm living the American Dream. I'm a lonely, self-reliant individual exploring a new frontier, just as immigrants have done for hundreds of years.

The American Dream. It's not in the fridge in a bottle marked vodka; it's not in a pound and a half of semi-cooked amphetamine; it's not a movie deal or a hanging chad or the right to remain silent. It's hidden in plain sight in a dusty corner of cyberspace on a little web site hosted by a fat, laughing, junkie cab driver. It's here; it's this. It's my new, hope-filled, ambitious life ...

I quit.

Incoming Email:

> To: <BritWriter>
> From: <Bubble>
> Subject: I found the perfect girl for you
>
> Before you quit, check out this girl's web site. I met her in Palm Springs last weekend. I think she's perfect for you. Unless of course you have a long lost sister you haven't told anyone about. She's gorgeous, a bit of an Anglophile and a lot of a nut. And – this is the killer – she's doing a PhD on number patterns or something and she thinks she's found a mathematical equation for the American Dream! Sounds weird, I know, but worth checking out. Just in case you're wrong about the self-reliant loner on the new frontier.
> I know you can't call her but send her an email (and a photo!)
> Your fairy godmother, Bubble

Bubble is asking me to buy into another popular myth. The 'love conquers all' myth that's as prevalent in American movies as the lone, misunderstood cowboy. Perhaps I'd be more inclined to buy into it if it weren't for Bubble's miserable track record at fixing me up on blind dates. A few months ago she had me meet the ex-wife of a well-known British TV presenter at a hotel bar in the Marina. She'd just flown in from North Africa and was looking for someone to show her a good time in LA.

'I'm a sexual tourist,' she says as we take our seats at the bar. I'm not sure what that means. 'It's a combination of the only two things I'm interested in,' she says. 'Travelling and fucking.'

She tells me how she's been shagged by three men today already, tupped in the searing heat of the Egyptian desert by a bunch of camel rustlers, passed between them like a damp spliff. It sounds seedy. I retreat to the bathroom. When I get back I'm surprised to see her still sitting there. I thought she would've found someone else in there to shag by now.

She looks up at me with tired, middle-aged eyes. She reminds me of my Auntie Brenda. 'That might be considered rude,' she says, 'since we're going to be fucking in the toilet later.'

There's a line outside the women's toilet. The men's is damp underfoot and smells of urine. And she reminds me of my Auntie Brenda. I decide to heed the judge's words and make an excuse about having a deadline for a story about a soap star with gonorrhoea, and drive home.

I don't much fancy a repeat of that date, thanks Bubble. I'm sure I can find a better way to spend my evening. Maybe I'll uncork another bottle and finish cooking up that methalymine.

Incoming Email:

>   To: <BritWriter>
>   From: <Ralph>
>   Subject: Quitting

> Bollocks you're quitting. Thirty days we agreed. Thirty days we paid you for. Just six more to go. Stick with it.

I've done it again. I've reduced the tweed-wearing, grey-haired patriarch of online journalism to cursing at me.

Incoming Email:

> To: <BritWriter>
> From: <Jim Womack, Warner Bros.>
> Subject: Re: Outline: To Live and Die Online
>
> I love this story. I pitched it to a couple of studios but it has more of an indie feel to it so I took it to Lion's Gate. They're very interested. They want to set up a meeting for us all next week and make a deal. Bring all your research with you. Then afterwards we'll celebrate with a few drinks. My liver has just about recovered from the last time. Well done,
> Jim

Just when I think things look bleak, LA's self-healing mechanism kicks in and balmy cheerfulness is restored. I'd almost forgotten about my email to Jim. I'd presumed he wasn't interested in the story. Then I receive a response like that.

It's seventy degrees outside. The sun is shining in Los Angeles. Optimism reigns. The American Dream is at hand.

Byte 25 – A Slight Hitch

Incoming Email:

> To: <BritWriter>
> From: <Abby>
> Subject: Byte 21
>
> I've been in Japan all week. Just got home. Caught up with your column. I know it's about a million years too late for all this, but for the record, I miss you too.
> Abby

Incoming Email:

> To: <BritWriter>
> From: <Bubble>
> Subject: I found the perfect girl for you
>
> Have you contacted this girl yet? I'm telling you, boy, you need to check out her web site. Don't be such a wuss.
> Bubble

I'm stuck. It's day Twenty-five and I can't decide if my search is over or not. It doesn't feel very satisfying if it is. I haven't logged off or stepped outside my door yet, but I don't much feel like surfing the Net in search of half-baked answers anymore. As far as I can tell, I've found the American Dream. And I've landed another screenwriting deal. What more is there to look for?

To appease Bubble and of course avoid the wrath of kindly old Uncle Ralph, I stick with it and check out this 'perfect' girl's web site. Maybe I'll give the 'love conquers all' myth one more shot.

Wow. I'm enthralled. To hell with her crackpot number equations and random sampling theories and photos of those legs that go allllllllll the way up ... this girl once met Hunter Thompson. Dr HST: icon, father of gonzo journalism, prolific consumer of narcotics and self-described 'lazy drunken hillbilly'.

Outgoing Email:

> To: <RandomSamplingChick>
> From: <BritWriter>
> Subject: Bubble gave me your email
>
> Bubble thinks we're so well matched you might be my long lost sister. I think it would be too dangerous to argue with her. Surfing your site, all these strange childhood memories came flooding back – the two of us skipping through corn fields together ... laughing at mother baking cakes in the kitchen ... stealing cars. And then one day you were gone. Alien abduction, the FBI said. But I always suspected you'd

joined the circus – I remember how much you loved eating fire and wearing large red shoes. I've been tracking those evil Ringling Brothers around the world so it's no coincidence we both ended up in LA. It's imperative that you write back to confirm this. I'm hunting for a photo of me taken before the disfigurement, but the techno-wobbles are getting the better of me and the scanner is refusing to co-operate. In the meantime, I found a photo of a very strange journalist gentleman with questionable taste in shirts.

You need to tell me how in the name of twisted Jehovah you got to meet the great HST – I need the whole sordid tale so I know it's really you, Dear Sister. I thought he never left Woody Creek these days.

Felicitations, your long lost sibling,

Captain America

Or as the good Doctor would say, Res ipsa loquitur. Let the good times roll.

That gibberish should scare her off. Especially accompanied by a photo of me standing in front of a headstone in a Japanese graveyard wearing dark glasses and a Hawaiian shirt, with my hands stuffed in my back pockets like my bottom is about to fall off.

Every film, every book in America pushes the same message. Intimate relationships are the only source of health and happiness; love is the only path to salvation. *Boy meets girl. And then he found love. The end. Happy days.*

Haven't I tried all this before?

*

My marriage comes at the end of the year. At the very end. Marriage, end. The words are synonymous. That's why weddings always fall at the end of all these stories and films. Nothing notable ever happens *after* marriage. It's the ultimate conspiracy, an evil pagan institution forced on the populace by devious government types out to weaken the resolve of the common man. Get married and we'll reduce your taxes. Get married and you can stay in the country. Family values? That's what Goebbels said about the Hitler Youth. Orwell was right: two legs good, four legs bad. The whole thing must have been devised by some vicious, man-hating lesbian. Margaret Thatcher probably. Nazi ...

My head is pounding with these wild, gibbering thoughts as I sit on the edge of the hotel bed, reflecting on the wreckage of my single life. The lights of Vegas twinkle through the window, taunting me. The largest New Year's Eve celebration on the West Coast is erupting on my doorstep. Thousands of people crowd along the six-lane Vegas Strip to celebrate. But I'm not one of them. I am – I can hardly even think it – I am married. Not just married, but married to someone I don't even know.

Every square inch of my body has broken out in angry red blotches. My chest feels tighter than a schoolgirl's brassiere. The alcohol that had so devotedly accompanied me throughout the day's events has now turned on me. I am in the midst of a fully-fledged panic attack. The only answer is sleep. Things will seem better in the morning.

I'm here – in Vegas, in a hotel room, wearing a wedding ring – because of a girl, a pub and a web site. No, not that girl, that pub or that web site. Three different horsemen of the apocalypse to accompany me this time. The web site is Vegasweddings4u.com, the pub is the Circle Bar on Main Street, and the girl is a twenty-something Californian.

Nervous, as always, meets her first. I'm sitting at home watching *Quadrophenia* and drinking strong tea, trying to prepare myself for life back in England. I still have the court order precluding me from frequenting bars so turn down Nervous's pleas to accompany him on a pub crawl along Main Street. He arrives at the Circle Bar on his own but in true Nervous style he goes ugly early and picks up an unfortunate-looking girl cruely known around Venice as 'Pumpkin Head' due to the size and shape of her cranium.

Abby joins them at the bar. She and Pumpkin know each other from AA meetings. They're both serving court sentences for driving under the influence. It seems to me they have both been punished enough – Pumpkin for her genetic misfortune, Abby for the three scars criss-crossing her face, reminders of where she was catapulted through the windshield when her car mounted the sidewalk and hit a traffic light. One is a half-moon shape from her left temple to the corner of her mouth, another runs the length of her left eyebrow and the third crosses the bridge of her nose. She seems intensely conscious of the scars and her hands flit nervously around her face as she talks to keep the lines in shadow. After Nervous plies them both with enough alcohol to float a battleship, Abby launches into a discourse on how difficult it is to meet decent guys in LA.

'Well,' Nervous says. 'There's a great guy in my apartment at the moment. He's getting deported soon.

He needs to get married to stay in the country.'

'Really? What's your address?' she says. 'I'll marry him.'

Nervous laughs and hands her his door key.

'Hi, I'm Abby,' she announces, her chestnut-brown eyes flicking round the room. 'I met your friend Bob in the Circle Bar. He said you needed to get married to stay in the country. I'll marry you.'

It's that simple. True, I'm only days away from Immigration running me out of the US like one of King George's redcoats. I've completed the anger management classes, pretended to attend AA, and am now just killing time until the final deportation hearing on the second of January. I have a little over a week left in this country. But marriage? To a complete stranger?

'Maybe you should choose your girlfriends a little more carefully,' the judge said.

I look Abby up and down. With her eyes closed, she is pure California: tall, blonde and sun-kissed. But those incongruous brown eyes make her skin appear paler, the freckles more pronounced. I'm choosing carefully. She has a flat stomach, pert breasts and all of her own teeth. With my rigid criteria for a life partner fulfilled, I accept. It may not exactly be the decision-making process the judge was advocating, but what the hell? What else do I have to lose?

'So that's settled then,' Abby says. 'What're you watching anyways?'

'*Quadrophenia*,' I say, shuffling along the couch so she can sit down. 'It's a British movie about–'

'Yeah, I've seen it,' she says. 'Jimmy and the Face.'

I stare at her a moment, not sure exactly what the protocol is after you've just accepted a marriage proposal from a stranger.

'Do my scars bother you?' she says.

'No.' She's so naturally pretty that if anything the scars enhance her looks, make her seem more real: the difference between an air-brushed magazine photo and the raw, flawed image of the negative. 'You want something to drink?'

'Sure. Whaddya got?'

'I don't know. I'll have a look.' I wander into the kitchen and dig up half a bottle of vodka and two glasses. By the time I walk back into the living room, Abby is asleep on the couch. I sit opposite her, down a vodka shot and watch her sleeping for a few minutes. Then I pull a blanket over her and go to bed.

I wake the next morning to someone shaking me. I growl and open my eyes. Abby is standing over me with a mug.

'Hope you don't mind, I helped myself to coffee. The milk in the fridge is off, though, so you'll have to take it black.'

I take the cup and sit up, still trying to squint the sleep from my eyes. 'What time is it?' I say.

'Just after nine.' She sits on the edge of the bed.

For someone who passed out on the couch the night before, she looks remarkably well. She's rinsed her makeup off and slicked the hair back from her face. The scars look pinker in the morning sunlight, snaking through the tiny freckles on her nose and cheeks. She's younger than I originally thought.

'I'm surprised you're still here,' I say.

'I didn't want to leave without saying goodbye.'

'How's your head?'

'Mmmm. Not great. Your friend drinks like a fiend.'

'Like a fiend?'

'Aha. I think Pumpkin threw up in the bar.' I smile and take a swig of coffee. 'So,' she says. 'Do you want to do dinner tonight?'

'Errr . . .'

'We should talk about this whole marriage thing.'

'Listen, it's OK. I really didn't take you seriously.'

'What? We're getting married, right?'

I stare at her, trying to figure out if she's being serious. She is. 'Yeah,' I say. 'OK.'

She kisses me on the cheek like we've been dating for years and bounces out of the room. And I know I should be scared. I expect to be; I almost want to be. But I'm not, not like I should.

'Hi Abby,' says the waiter, dropping two menus in front of us.

He's glassy-eyed and short and has a nasty habit of sniffing loudly before he speaks. We're in the Omelette Parlor and everything on the menu is some kind of omelette. It's a strange place to have dinner. Her choice.

The waiter sniffs. 'So what's going on?'

'Hey Danny,' she says. 'I'm engaged.'

Sniff. 'No shit?' And he looks at me. And sniffs. 'Congratulations. You wanna beer or somethin'?'

'What's up with his nose?' I say after he's taken our order.

'He's a coke fiend,' she says.

'A coke fiend?'

'Aha. You want some? I'm sure he's carrying.'

'No thanks.' I'm keen to keep the evening as sober

as possible. I want some straight answers to a couple of questions, namely why does she want to marry a total stranger?

'Why not?' becomes her standard riposte.

'There's no money in it for you,' I say. I'm working from home for some of my old JobPro clients, which pays enough to cover rent and attorney fees but not enough to buy myself a pretend wife.

'I know,' she says. I press her. 'You seem like a nice guy,' she says finally.

'You know I'm on probation for supposedly throwing my last girlfriend out of a car?'

'Nervous said it was a van,' she says. I look at her trying to work out if she's joking or not. 'He also said you didn't do it,' she adds with a smile.

'But aren't you the least bit concerned that–'

'It's George Costanza's Rule of Opposites,' she says.

'What?'

'From *Seinfeld*. George decides that every decision he's ever made in his entire life has been wrong.' She takes a sip of beer and does her best impression of a bald, stocky New Yorker. 'My life is the complete opposite of everything I want it to be. Every instinct I have, in every aspect of life, be it something to wear, something to eat ... It's all been wrong.' She sits back and finishes the beer. 'So he decides to do the opposite.'

'And that's what you're doing?'

'Maybe.'

'But–'

'But nothing. Now be quiet. And order some more beers.'

I smile. 'I'm not supposed to be drinking in public.'

'Me neither. Danny!' She says this last so loud that

I jump in my seat. 'Isn't breakfast the best meal?' she says. 'The English like breakfast, right?'

I nod. 'England: the land of embarrassment and breakfast.' She frowns. 'Julian Barnes,' I say.

She rolls her eyes and turns her attention back to ordering more beers.

We walk home along the bike path at the edge of the sand. An old homeless man steps out from the shadows, hand open for change. I leap back in surprise. He shivers in the ocean breeze. Abby hands him the doggy-bag from the Omelette Parlor, containing half a chicken and mushroom omelette and a handful of fries. His toothless mouth spreads into a grin. Abby then empties all the cash from her purse into his hands. I watch, amazed. As does the hobo – he looks like he's just won the lottery.

'Give him your jacket,' she tells me.

'What?'

'He's freezing,' she says. I slip off my jacket. She hands it to him then takes my hand and leads me away.

'What was that all about?' I ask.

'What?'

'The tramp. What is he, a relative or something?'

'Maybe.' And she falls strangely quiet.

It's only after she's repeated this with three or four other vagrants and I'm down to my last jacket that I learn why. Her father left her mother before Abby was born and no one has heard from him since. He was an unsuccessful screenwriter and her mother often jokes that he is probably living on a park bench somewhere. Abby has no idea what he looks like now so she takes care of any homeless person who looks about the right age.

I walk her home and pause on the doorstep.

'I have to fly to a meeting in New York tomorrow,' she says. 'Then I'm at my mum's for Christmas. You wanna get together the day after?'

'Yeah, sure,' I say. I kiss her goodnight and turn to leave.

'Where you going?' she says.

'I thought you were flying tomorrow.'

'Yeah, so? You can drop me off at the airport. We are going to get married, right?'

'Yeah.'

'OK. So we better have sex tonight then.'

I nod. It would be rude to argue.

I don't see her the day after Christmas. She calls to tell me she has to go back to New York for more client meetings and will have to stay there for the rest of the week. 'I'll meet you in Vegas, New Year's Eve,' she says. 'Did you book the chapel yet?'

'I've just got to confirm it,' I say.

'OK. So pick me up at the airport. I've bought a new dress but I still need some shoes to match.'

I hang up. So that's it, I think. Our courtship is over. The next time I see her will be on our wedding day. Everything is passing by me like a surreal dream.

That night the Baron emails me from some remote corner of the planet. He's just had a chemically induced revelation about the meaning of existence and feels compelled to share it with me. 'It's the Muppets, man, I'm telling you,' he begins in earnest with random words highlighted in bold capitals. 'I dropped some acid on the beach last night and suddenly realised that Jim Henson was God and that we are all

Muppets. The TV show is merely a sad metaphor for our lives. So when Henson died, it all became existential and God was really dead. That's why we're all winding aimlessly towards the end of the year – no one's controlling our strings.' He's right of course. And even if he wasn't, it's impossible to argue with a man on acid.

I book the wedding for 7pm and borrow a tie from Nervous.

Abby's mother calls up to confirm the name of the chapel. Apparently Abby's family has rearranged their New Year's Eve celebrations and will be flocking to Vegas to attend the wedding en masse. Someone has obviously forgotten to explain to them the true purpose of this union. This is no longer the breezy, carefree affair that I initially imagined. There will be in-laws, questions, polite talk of babies and mortgages. My chest is tightening. What the hell am I doing? And just as puzzling, what the hell is she doing?

I pick Abby up from Vegas airport in the early afternoon, my head foggy from a lack of REM sleep. She's tired and wants to take a nap before the wedding. I throw up and lay next to her on the hotel bed. I'm a nervous wreck. Sleep comes easily.

I wake to a pounding on the hotel room door. Abby is still asleep. It's 3pm, four hours 'til showdown. My head hurts. The pounding again. Nervous is at the door.

'You still haven't bought the rings,' he says. 'Maybe we should find a shopping mall before the stores close?'

*

'One last shot,' Nervous says. I nod and the bartender slips two enormous glasses of Jack Daniels in front of us.

We found a shopping mall. It's located next to a bar.

'Have you told your parents yet?' he says.

'No,' I say. 'I figured I'd let them know after the fact.'

Nervous chugs the Jack Daniels down in one and exhales loudly. 'My friend's getting married in an hour,' he tells the bartender.

'Congratulations,' he says and lines up two more shots. 'These are on the house.'

'He hasn't even bought the rings yet,' Nervous says.

The barman scowls. 'What time is the wedding?'

'Seven,' I say.

'Holy shit,' he says and slopes off to the other end of the bar to serve another customer.

Having enjoyed 'one last shot' another three times, Nervous and I stagger out of the bar with ten minutes to buy the rings, grab a taxi back to the hotel, get changed and meet the limousine outside. I'm almost too drunk to realise how impossible this is.

I hit the hotel room at a sprint, sweating bourbon from every pore, two $50 rings nestled in my pocket. I push open the door and skid to a halt, Road Runner-style. Abby is still curled up in bed, asleep. She pokes her head up from under the sheet as the door slams shut behind me.

'What are you doing?' I say.

'What?'

'We're late.'

'Oh. You shoulda woken me up.'
'Shit. Come one, let's go. Hurry.'

She slowly sits up and takes a sip of water from the bottle on the nightstand. I'm about to have an aneurysm. 'Abby!'

'You know, I still need to buy new shoes.'

'You're kidding. Can't you just wear some old ones?'

'No, I can't. I want to look nice. Call the chapel.'

'Fuck.'

I grab the phone and call the chapel, dizzy with panic and Jack Daniels.

My worry is completely unfounded. Booking a wedding chapel in Vegas carries no more obligation than ordering a pizza. Yes, I can reschedule. What about 11.20 or 11.35 or 11.50? I breathe a sigh of relief. Then Abby taps me on the shoulder, wiping the sleep from her eyes.

'You do love me, don't you?' she asks.

I freeze. It's an 'angina' moment. I hardly know her. It's like having an intimate conversation with the mailman. I gulp, nod perfunctorily and beat a hasty retreat to the hotel bar. Love, love? Nobody said anything to me about love. I've known her a week. One week. We've had dinner once. I don't even know her middle name. This isn't about love, it's about ... I'm beginning to forget exactly what it is about. Events have taken on a momentum of their own, racing like so many things haphazardly towards the end of the year. Thankfully, the bartender, clearly an insightful Doctor of the Human Condition, diagnoses my state perfectly and prescribes a magnum of cheap champagne to bolster my spirits.

It works. By the time we're crawling through the

throngs of partygoers converging onto the Strip, by the time I'm chugging more champagne in the back of a white limousine, I'm suitably oiled and the 'I love yous' are flowing freely. I love Abby; I love the whole idea of marriage; I even love the squat, bearded limousine driver. It's New Year's Eve and I'm sloshed. Cliff the counsellor would be horrified.

We stop at the city hall to apply for a marriage licence, a process that makes obtaining a pre-paid phone card look difficult. We each take a scrappy little form and an eraser-tipped pencil with 'I ♥ Vegas' written on the side from one of the boxes dotted around the dusty, wood-panelled room. Abby looks at the pencil then at the form.

'I don't believe this,' she mutters.

Each form requires just basic details: name, address, place of birth and intended spouse. Clearly ink would be too much of a commitment at this stage. Either a lot of people change the name of their intended spouse at the very last moment or Vegas officials are taking into consideration the general level of insobriety. Granted, it's the party night of the year, but the twenty-deep line of couples ahead of us is reminiscent of a conga at Mardi Gras.

We join the end of the queue and Abby slips her hand in mine and rests her head on my shoulder. 'These new shoes pinch,' she says.

'Then take them off,' I say.

'No. I might never get them back on. What did you do with that last bottle of champagne?'

'Left it in the limo. You want me to go and get it?'

'It's OK. We should probably stay sober enough to remember some of this.'

I smile and she rests her head on my shoulder again. It only really dawns on me at that moment how much of a traumatic experience this must be for her as well. After all, I'm the only one who has anything to gain from all this.

I squeeze her hand and she peeks up at me and smiles. And I feel something I haven't felt for a long, long time: the first few flutters of tickertape erupting.

'Next!' the Latina behind the counter bellows.

I nudge Abby's head up and we shuffle forward. She peers down at our forms, revealing bluey-green mascara daubed haphazardly over each eye.

'Birth certificates,' she says in a bored voice. Abby sifts through her handbag.

'Do you need to see a drivers licence or passports or anything?' I ask.

She shakes her head, oozing boredom. 'Just birth certificates.'

Abby hands them over.

'How d'you wanna pay?'

'Cash,' I say handing over a few screwed up bills from my pocket.

She takes the money and straightens it out. The bluey-green mascara blinks back at me. She stamps a piece of paper and pushes it over.

'You can call this number,' she says pointing to the back, 'in five working days and order additional copies of the marriage certificate.' Another flutter of bored bluey-green. 'Congratulations. Thank you for choosing to marry in Clark County, Nevada.'

The Candlelight Wedding Chapel is situated opposite the Circus-Circus Hotel and offers the facility to web cast the ceremony on the Net. My friends in England will be able to watch through their New Year hangovers.

The crowd on The Strip is growing as the limo pulls up outside, thousands upon thousands of people flocking in the same direction. I feel slightly envious. The first pangs of dread build in the pit of my stomach. The champagne has gone and my bravado is weakening. But there is still the family to meet: hordes of well-meaning people from places I've never heard of. I smile and shake hands and repeat names and try to remain upright. Abby's brother shakes my hand then immediately turns away. He's here under duress.

Her mother, a compact woman with a warm smile and a tweed business suit, hugs me tight.

'Welcome to the family,' she says.

I return her smile and look up to see the brother scowling at me.

'Thank you,' I say. Then there's an immediate uncomfortable silence.

I peer at the faces staring at me: uncles and aunts and family friends waiting for me to speak, to say something profound or at least something amusing to break the ice. But I freeze. I can't think of a single thing to say.

'So,' Nervous breaks in, 'who wants a glass of champagne while we're waiting?'

An officious woman with a clipboard barks out our names and quickly ushers Abby and me inside the chapel. The interior is dark and cold, with the faint scent of sweat lingering in the air. I stagger into a small room off to one side, sign a couple of forms, then offer the organist fifty bucks to play something a bit more upbeat than *The Wedding March*. Unfortunately, she's never heard of 'Born to Run'.

Abby's family walk past and take their seats in the chapel. Nervous, clutching more bottles of champagne, nudges my arm and indicates her family.

'Tough crowd, mate,' he says. 'Should've ordered that extra case.'

The clipboard woman smiles at us as we wait for our cue to walk up the aisle. 'First time?' she asks.

I nod. 'Yeah.' Then realise just what a strange question that is.

I look over at Abby but her eyes are fixed straight ahead like a greyhound in the slips. The first bar chimes out and she sprints up the aisle, dragging me with her. We come to a sudden stop at the altar and I notice her dress for the first time. It's cream and puffy and makes her look like a stale meringue.

Nervous buzzes around the altar with a video camera shooting footage for the web cast. The camera jiggles up and down as he tries to stifle his laughter. I imagine everyone watching in England getting nauseous from the shaky picture. Thankfully there's no sound, just blank faces and forced smiles.

Abby rolls her eyes each time the Minister uses the words 'respect and honour', then giggles 'I do.'

'I do too,' I blurt out instinctively.

The Minister touches my arm. 'Not yet,' he says.

Nervous snorts and the camera jiggles up and down on his shoulder again. The Minister finishes his delivery and nods at me.

'I do,' I say again and he smiles.

And that's it. It's all over in less than two minutes. My single life slips away with a whimper, a slurred 'I do.' I smile and pose for photos afterwards. The chapel's Elvis impersonator thanks me, thanks me very much and I bolt for the door, my hand still gripped in Abby's. The sight of The Strip hits me with the impact of a car wreck. The swelling crowd surges forward like hooligans at a football ground. I lead Abby into the mêlée, anxious to be lost in the crowd. The throng carries us forward. Someone hands me another bottle of champagne and I try desperately to take a swig. Warm amber trickles down my chin, soaking my shirt. Abby giggles.

It's time. Streaks of light fill the sky. Fireworks explode, people scream. Somewhere a voice crackles over a speaker. 'Happy New Year!' The familiar chorus of Auld Lang Syne seems curiously out of place in this heaving mass of bodies. I whoop and holler but can't shake the empty feeling inside. Nothing but lurid neon fills my line of sight. Cascading yellows, reds and blues all blur together. It's an explosion in a paint factory and it's swallowing me whole.

Abby gently touches my cheek. 'It's OK,' she whispers softly. 'It'll all be OK.'

I look down at her and she shoots me an unexpected smile. I go to speak, to say something reassuring but nothing comes out. Someone – Nervous, I think – grabs my arm and pulls me through the crowd towards the hotel entrance. I start to enter but Abby tugs me back. There's a homeless man crouched in the shadows.

The next thing I know I'm standing at the edge of the spinning Carousel Bar in Circus-Circus without a jacket or any cash. The scene is napalm on the senses: crude, vibrant, garish. We muscle seats at the edge of the revolving bar and knock back rusty bourbon. The sights flashing in front of us change at the speed of a TV remote in the grip of a dangerous lunatic. Trapeze artists swing above the howling craps tables, obese housewives wrestle with buckets of coins, and brutes in sequinned waistcoats pimp the circus sideshows. The bar revolves and the images storm back again, each time louder and brighter. And the bourbon flows, ushered down by a stomach full of champagne. Then I notice the first red blotch on my hand. I peek under the sleeve and see that my arm is covered in a carpet of hives. The liquid courage has vanished, leaving me a quivering, nervous wreck. I just want my bed. This is the new year, my fresh start. The old year, my old life has faded into nothing. But all I crave is sleep ...

The black cloud of doom that so gripped me the night before lifts with the sun. Morning arrives just as it did when I was single. I haven't developed a paunch, started to wear pyjamas or been drained of the will to live. Abby rolls over and slips her arm over my chest.

'Morning, husband,' she says without opening her eyes.

'Morning, missus.'

She hugs me tighter and I take a deep breath and stare at the ceiling. Maybe I can do this. Just maybe I can.

We drive slowly to the edge of Vegas, marvelling at the aftermath. Everything from my headache to the mounds of litter hanging over the city are testaments to the night before. The desert beckons and we begin the monotonous drive back to LA. Only the odd line of cattle fence shimmering in the desert heat haze betrays any human existence; nothing but dust and Joshua trees all the way to Barstow.

We speak little. Through the corner of my eye I catch Abby snatching glances at me. We're married but not yet at the stage of being comfortable with the silence between us. I fiddle with the rental car radio to give my hands something to do.

'So,' she says at last. 'What do you do for a living?'

Byte 26 – My So-Called Wife

Incoming Email:

> To: <BritWriter>
> From: <RandomSamplingChick>
> Subject: You found me!

I can't believe you finally found me, Captain, after all these years! I abandoned my life on the road with the Ringlings and elephants and fire-eating dwarves after I developed a mortal fear of clowns. The sight of rainbow wigs and the smell of greasepaint would send me recoiling in horror. I'd wake up in a pool of sweat screaming 'Coco! Argh!' only to discover it wasn't my sweat.

So dear Bubble sent you my web address? The site isn't finished yet and there's a lot of crap on there about my hobbies and interests and very weird streams of consciousness that double for thought-provoking research, but, (deep breath) yes, I think I have found the American Dream. I'm writing my thesis on randomness and number patterns. The American dream is a percentage. Somewhere between 95.75 and 100 per cent. I'm narrowing it down to a precise figure.

I hope there were no new photos of my prosthetic leg posted on the site. It doubles as a truncheon, so I can defend my country on any domestic or international flight.

I liked the photo of the journalist in the fancy shirt. Tell me, is it Paul Smith? Delia Smith? Ben Sherman? Sherman Hemsley? Unfortunately, most of my attire comes from those stores in North Hollywood where the sizes aren't labelled as small, medium and large, but rather chico, medio, and grande (the other Marx Brothers). But back to the photo, where exactly is this handsome young man standing? And where did he come from and where is he going, at what speed, heading in which direction?

Oh, good grief, I have to stop this so I can get a normal conversation started. Tell me about yourself in 300 words or less ...

Somewhere between 95.75 and 100, huh? I never considered the possibility that the American Dream might be a number. Then again, according to Douglas Adams' *Hitchhiker's Guide to the Galaxy*, the meaning of life is 42. That means the American dream is three times the size of the meaning of life. Typical. Everything has to be BIGGER here.

Relationships in the Internet age: you meet by exchanging lies and flirt by arguing over who has the biggest hard drive (wink, wink, nudge, nudge).

Progressively racier exchanges lead to the scanning and swapping of photos. If you're honest enough to send a picture of yourself, it's probably a hazy, slightly-out-of-focus long shot in black-and-white that was taken at least ten years ago when you were twenty pounds lighter and didn't wear inch-thick bifocals. More likely it's not a photo of you at all, but rather a raunchy shot of your much more attractive younger sibling or a clipping from a fashion magazine. Either way, photos are exchanged and it's on to that first tentative phone call. After smoking a dozen unfiltered cigarettes to give you that husky, oh-so-sexy voice, you pick up the phone. If all goes well, if the stammer is kept in check and you remember to take your Tourette's medication to quell the involuntary cursing, a first date is arranged.

Even with online dating there is at least a process, a recognisable pattern to the thing. Which is more than I can say for my relationship with Abby.

We arrive back from Vegas late on New Year's Day. Abby's roommate is away so we spend our first married night in LA at her place. The next morning I have to be in criminal court at nine o'clock, then Immigration Court at noon. Howard suggests I come to the former without Abby; he doesn't want the DA to know I'm married. After all, the deal has always been that if she drops the case against me, I will quietly disappear back to England.

The fat little judge examines my discharge form from the Therapy Center. I attended all the required sessions, I'm paid up to date and even Cliff the Counsellor has to admit that I present no danger to society. The judge doesn't ask about AA. Instead he exchanges a few quiet words with Howard and the DA. I look around the courtroom, half expecting to see Roxy come bounding in, ready to spring some final surprise.

I turn back to the judge as he hammers his gavel. The case is dismissed. All charges against me are dropped. I step outside and shake hands with Howard. The DA walks past and smiles. She stops and doubles back.

'Look,' she says, her eyes flicking between Howard and me. 'I know you didn't deserve all this. Sometimes the system doesn't work as well as it should.' She looks genuinely apologetic. 'Good luck back in England. I hope everything works out for you.'

I nod and she heads back down the corridor, the click-clack of her heels fading into the background hum of the court building.

I press the buzzer again and check my watch. It's after eleven already. I buzz again. Abby's voice croaks over the intercom.

'Who is it?' She's obviously just woken up.

'It's me,' I yell. 'We're due in immigration at twelve!'

She groans and buzzes the door open. By the time I run up to her second floor apartment, she's spinning around the bedroom in an unbuttoned dress, hunting for some matching shoes. She settles on a pair and grabs her purse.

'Ready,' she says, out of breath.

'Passport, ID, birth certificate,' I remind her.

She doubles back to the kitchen and snatches up a clear plastic folder. Then a make-up bag. And comes scuttling out the front door. She follows me down the stairs buttoning her dress as she goes. Twenty minutes later, I pull into the shopping mall car park opposite the Immigration building downtown. Abby flicks the vanity mirror up and turns her face to me.

'How do I look?' she says. She has a little eyeliner and a touch of blusher on. She looks great.

'You look great,' I say. 'And we're early.'

'Are you kidding me? How early?'

I check my watch. 'Twenty minutes. But let's wait in the car, I hate being in that building. When did we meet?'

'July fourth,' she says. 'At Nervous's party. But they're not gonna ask that today.'

'I just want to make sure we say the same things. Just in case.'

'Are you always this uptight?' she says.

'Only when it comes to dealing with Immigration. You don't know what they're like. What's your brother's name again?'

She smiles and leans over and unzips my fly. I look at her and she shoots me a wicked grin. 'Just relax ...' she says. And I do.

'Carl, this is Abby.'

My immigration attorney hasn't taken his eyes off her since he saw us approaching the courtroom from the far end of the corridor. He straightens his grey linen suit, adjusts his ponytail and takes her hand.

'Well, OK,' he says to me, his eyes still fixed on Abby. 'We'll file for a motion to change your status based on marriage to a citizen. You are a citizen I take it?' Abby nods. 'Good. Have you got a wedding certificate?' He's talking to me again but his eyes don't waver from Abby. 'And do you have your passport, Abby, and your birth certificate with you?' She hands him the plastic folder. 'Great. That's just great.'

There's a moment's silence. My beat poet-attorney is still staring at my wife-stranger. I clear my throat. 'Shouldn't we be going into the court now?'

'What?' says Carl. 'Oh, yeah, right.' And he finally looks at me. 'Nice tie.'

'Do I have time to run to the restroom?' Abby says. I look at her. 'I need to, you know . . . freshen up.'

'Oh,' I say, suddenly realising what she's talking about. 'We'll see you in there.'

Carl watches her run off. 'Yeah, man, she seems . . . yeah.' And he opens the courtroom door.

Abby giggles every time Carl addresses the judge and refers to her as my 'lovely young wife'. The judge seems less impressed, particularly by the timing of the marriage.

'I see,' he says, looking over his glasses at Carl. 'We delay the deportation hearing for nearly a year so he can resolve the criminal charges. And on the last day he turns up with a wife.'

'You know how these things happen, your Honour,' says Carl. 'It's easy to meet and fall in love with someone in a year. I think you can see why he's fallen for her.'

Abby giggles again. I squeeze her hand tighter, hoping it'll act like a volume control.

The judge makes a growling sound in the back of his throat and glances over at me. 'You just got in under the wire, huh?'

'What?' Abby whispers to me. 'What is he saying?'

I squeeze her hand as tight as possible; the volume control appears to be broken.

'I'm an American citizen,' she says louder still. 'I can marry who the hell I like. No one is gonna tell me who I can and can't marry.'

'OK,' I whisper. 'Keep it down. This is a courtroom. Please be polite.'

I really want to remove my hand from hers and place it over her mouth, but decide under the circumstances that wouldn't be a smart idea.

'I'll be polite as long as they don't try to tell me I can't marry you. Look at these people. They don't even speak English.'

She has a point. There's only one other couple in there that isn't accompanied by a translator. I smile and nod my head across the room at Franco, the Italian bodybuilder. His wife is sitting next to him, although it wouldn't be unreasonable to presume she was his mother, or even his grandmother. She's easily sixty-five and has tight, drawn skin around her mouth that suggests her teeth are no longer her own. He married his landlady.

'Are you kidding me?' Abby goes on. 'They can come into this country but they're gonna hassle me for marrying you? I don't think so. Your hands are sweating by the way.'

The judge clears his throat and at last she falls silent. He tells us we have to return in two months for an interview with an INS agent to establish whether or not our marriage is real. I wipe my hand on my leg and mutter a 'thank you'.

The next two months pass easily enough. We move into the apartment on Montana. Abby, when she isn't handing out my clothing to the multitude of homeless men that live in the park along Ocean Avenue, travels a lot with work. I work from home, writing for magazines and a few old JobPro clients and land another screenwriting gig. And I try to work out at what point the marriage becomes 'real'. I just seem to suddenly find myself in the middle of a domestic scene. It's like an episode of *The Twilight Zone*. I wake up one morning to find everything I imagined my life to be is in fact just a dream, and I am really someone I hardly recognise. I fall asleep one night thinking I'm a single bloke with more legal problems than OJ Simpson and Roman Polanski combined, then wake up to find I am in fact a married man and a working screenwriter and, however temporary, a legal resident.

But there is still this stranger lying next to me every morning; this person that behaves like this is the most natural situation in the world. One afternoon, with my head pounding with plot points and act breaks, I search the bathroom cupboards for an aspirin. Instead, I uncover twenty-seven sticks of Lady Fresh deodorant and a dozen bottles of Prozac. I have no idea she's on antidepressants and even less idea they might be responsible for generating that level of perspiration. And I know now that David Byrne wrote that song for me. *Abby is not my beautiful wife, this is not my beautiful house* . . .

'Favourite band?' she says.

'Mmm, tough one,' I say. 'It changes weekly. I'm listening to a lot of Talking Heads at the moment.' I cover her eyes. 'Colour of the bedroom curtains?'

'We call them drapes. And what the hell is it with you and window dressings anyway?'

'They'll ask,' I say. 'They always do. So what colour are "the drapes"?'

'Blue,' she says.

I drop my hand and she takes another sip of champagne. It's her birthday and we're waiting for the results of her annual oncology test. She fluffs up her cushion.

'We need a couch,' she says.

'Not much point if I get deported.'

The only furniture we have in the entire apartment is a bed, my desk and a few throw cushions that double as a sofa. We decide we'll go furniture shopping if my green card application is approved at the INS interview.

'Point taken,' she says. 'Next question.'

'What deodorant do you use?'

'That's really freaked you out, huh?'

'It's ... it's just a little weird.'

'Like you're Mr Normal the way you talk to your computer.'

I smile. 'How long have you been on Prozac?'

'All my life.'

'Seriously.'

'I only take it when I can't face getting up in the morning,' she says.

'Which is how often?'

She looks down at the champagne bubbles dying in her glass. 'Every day,' she says, then quickly asks me to open another bottle.

I refill her glass and she asks me about Katie. Just telling people my sister died from cancer in her early thirties always elicits the same response. 'I'm sorry,' they say, then there are a few uncomfortable moments of silence. It isn't like that with Abby, though, so I tell her the whole story, something I've never done before.

'What kind of chemo was she on?' she asks. I don't know. 'How long was she sick for?' I know to the very hour. 'When did she die?' It was just as Roxy and I were turning from the A1 onto the North Circular Road on our way back from my parents' house. 'Why didn't the doctors tell you to have regular check-ups?'

'It started off as ovarian cancer then moved to her stomach,' I say. 'I guess they don't think that puts me at risk.'

She nods. There's no fake sincerity, no exaggerated sympathy, just a tacit understanding. 'Do you miss being able to visit her grave?'

'No. I never went when I lived there.' She stares at me. She wants more. But only if I'm prepared to give it. 'I don't know,' I say. 'It's not where Katie is.'

She nods again. But I don't want to say anymore. She understands and asks me if I want some more champagne.

'Do you?' I ask.

'Yeah,' she says and checks her watch. 'They should call soon. I don't like to be more than one glass away from drunk when I answer it.'

The INS interview is on a Monday morning. We bicker all the way there: I'm convinced we haven't practised enough and Abby is adamant that it doesn't matter because no one can tell her who she can and can't marry. We take a number and sit in a packed waiting room. Somewhere a baby is crying. It makes me acutely aware of the silence between us.

'I'm sorry,' I say at last. 'I'm just a little tense.'

She finally looks across at me. 'Yeah, well,' she says. 'I'm not going to give you a blow job in here.'

A frosty immigration officer eventually calls out our number. She glares at us as we approach.

'I'll interview your wife first,' she says. 'Then come back for you and compare answers.'

Abby follows her out and I'm left stewing in the waiting room.

The baby's crying again. I pace the room, reciting the facts we crammed last night. We met July fourth, at a party, our first date was dinner at Mario's, her mum's name is Audrey, her brother's name is ... Bugger, what is her brother's name? This is worse than O-Level History. Archduke Franz Ferdinand, the Ottoman Empire and 1914 have been replaced by details of L'Oreal moisturiser, blue velvet curtains – drapes – and a dozen names like Uncle Chuck and Auntie Babs from Hoboken, New Jersey. Or is it Wichita Falls?

I wait for what seems like three days, my palms dripping sweat like leaky faucets. If they decide this marriage is anything but legitimate, I won't be allowed back in the US for at least seven years, maybe never. Talk about pressure. It's like a Mad Max version of *Mr & Mrs* or *The Newlywed Show*. The warm and cuddly Derek Beattie has been replaced by a Nazi cyborg and the only consolation prize is immediate deportation.

I hear my name called and turn to see the cyborg at the door. She beckons me to follow her. We walk down a carpeted corridor and into an interview room. The sound of the baby's crying fades as I close the door.

The cyborg tells Abby to move to a seat at the back of

the room. She glances at me briefly but I can read little from her expression. The cyborg orders me to sit directly in front of Abby so we can't make any eye contact. Evidence of our marital shackles – photos of the wedding, joint bank account statements, the apartment lease proving we live together – are sprayed across the cyborg's desk. There's a video camera resting on a tripod next to her. She catches me looking at it. 'We only use that if we have any doubts,' she says.

I nod and swallow nervously and the interrogation begins.

'When was the last time you kissed your wife?' The cyborg peers over her clipboard at me.

My wife. The term still takes me back every time I hear it. The cyborg wipes her thin lips and repeats the question. Bugger, we haven't rehearsed this one. I'm expecting questions about the colour of the bedroom drapes, who sleeps on which side of the bed, that kind of stuff. But kissing?

'I kissed her on the cheek about an hour ago,' I finally say.

Abby shifts in the chair behind me. 'Oh, yeah, I forgot about that,' she mumbles. Great, my answer doesn't match hers. I look at the video camera.

'When did you last share a home-cooked meal, what was it and who prepared the meal?'

I know this one. 'Thursday,' I say with some confidence. 'I cooked a chilli.'

'Are you sure?'

'Yes.'

I hear Abby shift in the chair behind me again. 'I thought I did a chicken stir-fry?' she says.

'No,' I say, without looking round. 'That was Wednesday night.'

'Oh, yeah.'

The cyborg makes another note on her sheet. Shit. This isn't going well. I feel like Dickie Attenborough in *The Great Escape*. She can only have my name, rank and serial number. And possibly details about the bedroom drapes. That's OK, Dickie would have done the same.

All I know about these interviews stems from the movie *Green Card*, where the emphasis seems to be on remembering the name of her face cream, as well as the little Carl has told me. The only subject definitely off-limits is sex, although they have cunning ways of skirting round the issue. The kissing question is followed-up by 'What part of your wife's body do you compliment the most?'

The part that said 'I'll marry you to keep you in the country,' I think. But that's no good, it has to be what Abby would say. Her eyes? Possibly. Ears? Unlikely. Breasts? Probably, but do I really want to go down that road?

'I ... err ... I like all of her.' I say and it sounds so lame.

'Specifically,' the cyborg orders.

Damn, this *is* O-Level History. I've revised all about World War One only to find the exam is on the General Strike. The cyborg shoots me another impatient look. Why can't she ask me about the damn drapes or at least make it multiple choice, give me a fighting chance?

'Well, I've never been one to get into specifics. It's more of a general compliment thing.'

I'm really fluffing now, but to my surprise the cyborg exchanges a knowing smile with Abby and then ticks her notes. It's the right answer. Apparently

Abby's response had been: 'He never compliments me. He's very English.'

I have the hang of it now: the phone's on my side of the bed, her boss's name is Ken, I'm allergic to Tequila *not* tuna, her brother doesn't like me – probably because I can never remember his name – I do the laundry, she does the bills, and no, she's a horrible cook. The secret isn't to have the same answers and agree on everything, after all most married couples can't agree on which TV channel to watch. The real secret to feigning married status is to exude a subtle air of disappointment. Disappointment that I forgot her favourite perfume, disappointment that she can't remember who scored the winning goal in the '91 Cup Final. Trivial disappointments, granted, but enough to one day wreck the strongest relationship, screw up any kids and keep an army of lawyers and analysts gainfully employed.

The cyborg seems satisfied that the marriage is real and says she will approve my Green Card application. Relief flushes over me but I decide to save the lap of honour for the parking lot.

As we get up to leave, the cyborg glances at her notes again. 'Oh, I forgot one question,' she says. 'What colour are your bedroom drapes?'

Outgoing Email:

> To: <RandomSamplingChick>
> From: <BritWriter>
> Subject: Re: You found me!
>
> Are you suggesting this isn't a normal conversation? OK, I'll do my best to write something

normal. The journalist is Dr Oranjeboom, aspiring gonzo, and his shirt is Emporio Thrift, size medio, won from a homeless person in a rigged card game. I believe he's standing in a Buddhist graveyard somewhere outside Tokyo. He's one of the world's great standers. He travels the world looking for new and interesting places to stand. In this instance he'd mistaken the crypt for a Japanese pub and was standing there for several hours waiting for it to open, desperately trying to hold his prosthetic bottom on. Moments after the photo was taken, it finally fell off, and he was forced to return to LA for a replacement. But then you've probably had similar trouble with your leg, right?

Ah, and there I go again. I said I was going to be normal and then I go and write more gibberish. Normal . . normal . . in 300 words or less. I was brought up in Hertfordshire but moved to London as soon as they'd let me on the train. Came to LA eight years ago for a holiday, lost my return ticket, decided to stay. I freelance for magazines under a variety of names depending on:

(a) how crap the material is (b) whether it's likely to land me in jail or (c) if it's just funnier doing it under someone else's name.

I'm currently living online writing a daily column. I have no diseases that I'm aware of – fuck, bollocks, wank – apart from the Tourette's. When I grow up I'd like to be an astronaut or a mountain yodeller. I don't often smoke (unusual for an Englishman) but do enjoy the odd tipple (less unusual) and, of course, I don't much care for the French.

And that's about all I can manage in one sitting (on a plastic bottom). Now your turn.

Yours in prosthetic turmoil.

Byte 27 – Scenes From a Fake Marriage

INTERIOR. PRODUCER'S OFFICE – DAY

'It's a romantic comedy called *Wife Dot Com*,' I say. 'A lonely English teacher at a prestigious boys' school needs a wife in order to be considered for the position of headmaster, so he orders one from the Internet. Only she turns out to be an escaped mental patient. Sort of *Goodbye Mr. Chips* meets *One Flew Over the Cuckoo's Nest*.'

'And then they get eaten by an alien?'

'No, I was kidding about that bit. I've just got this weird obsession with alien movies.'

Bob Metz leans back in his chair and makes a clicking sound with his tongue. He's a round, ruddy-faced man in what is an unmistakeably expensive suit.

'I have a three page outline,' I add.

His tongue clicks again. 'Man orders a wife from the Internet,' he says, mulling it over like a sommelier tasting wine.

'It's very now,' I say. 'Look at the statistics on how many people are meeting over the Internet these days.'

'How many?'

'I don't know. But it's a lot. People don't meet how they used to.'

'How did you meet Abby?' he asks.

I hesitate. 'A friend introduced us.'

'You know how I met her?' I nod but he decides to tell me anyway. 'I was sitting next to her on a plane. New York to LA. They were showing my last movie. I told her I produced it and she proceeded to tell me what a pile of horseshit it was and why.'

I flinch with embarrassment. Maybe he's only asked me here so he can pull my script idea apart and take revenge on Abby. But he breaks into a smile and says, 'That kind of honesty is rare in this town. She's one spunky broad your wife. Did you see it?'

I nod.

'And?' he says.

'Not really my cup of tea,' I say.

He shrugs. 'No, you're right. It was the director's fault. He's a total prick. You have any idea how good the original script was? I'll let you read it sometime. Then he came on board and the whole project went to shit. So d'you own the domain name wife dot com?'

'No,' I say. 'But it shouldn't be too hard to get. It hosts a really bad personals site at the moment, one that charges seven hundred and fifty dollars to place an ad.'

'Seven fifty? Jeez. How many ads on there?'

'Last time I checked, exactly none. That's why I think they'll be willing to sell it for a few bucks.'

He leans back in his chair and resumes the clicking sound with his tongue. 'Man orders a wife from the Internet,' he says again. 'I like it.'

EXTERIOR/INTERIOR. SANTA MONICA
APARTMENT – EVENING.

'Well?' says Abby, shifting excitedly in the doorway.
'Well what?'
'Well, how'd it go, you big jerk? What did he say?'
'He said you're a spunky broad.'
'Is that because I dissed his movie?' she says. I nod. 'Huh. Spunky broad. Who the hell talks like that anyways?'
'Dissed movie producers,' I say, finally making it past her and into the apartment.
She jumps onto my back and tries to bite my ear. 'Stop teasing me and tell me what he said about *Wife Dot Com*.'
'He said he wants to option it.'
'Really?' She bounces up and down like a jockey on a reluctant steed.
'Owww.'
She jumps off and looks up at me. 'That's fantastic. So why aren't you jumping up and down? Why aren't you excited?'
'I am really. It's just superstition. I'll jump up and down when the contract's signed and the cheque clears.'
The buzzer on the oven sounds. 'It'll get signed,' she says, moving into the kitchen. 'You hungry? I made a celebration dinner.'
I laugh. 'A celebration dinner? And what would you've done if it was bad news?'
'Called it a commiseration dinner,' she says, grinning. 'But I knew it'd go well. I have faith in you.'

INTERIOR. SANTA MONICA APARTMENT –
NIGHT

I lean back and push the empty plate away from me. 'Thank you,' I say.

Abby shrugs. 'It was kinda burned, huh?'

'No, it was good,' I lie.

'Really?'

'Really.'

She offers me the bottle of wine resting on our new Ikea dining table. 'You wanna finish it?' I nod and she pours the last half a glass. 'Penny for them?'

'Hmm?'

'Your thoughts?'

'I told you, it was good.'

'I didn't mean dinner.'

'Oh,' I say. 'I'm good too.'

She drags her chair closer to mine and clinks wine glasses. 'Here's to your movie getting made.'

'Thanks, Ab. For everything. You've . . . changed my life you know. You didn't have to do half the things you've done.'

She frowns. 'You're my husband. Why wouldn't I?'

I stare at her a moment. A husband looking at his wife. A man eying a stranger.

'What?'

'Nothing.'

She takes another sip of wine. 'My mum wants to throw us a wedding reception next month.'

'A what?'

'You know, for all my family that didn't make it to Vegas for the wedding. Maybe your parents can fly over. There's this hotel near my mum's with a great reception room overlooking the ocean.'

I shake my head and carry the plates into the kitchen. Abby follows me out. 'Well?'

I fill the sink with scalding water and flinch as I lower the dishes beneath the suds.

'Helloooo,' Abby says. 'Will you talk to me?'

I pull my hands out and dry the red skin. 'A wedding reception? What are you doing?'

'What d'you mean?'

'You know exactly what I mean. Abby, we've known each other for a couple of months.'

'Yeah, so?'

'So ... so, we hardly know each other. And you want to have a big reception, hire out a hotel. What is this?'

'We're married.'

'And why are we married?'

She turns away. 'So that's a no, then?'

'You're damn right it's a no. You're freaking me out. What's wrong with you?'

'You're supposed to be my husband,' she sniffs and walks off.

By the time I've finished cleaning the dishes, Abby's curled up on the bed drying her eyes and watching *Seinfeld* on TV. It's the 'Rule of Opposites' episode.

George is in his car with a beautiful woman. *'Are you sure you don't wanna come up?' the woman says. 'I mean it's only nine thirty.'*

'I don't think we should,' George says. 'We really don't know each other very well.'

'Who are you, George Costanza?' the woman says.

'I'm the opposite of every guy you've ever met.'

I sit down on the edge of the bed. 'Oh God, I'm George Costanza,' I say.

Abby doesn't smile. 'We all are,' she says. 'A little

bit. I think that's the point.' She flicks off the TV and wipes her eyes again.

'Listen, Ab,' I say. 'This is all ... new. For both of us. It just freaks me out, that's all. Everything's happening so fast.'

'You still love her don't you?'

'What? Jesus, no. No, not at all. Are you kidding?'

'You don't love me.'

'Abby–'

'You never say it. At least not when you're sober.'

I finger the ball of pot pourri hanging from the window latch. Then check my watch. 'You want to catch the late show?'

'Where?'

'AMC on Third Street.'

'What's playing?'

'*Alien Resurrection*.'

She smiles and wipes her eyes again. 'Sure.'

EXTERIOR. THIRD STREET PROMENADE – NIGHT.

It's nearly two am as we walk back from the cinema. 'I know you like those movies,' she says. 'But that was really crappy, huh?'

'Yeah, it was,' I say. 'That's OK though. I'm sort of glad.'

'You're–? Oh, I see. She saw the best two you mean? Your sister?'

'Yeah. The third one was OK I suppose. But that one ... she would've hated it.'

'So there's no alien in *Wife Dot Com* now?'

'Naaa,' I smile. 'Bob didn't seem too keen on the idea.'

'Ahhh, what does he know? His last movie sucked.'

I squeeze her hand then put my arm around her and pull her close. 'You're great,' I say.

She stretches her neck and plants a wet kiss on my cheek. 'I'm great?'

'You're great.'

I want to tell her I love her. I nearly do. But something holds me back. A feeling that somehow now isn't the right time. I decide to save it for another day, a day when it fits better: a fully-fledged 'I love you' kind of day. So I just kiss her instead. And the 'I love you' goes unused.

Byte 28 – A Click Apart

Everything changes the morning my green card arrives.

Abby's lying on the couch surrounded by the Saturday papers. She looks up as I carry the mail into the apartment, a fly buzzing around my face.

'Kiss me,' she says.

'Huh?' I wave the fly away.

'I want you to kiss me. To see if we kiss to the left or the right.'

'What are you talking about?'

She stands up still clutching the Travel section. 'I've just been reading about this guy who's travelling the world to find out if people put their heads to the right or the left when they kiss.'

'And?'

'It's mainly to the right. So come here and give me a kiss.'

'I think I go left,' I say.

'So show me.'

'Naa, you've made me all self-conscious now.'

'You–!'

I lean forward and peck her on the mouth, head

straight, my nose touching hers. She smiles and whacks me playfully on the arm.

'You're no fun,' she says, then sees the envelope in my hand. 'Anything good?'

I use the envelope to swipe at the fly again, then hold it out to her.

'It's my green card.' She withdraws her hand as if I'd just told her the letter was packed with anthrax. 'What's wrong?'

'You know what's wrong,' she says. 'So that's it then? When were you going to tell me?'

'What are you getting mad about? I've only just opened it.' The fly's back again.

'So we're getting a divorce now?'

'Did I say that?'

'You didn't have to. What about my job?' Last week she was offered a promotion that would mean moving to New York. She hadn't seemed interested before now.

'What about it?' I say.

'Do I take it?'

'That's up to you.'

'No, it's up to us.'

'It's your career.'

'But what do you think? Should I take it or not?'

'Abby, I really don't–'

'Can't you just give me a straight answer?!'

'Yes, then!' I yell and immediately regret it. She looks down, pretending to read the paper again. 'It's a great opportunity, Abby,' I say. 'I don't want to stand in the way of that.'

'So you won't move with me then?' She looks up, her eyes glistening.

'Ab, my work's here–'

She holds up her hand. 'Don't. Let's not pretend. It's the easy way out, isn't it?'

I finally squash the fly against the corner of the coffee table. It leaves a black and crimson stain on the envelope.

'It isn't like that,' I say.

But it is. It's exactly like that. She knows that with three thousand miles between us, we'll see less and less of each other until everything simply withers and dies like a neglected houseplant. And part of me secretly hopes that she's right.

We argue for the rest of the afternoon. Then we don't speak for a day. Then we argue some more. She takes the job in New York. And I stay in LA. And that's the beginning of the end. We commute back and forth at weekends for a while but it's expensive and tiring and always seems a long way to travel for an argument.

She calls me up from work one afternoon and suggests we seek guidance counselling. I laugh. She's been talking to someone; Abby would never come up with an idea like that on her own. She always refers to the self-help movement as the self-self cult. 'That's where these self-absorbed people go wrong,' she'll say. 'They're unhappy so they spend all their time analysing themselves. Spending all that time with someone so unhappy only makes them more miserable. They'd be much happier if they just spent that time thinking about someone else.' No, guidance counselling isn't her idea. It's a test. One that she knows I'll fail.

'I'm serious,' she says when I finally stop laughing.

I tell her I know she is. Then suggest we get a dog

instead. She likes the idea and we talk about it for several weeks but we can't even agree on that. She wants a terrier; I want a retriever. She suggests counselling again. I tell her I can't see the benefit of a five-hour flight followed by two hours in a church hall listening to some pious hippie in corduroys tell me I'm crap at relationships. She starts to cry and hangs up the phone and we don't talk for days. Then she emails me with a compromise: online marriage counselling. No flights, no church halls, no corduroy. Maybe she is serious; maybe I'm wrong about it being someone else's idea. I agree to a series of email seminars called 'Learn to Listen – and Enjoy It'. It seems better than making her cry again.

The first session consists of an hour of 'fun exercises' via Instant Messaging aimed at helping us 'communicate more openly'. She gets annoyed because I type so fast she never knows where I am at. I get annoyed because she keeps ending sentences with a preposition. I'm not sure how much either of us enjoys it.

We struggle through the next two seminars. They're email sessions this time to 'slow the process down' and allow us to 'craft more capable contributions'. I see them more as further vicious attempts to get me to write down my feelings. I feel ... hounded. I feel ... homesick. I feel ... hopeless. More h's. It's difficult to imagine someone like Clint Eastwood ever stooping to this. Dirty Harry puts down his Magnum and writes something touchy-feely about how his emotional needs aren't being fully met in his current relationship.

Maybe I should turn the TV off while I'm doing this. As I type I watch old movies and basketball games I have no real interest in and suspect she is equally distracted. She keeps going off on long tangents that don't seem particularly helpful or interesting. That's the downside to Internet counselling. There's no pious hippie to politely clear his throat and tell us to stop rambling.

The fourth session we complete from opposite ends of her New York apartment. We're supposed to be airing all our grievances in 'the safety of cyberspace'. We end up shouting at each other through the bedroom wall. I type 'bollocks' a lot and slam the laptop shut and go out for a walk.

I stroll through the Village, past the brownstones and boutiques. Two men kiss in the doorway of a leather and love shop on Christopher Street. Their heads are tilted to the right. A woman in a faux fur coat streaked pink and black like a psychedelic tiger struggles to control a Dalmatian. The dog tugs hard on its leash dragging her tottering past me in dangerously high heels and I feel like I've stepped into the pages of a Tama Janowitz novel.

I turn along West Fourth to Washington Square, sit in the park with the tourists and students and bums. A man with torn red pants and a soiled shirt that has 'The Death Penalty is Dead Wrong' written on the front battles a pigeon and the voices inside his head over a corner of stale loaf. It starts to rain and I instinctively go to hand him my jacket, then stop. Abby isn't here; for once I can enjoy the luxury of returning home from a walk with all the clothes I started with. I turn the jacket collar up and walk back to the apartment.

She's curled up asleep on the bed. I never understand how she can sleep like that, curled into a tight foetal ball.

Me, I need to be stretched out from one corner of the bed to another, limbs spread-eagled like a just-arrested felon in a 70s cop show. I sit on the edge of the bed and watch her dozing. It's stopped raining and the late morning sun streams through the drapeless windows, licking at her pale skin. The city mumbles in the distance. I stroke her face, my fingers gently running the length of her scars. She stirs and slowly opens her eyes. Her eyes settle on mine and she smiles.

I ask if she wants to get out of the city for the afternoon.

She nods. 'Where d'you wanna go?'

'I don't know. Let's just drive, see where we end up.'

'OK.'

A few hours later we've broken the tight net of Manhattan traffic and are driving along a green, tree-lined highway in New Jersey. We cross the state line and stop for a coffee in a Pennsylvania tea shop at the edge of the Delaware. We spend the rest of the afternoon walking along the river's banks and get accidentally drenched by a waterfall. We sit on a stone wall to dry off in the fading sunlight.

An old couple approaches with their dog. They're both wearing identical black berets and are so arthritic they have to lean on each other for support. Their dog hobbles over, equally arthritic, tongue hanging out from the mere exertion of living. Abby pets his greying muzzle and makes a point of telling me he's a terrier.

The old lady calls out 'Teddy' and the dog hobbles back, shuffling from side-to-side on his old hips. We smile and wave and watch the three figures slowly, slowly disappear from view.

'That's still my favourite dog,' Abby says at last.

I smile and nod and don't say anything. Maybe I'm learning to listen.

Rather than drive back to the city, we check into an old slate and red tile hotel straddling the river. A water wheel turns by the entrance. The bell hop shows us to a small room dominated by a four-poster bed and flowery drapes. He tells us Paul Revere once stayed there when he was hiding out from the British. Abby sneaks a glance at me and smiles.

'Down with the British,' she says.

I tip the bell hop and thank him in my best American accent.

I flop on the bed while she takes a bath. By the time she's done I'm already asleep, dreaming of red coats and arthritic dogs. I awake first the next morning and let her sleep in while I take another walk along the river. She meets me for breakfast outside. She ruffles my hair and pecks me on the cheek as she sits down and part of me wishes I didn't have to fly back to LA today.

The car breaks down on the return drive to New York. I pull over onto the hard shoulder and call AAA. We sit on a grass bank at the side of the road for hours waiting for the truck to arrive. We count the number of cars that nearly rear-end her BMW.

'Maybe we should push it further off the road?' she says.

I shrug. 'If someone's going to hit it, they're going to hit it.'

She shakes her head at me. 'That's a helluvan attitude. Whatever will be, will be, huh?'

'Something like that.'

'That's you to a tee, isn't it?' She tucks her knees

under her chin and doesn't speak again until the tow truck arrives.

The driver pops the hood of the car. He's says it's just a loose cable on the alternator or something. It takes him thirty seconds to fix it and get the car running again. Abby looks at me but doesn't say anything.

'Just a loose cable,' I say. She nods.

There isn't time before my flight to stop off at her apartment so she drives me straight to the airport. We hit the Sunday evening traffic flooding back into Manhattan. She pulls up outside the terminal. I'm late. She touches my arm as I go to jump out of the car.

'I'm glad you came up,' she says. 'I'm glad we had this weekend.'

I put my arm around her and tell her I'm willing to try another counselling site. We kiss goodbye. My head falls to the right and things feel better.

That was over a year ago. I haven't seen or touched Abby since. I call her when I get back to LA, then again the next day and leave messages both times. She doesn't call me back until the following weekend. She tells me she needed time to think about things.

'It isn't going to work out, is it?' she says.

'I don't know,' I say. 'Maybe not.'

Still, I pay for a month of unlimited email consultations at a South African counselling site in the hope that a foreign perspective might help. It doesn't. We hardly bother to use it. Everything is slipping away, just as she thought it would. MarriageSavers.com claims that 'even terrible marriages can be saved in four out of five cases' but I don't believe that anymore.

Months pass without us exchanging more than an

occasional email. We both start seeing other people. We never mention it of course. But we both know. I think you always know about things like that. Then she calls me. And suggests it's time we move on with our lives.

I find an attorney that offers quick, painless divorces online. We have no children and no property, so for two hundred and forty-nine dollars and a hundred or so in court fees it can all be over within ninety days. There's no need for either of us to appear in front of a judge or even each other for that matter. Everything can be done online and through the mail. It's nearly as quick and pain-free as the process of getting hitched in the first place. A few clicks, a signature and four years of marriage are over.

A few months later I receive the letter from the courthouse: that single sheet of plain white paper with 12-point courier type. And it's done. It's clean, it's amicable, it's virtual. And it leaves me with the thought that maybe a terrier wouldn't have been so bad after all.

I Instant Message her the first day of my month online to let her know it's settled.

'That's it, then,' she types back eventually.

'Yeah,' I write.

'Keep in touch.'

'And you.'

'Even if it's just an email every now and then.'

'I will.'

'You know, I really didn't think it would happen to us,' she writes. 'Not us. I always thought we were different, you know. Because of how we started out. But we're not, are we?'

'No,' I write back. 'We're not.'

Byte 29 – The Rule of Opposites

Incoming Email:

> To: <BritWriter>
> From: <Nervous>
> Subject: Look Who I Found!
>
> As a newly single chap, I too have been surfing the online personals. And I haven't been limiting myself to a single city, either. Louisville, Atlanta, New York, DC. I have air miles. LA, San Francisco, Seattle ...
> Anyway, came across this girl: link.
> She still looks great. Funny as ever. And obviously still single. What did the Baron say about being a collection of bad decisions?

I click on the link.
 I see the photo first. It loads slowly, gradually revealing her face from top to bottom, like a cover slipping in slow motion to unveil a bust. Maybe because it's been such a long time since I've seen her and the photo is not one I remember, but I almost don't

recognise her. She's standing in the dappled shade of a tree, smiling so broadly at the camera that I wonder who's taking the picture. Her hair is shorter, almost boyish, making her look even younger than I remember. The freckles and scars have faded, or maybe it's just that her skin is paler away from the year-round California sun. The eyes are the same, though – silky brown, warm like chocolate. And so is her smile, her 'life-is-endlessly-bizarre-so-you-may-as-well-enjoy-it' smile. Abby.

Abby, Abby, Abby.

I scan down the page and read her ad:

'What Would George Costanza Do?'

In the words of George Constanza, 'It's not working, Jerry. It's just not working. Why did it all turn out like this for me? I had so much promise. I was personable, I was bright. Oh, maybe not academically speaking, but ... I was perceptive. I always know when someone's uncomfortable at a party. It all became very clear to me today, that every decision I've ever made, in my entire life, has been wrong. My life is the complete opposite of everything I want it to be. Every instinct I have, in every aspect of life, be it something to wear, something to eat ... It's all been wrong.'

With this in mind, I too am now going to try the opposite. So listen up, guys, here's what I am looking for in a man. Any of these will set my heart a flutter, or better still, how about being a combination of all five? Oh, deep joy.

Mr Gym Monkey: If your pecs or decs or whatever-ecs weigh more than my car, you're just the hunk o' steaming love I've been searching for. You're as wide as you are tall, with no neck but enough back hair to braid like a schoolgirl. I love endless conversations about how much iron you can curl, how much protein Arnie could eat back in the day and why steroids should be legalized. I want to have baby meat heads with you while you oil up your arm thighs and gaze longingly into that full-length mirror.

Old Lothario: Sure, the Just-For-Men gel works fine, even on hair plugs. The only silver on you is wrapped around those well-manicured hands of yours. But you're refined, you're self-confident and heck every girl loves a fifty-year-old in a bright red convertible. Money, fast cars, B-list celebrity friends ... you've got it all. You get your rocks off by taking me shopping and you hate kids (even your own) unless of course you're dating one. Perhaps I can fulfill that little schoolgirl fantasy of yours?

The Illegal Alien: No, you're not supposed to even be in the country but hell, I'm an American citizen, what more do we need? Of course I'll marry you, lie for you, support you, risk jail for you. But don't even think of doing something in return. After all, I'm just a dumb Californian blonde who lives to serve. Let me hear you say it: 'I do ...'

Mr Brewski: Is that stale beer I smell on your breath? Never mind, you are one funny guy and yes, the lines of coke make you even funnier.

English as well? I love accents, especially when they're slurred. Irish, Scottish or Australian, even? Hell, us Yanks can't tell the difference anyway, especially when you breathe that sweet hoppy breath of yours. I'd love to be the mother of your children, but I fear that your strict diet of alcohol and narcotics has killed off any fertile sperm. Still, we can look forward to lots of sloppy sex, vomiting and grievous hangovers.

Struggling Artiste: No job, no income? That's OK. I understand you can't put a price on your art. And whoever heard of an aspiring writer or actor paying his own rent? You're the sensitive type, clearly not jaded by years of professional and personal rejection. That ex of yours certainly fucked you over but I find it endearing that you still remember to call me by her name. After all, we both know you're over her.

So, in adherence to George Costanza's Rule of Opposites, I'm completely ignoring every urge towards common sense and good judgment I've ever had and am making these my top choices. If you fit any of these descriptions, you must contact me immediately. And don't forget to include a photo, preferably one of your genitalia, your car, or of you and your ex together. Should you be witty, intelligent, good looking and emotionally stable, please don't respond. Your kind has lost its appeal.
Abby

I briefly consider responding, if only because I'm self-aware enough to recognise myself, however painful it might be, in at least three of the categories.

But I decide against it. I know how hard it must have been for her to have placed a personal in the first place, even one with such a vicious, unforgiving tone.

Is that really how she sees me: Mr-Brewski-the-Illegal-Alien-with-a-splash-of-Struggling-Artiste-who's-dangerously-close-to-becoming-Old-Lothario? I wonder how many Mr Gym Monkeys she's dated. I feel that pang again, the one deep down in my stomach that feels like a tickertape parade grinding to a soggy halt in the rain. It's the solitude, I tell myself, burning like furious indigestion again.

Loneliness and change, I remind myself. I'm the self-reliant loner exploring a wild new frontier. There's no place for regret or self-pity – certainly not in a city like Los Angeles, a city with such a well-oiled self-healing mechanism. Just turn the next corner and see what's there.

Incoming Email:

> To: <BritWriter>
> From: <RandomSamplingChick>
> Subject: Re: You found me!
>
> Let's scrap normal. For a start my email is misbehaving. Every time I try to email you my PC crashes. You'll have to take my word for it that the email I sent you yesterday was hilarious. And poignant, filled with witty anecdotes from our childhood about Mama and the fire-eating dwarves. I'd tell you more about me (and how I came to meet the good Doctor) but then there would be no incentive for you to drive out to Palm Springs to meet me. And you must.

For you have my web site address, you know all my deep dark secrets. I need to meet you in person so that I can stick a chip in the back of your neck and make you forget my existence.
Your long lost sister

Outgoing Email:

> To: <RandomSamplingChick>
> From: <BritWriter >
> Subject: Re: You found me!

> I concur. We have to meet – under the cover of darkness of course. The sun does strange things to my eyes. Bring a pocket knife, a magnifying glass and $1.75 so we can compare DNA. I have to be sure.
> Just one question: are you familiar with the term 'sexual tourist'?

Incoming Email:

> To: <BritWriter>
> From: <RandomSamplingChick>
> Subject: Re: You found me!

> No.

Outgoing Email:

> To: <RandomSamplingChick>
> From: <BritWriter >
> Subject: Re: You found me!

Good.

By tomorrow evening my mission here will be complete. I will race through the desert as soon as I'm done. It should be easy to recognise me – I'll be the one without buttocks skulking in the corner singing 'The Rubberband Man' in dull monotone – do-do-do-do-do-do.

Incoming Email:

> To: <BritWriter>
> From: <RandomSamplingChick>
> Subject: Re: You found me!

Tomorrow evening it is.

Incoming Email:

> To: <BritWriter >
> From: <The Baron>
> Subject: Change of Plans

Buddy, change of plans. Won't be coming in to LA. Doing some real funky shit here ... too many stories. You'd love it. In Chiang Mai, northern Thailand, now. Tomorrow I'm going through the jungle, down the Mekong River on a bamboo houseboat for four days, stopping overnight at different villages that have little Opium dens ... gonna be a trip!

Have fun online, brother. Come and meet me somewhere when you're done. And stop with the solitude crap, you sad bastard. Get a pet or a girlfriend or something.

The Baron.

Byte 30 – Random Sampling

Incoming Email:

> To: <BritWriter>
> From: <Abby>
> Subject: LA here I come
>
> Hey you. I'm flying back to Tokyo today. Looks like I might have to layover tonight in LA. If I do, do you want to meet up? I know your month is up today and I'd love to see you. Might be fun to talk in person for once rather than on the phone or email. Understand if you don't want to.
> Abby

Outgoing Email:

> To: <Abby>
> From: <BritWriter>
> Subject: Re: LA here I come
> Of course I want to. Just let me know where and when.

I'm still logged on. Day Thirty. I'm supposed to leave for Palm Springs soon. I'm still logged on. I could log off now. It's been thirty days. But something in me is wary about what I might find out there. My inbox is brimming with spam hawking military-grade gas masks for nuclear, biological and chemical protection. *Chin mounted canister; comfortable, lightweight rubber; full-face vision; small, medium, large available; protection for the entire family.*

Maybe it's a reflection of the America awaiting me out there, but a Pennsylvania-based consulting firm has just launched its 'layoff calculator', a program to determine the chances an individual will be made redundant within the next year. Subscribers enter their zip code, industry and occupation, how they fared in their last performance review and, if applicable, their company's stock symbol. The calculator then assesses their chances, in percentage terms, of being laid off before the end of the year. Fortunately, it doesn't work for freelance columnists of UK magazines unable to live without the Internet.

I stay logged on while I clean the scrawled *Lou 'Cherry Nose' Browns* from my bedroom wall.

Thirty days and four hours. The wall is clean. I wonder if Uncle Ralph will pay me overtime for this? I haven't heard back from Abby. Maybe she won't be stopping in LA. I'm still logged on.

My PDA has Net access again. I've been meaning to subscribe to a service since the free trial expired a few months ago. A couple of clicks on Go America's site and the Blackberry is back online. Go-anywhere Internet in the palm of my hand. All my emails are forwarded to the PDA; I can access just about any web site. Why didn't I think of this earlier?

I'm still logged on.

Thirty days and seven hours and counting. I can log off anytime now. But I don't. I'm still connected as I finally push the front door open and try to step outside. My path is blocked by three boxes of groceries from E-Deliveries. They're filled with enough fried chicken, meatballs and fettuccine, ham sandwiches, aspirin, cellophane, olive oil and vodka to keep me fuelled for at least another thirty days. I take the oil and cellophane with me, just in case the evening should exceed all my wildest expectations, and push the rest inside the door. I then step outside for the first time in a month.

I fill my lungs with the muggy evening air – about as close to fresh air as you can get in Southern California – and drag the sunglasses down from the top of my head. The sun is already dipping beyond the ocean but it's still too strong for my sun-starved retinas. I can hear the distant rumble of the first evening commuters on Ocean Boulevard trying to get a break on rush hour traffic, but the apartment building and this corner of Montana Avenue are strangely quiet. There's no one around to greet my rebirth, not even Mr Upside-Down-Potato-Head. Oh, there he is: in the laundry room downstairs, sharing a quiet moment with a pile of sweaty undergarments. He glances up through the open door as I descend the steps towards him, a pair of yellowed jockeys clutched in his hands.

I nod and say, 'Hello.'

He stares at me a beat, then uses his foot to kick the door shut. The real world equivalent of having my email blocked. I shrug and continue down to the garage.

The Jeep doesn't start straight away. The radio crackles and fizzles as it tends to do and it takes four or five urgent twists of the ignition key before the engine shudders to life. A red light on the Blackberry flashes. I have email. I check the messages. Three new emails: all spam. I delete them then check the traffic on Yahoo! There are no delays on the 10 freeway; my route through the desert is clear. I crunch the Jeep into reverse and try to forget about email and web sites, at least for a couple of hours. There's a living, breathing human being waiting for me in a Palm Springs restaurant. She seems smart and funny and, in the photos on her web site at least, rather saucy. I've done my time online and this is my reward, I tell myself, an evening with a girl. A few drinks, a good laugh and who knows what else. Welcome back. See, there's just no reason for me to be online anymore, no reason at all.

I pull out onto Fourth Street and head towards the freeway and the Blackberry flashes again. I'm still logged on.

Incoming Email:

> To: <BritWriter>
> From: <The Baron>
> Subject: Two Theories
>
> Forgot to say: Remember I once told you I had two theories to arguing with women?
> Well, neither one works.

It's sometime after ten when I snap. Numbers tend do that to me. I paid the bill about an hour ago but she's still jabbering on, nearly a full glass of wine in front of her. The waiter flits about behind us, anxious to clear the table. I can feel his gaze burning the back of my head.

'Come on, drink up,' I tell her again.

She pauses and makes another note on the clipboard resting next to the dark green stain on the tablecloth that I've been staring at since she started talking.

'Now what are you doing?' I ask.

'Counting,' she says without looking up. Dear God, she is totally oblivious to how bored I am. 'You've asked me seven times to finish my drink,' she says, 'rolled your eyes twelve times and sneaked a glance at your Blackberry nine times. Ten times now.'

I'm still logged on.

'I'm not sure you're even listening to what I'm saying,' she says.

I'm not, of course. I'm wondering how she could turn out to be such a different person to the one I was expecting to meet. That, and how badly I need a very large vodka and tonic. My eyes move from the green stain back to her. She's talking again. I study her face. She's very pretty. When we first met up earlier that evening, I couldn't believe my luck. Tall brunette, short skirt, thigh-high boots, no bra. Then she started talking, and she only ever pauses to count.

She counts the time it takes each person in the restaurant to order, the number of times diners ask for the wine list, even the number of times each one visits the restroom. She can't look at the world without needing to count it. UFO sightings, outbreaks of computer viruses, dot com collapses –

each random sampling points to a larger pattern, she tells me. She believes that nothing is random, everything has a pattern, even the American Dream and randomness itself. That much I understand. That much I find interesting, up to the point when she begins applying number patterns to endless diatribes about her feelings and how probability calculus affects her relationships and how statistical analysis enables her to 'look deep within herself' and 'work on certain areas of her psyche'.

All those witty emails were just a trap, a vicious ruse to lure me here to listen to more vapid bollocks about relationships. I swear if she asks me to write down my feelings I'll throw up right here in the middle of this Zaggat's-recommended restaurant. Why does every conversation with a girl in Southern California, even one that starts off about the Internet and the American Dream, have to deteriorate into a tedious monologue about relationships and personal growth? She tells me she was originally from New Jersey but moved west three years ago. I strongly suspect it was because she ran out of things to count and people to bore up there.

I hold the Blackberry at arm's length under the table. The light isn't flashing but I check my email all the same, just in case.

The inbox is empty.

She's talking about her 'inner child' again and making notes on the clipboard. There's a commotion at a table somewhere behind me. The sound of shattering glass and a woman shrieking. I briefly wonder if she's been eavesdropping on Random Sampling Chick's conversation.

'Tell me, you fucking cunt!' the woman yells.

I don't turn around. I don't need to. Some voices you never forget.

'I'll smash this in your fucking face!' Another glass shatters on the table.

I can't hear what the guy she's screaming at says. Goodbye, if he's got any sense. The full-volume expletives continue as several waiters bravely usher the couple outside.

Random Sampling Chick makes another note on the clipboard and looks up at me. 'You've gone pale,' she says.

'Drink up,' I tell her. 'I need to get out of here.'

'Just let me finish my story,' she says. And she's back to her inner child and 'the inevitability of everyday life'.

I'm here because I responded to an email from Bubble. I'm here because my assignment finished and I needed a night out of LA and out of my own head. And I had the means and the desire to drive two hours through the desert to meet her. It all seems pretty random to me, but to her it's nothing but pattern and probability. Meeting strangers off the Net has a direct correlation to the amount of time you spend online. The more time you spend online, the more likely you are to chat with strangers. More chatting leads to more meetings. She holds up a graph and shows me how many more evenings like this I can expect in the next five years based on my current and projected levels of Internet use.

I make a mental note to rip out the modem from my PC when I get home.

The red light flashes in my palm. More spam. What am I waiting for? Why don't I just log off now and be done with it?

We step outside the restaurant. Two black-and-whites, lights blinking silently, sit either side of the valet parking kiosk as an ambulance disappears into the night, siren shattering the still calm of the desert. The maître d' talks animatedly with a cop. I hand my ticket to a valet and notice his colleague sweeping shards of broken glass up from the driveway. I can only imagine what happened out here.

I offer Random Sampling Chick a ride home. Unfortunately, she accepts. She starts to say something as she gets in the Jeep so I turn the radio up. It whines with static again. The weak signal fades in and out on a Counting Crows song. 'A Long December'. I haven't heard that track in years. I turn it up even louder and the spitting and crackling drowns out her voice completely.

I pull past one of the squad cars and the Jeep headlights arc across a face slumped uncomfortably in the rear seat. She screws her eyes up to avoid the sharp light but not before I glimpse their piercing blue. All that's missing is the dangerous smile.

I'm back at Random Sampling Chick's apartment now, still dreaming of that vodka and tonic. She offers me a choice of herbal tea or mineral water. I take the water and gaze at the living room walls. They are covered in multicoloured graphs, some computer-generated, others hand drawn, giving the place the look of a kindergarten classroom on parents' evening.

I'm still smiling at the thought when she suddenly announces, 'I'm eighty-seven per cent happy this week, my highest level for three years.'

She's at the computer with a mock-up of her new

web site on the screen. It doesn't have a name – she prefers a URL of just numbers, numbers I quickly forget. It's basically a program she's developed to measure happiness. It helps users grade the quality of their lives in several different categories before reaching a 'happiness quotient'.

She scores 88 out of 100 in the Career category, more in Physical Health, less in Mental Health. The whopping 95 under Financial Security makes me wonder why I didn't let her pay for dinner, and the respectable 80 in the Sex Life category gives me a brief flutter of hope. I stare at her thighs for a moment but it's no use, she's still talking and I'm slowly losing the will to live.

She enters the data into the computer and it spews back the eighty-seven per cent figure. She seems very pleased and looks up at me for a reaction. It feels like it's been several hours since I last spoke. My voice croaks and I ask her how this applies to the American Dream.

'The American Dream is all about personal growth,' she says. I really should have seen this coming. 'And the attainment of happiness,' she continues. 'Happiness, like everything else, has a pattern, a series of numbers. Forget e-commerce and making money, the Internet is going to become the greatest tool for personal growth. People will use it to find out how happy they are.'

The Blackberry flashes. I have a message.

Incoming Email:

> To: < BritWriter >
> From: < Abby >
> Subject: I'm in LA!
>
> Just arrived at LAX. I'm here overnight, staying at the Marriot. Have some work to finish, then plan to have a few drinks in the bar. I'd love to see you if you can make it down. I'll have a vodka and tonic waiting for you ...
> Love, Abby

Random Sampling Chick is still talking. 'Therefore, the level at which true happiness is attained is the numerical interpretation of the American Dream. Like I said it's somewhere between ninety-five point seven-five and one hundred per cent. So I'm getting close this week.'

She's either brilliant or insane, I can't decide which but just to be on the safe side I get up to leave. She's still talking when I slip out the door and I wonder how long it'll be before she notices I'm gone.

I type on the Blackberry as I walk to the car.

Outgoing Email:

> To: < Abby >
> From: < BritWriter >
> Subject: Re: I'm in LA!
>
> I'll be there in two hours. Make the vodka and tonic a gentleman's size, ice and a slice. I need it.

I'm still online.

The drive back through the desert actually takes one hour forty-seven minutes. I pass nine gas stations, six Ford Broncos, three police cars, two multiplex cinemas, four Burger King's, a Denny's diner and eleven traffic lights, five of which are red. The radio works clearly for exactly seventeen minutes. And I estimate that I am ninety-nine per cent happy to be back in LA.

I don't notice my hands are shaking until I pull the Jeep into the Marriot parking lot. I put it down to aggravation at the poor radio reception or fatigue from the monotonous drive. But it's not. It's something else. Something ended tonight. I can't quite put my finger on what it was but for the first time in eight years of rattling around this crazy town, I feel a sense of clarity; the sense of peace that comes at the end of a long search. Even the static and gibberish on the radio have fallen silent. I've finally locked on to a clear signal. *Arrow ninety-three point one. Classic rock. All day, every day.*

I feel like I did in those first dizzy hours of being in LA. Optimistic.

But this time everything feels unscripted. The movie writing itself in my head has spooled out of control so many times, it needs to be rewound and re-cut. All the way from the beginning. I have no idea where this new movie is headed or what kind of role I'm going to play. From now on I'll just have to improvise.

I take a deep breath and step out of the Jeep. I check my reflection in the side mirror, slick down my hair and straighten my jacket. I'm just yards away now. The hotel doorman has his face pressed against the glass door, eyeing a homeless man hovering on the sidewalk outside.

'Spare any change?' the homeless man says as I walk past.

I hesitate for a moment and glance at the crinkled leather face hidden under a baseball cap that once had 'LA' stitched to the front. I slip off my jacket and hand it to him.

He frowns. 'What size is that?'

'I'm not sure,' I say. 'A forty-two I think.'

'Hmmm,' he says, fingering the buttons. 'You don't have one in a forty-four do ya?'

I smile. Abby never had this trouble giving away my clothing.

'Listen, it's late,' I say. 'Do you want it or not?'

'Yeah, yeah, I want it. Of course I want it. I guess I'll just have to lose some weight,' he says and pats his stomach. 'What about some change?'

The Marriot lobby is quiet and chilly with too much air conditioning. I march through then pause at the entrance to the bar and peer in. Steel grates have been lowered on two of the bar's three sides. The bartender is busy pulling cash from the register. Leaning on the open side of the bar is a lone figure reading from a laptop and nursing what are unmistakeably two large vodka and tonics.

I think about emailing her to let her know I'm standing less than ten yards away but when I reach for the Blackberry I remember I left it in the car. So I have no way of emailing her and no way of seeing the error message repeated across the Blackberry's tiny screen: *Internet Explorer Script Error. Cannot find 'x-%24home%24://null/.' Make sure the path or Internet address is correct. Internet Explorer Script Error. Cannot find 'x-%24home%24://null/.' Make sure the path or Internet address is correct . . .*

As I walk to the bar, she starts to turn towards me. And I have no way of knowing that I'm finally logged off.

But I am.

Slick
Daniel Price

'I work in the field of perception management, although the less colourful term is 'media manipulation.' We're the CIA of PR, the sublime little gremlins who live just outside your senses, selling you products and concepts without you even knowing.'

Scott Singer is a publicist, expert spin doctor and media assassin, killing scandals and selling the unsellable - be it guns, porn or reputations. Now he's the hired gun in a record company's attempt to save the public character of their major artist, rap star Jeremy Sharpe, a.k.a. Hunta. Hunta is no stranger to controversy. He currently stands accused by the media of inciting criminal acts among his teenage fans and his staff is fighting to stop a former assistant going to the press with her own accusations.

Instead of getting nasty, Scott gets creative. One way to avoid a scandal is to create a bigger one – a grand and epic hoax that will dominate the news cycle, and eclipse the truth. It will be his greatest achievement to date, if it works ...

'Bitterly comic ... as polished and precise as anything by Will Self' *Time Out*

Safelight
Shannon Burke

Struggling to come to terms with his father's death, paramedic and photographer Frank descends into the chaos and misery of Harlem, taking photographs of the ill, the wounded, the dying, and the down-and-out. Accompanying him on his wanderings are his loudmouthed partner, Burnett; his best friend, Hock, who boosts drugs from the hospital; and his brother, Norman, a surgeon who can't understand why Frank is in such pain. Frank's ruin seems inevitable, but then he meets Emily, who offers him a chance at redemption. Against everyone's advice, Frank and Emily fall in love. Together, they try to find a way out of the shadows and sadness, and it is through this connection that Frank begins to recover his ability to see the beauty of life.

In short, cinematic scenes, with not a word wasted and nothing told that can be shown, Shannon Burke leads us on a powerful journey through the darkest precincts of the street and of the soul.

'... provoking and disturbing ... a work of nerveless intelligence, disarming tenderness and hard-won optimism.' Jim Crace

'An accomplished and haunting debut ... a tour de force' *New York Times*

A SELECTION OF NOVELS AVAILABLE FROM PIATKUS BOOKS

THE PRICES BELOW WERE CORRECT AT THE TIME OF GOING TO PRESS. HOWEVER PIATKUS BOOKS RESERVE THE RIGHT TO SHOW NEW RETAIL PRICES ON COVERS WHICH MAY DIFFER FROM THOSE PREVIOUSLY ADVERTISED IN THE TEXT OR ELSEWHERE.

0 7499 3605 3	Slick	Daniel Price	£6.99
0 7499 3512 X	Safelight	Shannon Burke	£6.99
0 7499 3562 6	The Outside World	Tova Mirvis	£6.99
0 7499 3589 8	Home	Tim Relf	£6.99
0 7499 3602 9	The Man From Perfect	Andrea Semple	£6.99
0 7499 3565 0	Wedding Season	Darcy Cosper	£6.99

ALL PIATKUS TITLES ARE AVAILABLE FROM:
PIATKUS BOOKS C/O BOOKPOST
PO Box 29, Douglas, Isle Of Man, IM99 1BQ
Telephone (+44) 01624 677237
Fax (+44) 01624 670923
Email; bookshop@enterprise.net
Free Postage and Packing in the United Kingdom.
Credit Cards accepted. All Cheques payable to Bookpost.
(Prices and availability subject to change without prior notice.
Allow 14 days for delivery. When placing orders please state if
you do not wish to receive any additional information.)

OR ORDER ONLINE FROM:
www.piatkus.co.uk
Free postage and packing in the UK (on orders of two
books or more)